"Susan? Did you find the camera?" Jed appeared in the doorway behind her. "I got hold of a plumber. And Kathleen says it's important that you call her back—she just heard something about Simon Fairway. . . ."

"Simon Fairweather," Susan corrected her husband. "You met him when we wanted to build the workshop over the garage. He's the building inspector. . . ."

"That ass."

"You might not want to insult him," Susan interrupted. "Apparently he's been murdered."

That stopped him. "Hon, we've only been home fifteen minutes. How did you end up in the middle of a murder investigation so quickly?"

"I'm not in the middle of anything! I just happened to get some interesting messages on the machine." She reached for the phone. "I guess I should call Brett back first."

Jed sighed and left her to it. When the chief of police called, his wife usually answered.

By Valerie Wolzien
Published by Fawcett Books:

MURDER AT THE PTA LUNCHEON
THE FORTIETH BIRTHDAY BODY
WE WISH YOU A MERRY MURDER
AN OLD FAITHFUL MURDER
ALL HALLOWS' EVIL
A STAR-SPANGLED MURDER
A GOOD YEAR FOR A CORPSE
'TIS THE SEASON TO BE MURDERED
REMODELED TO DEATH

REMODELED
TO DEATH

VALERIE WOLZIEN

FAWCETT GOLD MEDAL • NEW YORK

A Fawcett Gold Medal Book
Published by Ballantine Books
Copyright © 1995 by Valerie Wolzien

Library of Congress Catalog Card Number: 95-90343

ISBN 0-449-14921-8

Manufactured in the United States of America

First Edition: September 1995

10 9 8 7 6 5 4 3 2 1

ONE

"DO YOU THINK THEY'LL BE ALL RIGHT?" SUSAN ASKED HER husband, lowering the car window to wave at a neighbor who was out walking the dog.

"Hon, this is the first time in almost twenty years that we're going to have a whole month to ourselves. You're not going to spend all August worrying about the kids, are you?" Jed Henshaw asked as he turned the car down the road on which they had lived for the past fifteen years.

"Not a chance! I've made plans. I'm going to get up early each day and do yoga with the lady on public TV, then run at least two miles in the morning, swim laps at the club in the afternoon, get lots of reading done, clean out the basement, the garage, and the attic, and paint both upstairs bathrooms. What do you think about apricot?"

"Sounds like you're going to be busy. You know, I was hoping we'd be spending more time together," Jed suggested, placing his hand on his wife's knee.

"I just happened to put a bottle of champagne in the refrigerator while you and Chad were filling his backpack this morning." She smiled and patted his hand. "But you didn't answer my question. What do you think about apricot?"

"I like them. But it's been a long day, why don't we eat out tonight?"

"Not the fruit, the color. I was thinking about painting the walls in our bathroom light apricot," she explained as they entered their driveway. "And maybe lemon yellow in the other bath."

"Sounds pretty."

"Too feminine?"

Jed moved his hand off his wife's knee and pressed the garage-door opener. "Why don't we take a nice cool shower and think about it?"

"Okay. But someone has to walk Clue first. She's been alone for hours."

"Why don't I walk her and you can get the champagne and glasses out," Jed suggested, putting his foot on the brake and opening the car door in almost one movement.

"No one would ever guess that we've been married for nearly a quarter of a century, would they?" Susan answered, getting out of the car and following him to the door between the garage and the kitchen.

"It gets better every day. What the . . . ?"

Susan ran smack into her husband's back. "What's wrong? Is it Clue . . . ?" But the golden retriever bounded by Jed and leaped up on Susan. "What's this gooey stuff on her paws?" she asked, realizing that the dog was covering her beige shorts with globs of grayish slime. "Down, Clue! Jed, this stuff reeks!" She grabbed the big animal's collar and peered around her husband. "Oh, no!" she wailed. "What happened?"

The Henshaws stood and stared at their kitchen. When they'd left home this morning, there had been dirty dishes cluttering the counters, coffee grounds tossed in the sink, and half-full boxes of dry cereal standing in the middle of the kitchen table. Now there was also a gaping hole in the plaster ceiling and the quarry tile floor was covered with rusty water and slimy muck.

"What happened?" Susan repeated.

"I think," Jed began slowly, "that we're going to have to worry about more than the color of the bathroom walls."

"What?"

"Why don't you put Clue in the backyard and I'll go upstairs and look around?" he urged, then hurried off without waiting for a response.

Susan stood still, scratching behind the dog's ears and trying to assimilate what had happened.

"Hon! You better find the number of that plumber we used when we had the hot-water heater replaced last winter!"

Susan looked down. There were about twenty gallons of filthy water on the floor between her and the address book, which was lying on the counter under the wall phone. She reached out to get a mop from the broom closet.

"And don't touch anything until we take photographs for the insurance investigators!"

Susan put her hand down, realizing that her husband's voice was coming through the hole in the ceiling. She sighed. "Come on, Clue, why don't you go terrorize the squirrels in the yard?"

The dog dashed out the door that Susan opened as Jed called down from above, "Would you turn off the main shutoff valve?"

"The what?" Susan called back up, wondering why they had an expensive intercom system if everyone was going to rely on yelling to get messages between floors. Of course, in this case, Jed was actually yelling through the floor.

"The main water shutoff—it's in the basement. Above the washing machine. I've shown it to you more than once—"

"I remember! I remember!" All she actually remembered was that Jed had insisted on showing her something hidden in the ceiling over the clothes dryer, but she wasn't going to admit that now. "Turn it off, right?"

"It turns off left!"

Susan frowned and hurried to the basement. First she'd find it, then she would worry about which way to turn it. Water had run across the floor and was dripping down the basement stairs, so she was careful not to slip on her way down. Loud noises were coming from above and she could only hope that Jed was in control of whatever was happening up there. She didn't relish any of that sludge pouring down on her head.

There were two knobs sticking out of the many copper pipes hidden in the ceiling of the laundry room. One was red and one green. Susan shrugged and twisted the red knob to the left until it would turn no more. Then she moved everything out of the path of the sludge before she returned upstairs. Jed was still yelling, but it was difficult to understand his words as the dog was scratching on the door and the phone began ringing. Assuming the answering machine was on, she decided to ignore the dog and ran upstairs to see exactly what was happening to her house.

Jed wasn't on the second floor, but she didn't have any trouble finding him. She just followed the squishy footprints leading down the hallway to the attic entrance. "Jed?"

"Up here."

Susan opened the door and climbed the maroon-painted steps to the space under the roof. Before they had moved into the house, a previous owner had made some half-hearted attempts to turn this area into a living space, even adding a tiny half-bath under the eaves. The Henshaws used the area mainly for storage, although Susan had once set up a sewing machine in one corner and there was still evidence of Chad's enchantment with HO scale trains many years ago. Jed's footprints led across the wide wood planks to the bathroom.

"Jed? What are you doing?" The loud noises had resumed.

"Look at that," he insisted without answering her question.

"I can't see." She moved around him and peered down into the hole he had ripped in the floor of the bathroom. "What is it?"

"The top of our cracked main drainpipe. Who would have thought they were still using cast iron when this house was built?"

Susan assumed that was a rhetorical question.

But his next one wasn't. "When is the plumber arriving?"

"Ah . . . I couldn't find his number. . . ." Susan lied.

"Call Jerry then. He told me they were going to have a new dishwasher installed before the baby came. Maybe they have the name of a good plumber."

"Okay. But I have to go to the bathroom . . ."

"You can't flush the toilets."

"I can't?"

"You turned off the water, didn't you? Susan, I hope—"

"I did—if you're talking about the red knob in the ceiling of the laundry room. But I better go call Kathleen about that plumber, hadn't I?" Susan asked, trotting down the stairs toward her bedroom to phone.

She quickly dialed her best friend's phone number, more anxious to discover if Kathleen (nine months and eleven days pregnant) had started labor than to acquire the name of a good plumber.

Kathleen answered on the first ring. "Hello? Susan?"

"Hi! How did you know it was me?"

"I've been leaving messages on your machine all morning," Kathleen explained.

"Your contractions have started! You need me to drive you to the hospital. Where's Jerry?" Susan wondered where she had stashed her purse as she talked.

"Don't get excited. Not a chance. I think this baby is planning on attending college in utero. I've been calling all day. Where have you been?"

"At the airport. We thought we were going to be able to get Chad off to Bangor and Chrissy on her way to Kennedy airport in less than an hour. But Chrissy's plane was grounded because of some sort of mechanical problem and we had to make other arrangements for her to connect with a flight to Barcelona—and while we were doing that, Chad missed his flight to Maine. So we had to contact the Outward Bound people to see that their van picked him up from the later flight and . . ."

"But they both got out okay?"

"Yes," Susan said, surprised by Kathleen's lack of interest. "But what I called for," she continued, "is the name of your plumber. We just got home and one of the pipes broke on the third floor and water came through the kitchen ceiling and—"

"It missed the second floor?"

"Excuse me?"

"You have water on the first floor that came from the attic without hitting the second floor—"

"Wait a second," Susan interrupted, putting the receiver down on the bed and hurrying over to the adjoining bedroom. She left the small room more slowly. "Kathleen? Are you still there?" she asked, picking up the receiver.

"Yes. Susan—"

"It's a mess! The ceiling fell into the tub. The tub enclosure is smashed. There's glass all over the floor. Oh, God, the other bathroom shares that wall. Kath, I'll call you back." She hung up without waiting for a response.

The second bathroom on the floor was worse than the first. The wall had collapsed as well as the ceiling, and the toilet was cracked and leaking water onto the green and white tile floor. Susan was beginning to feel overwhelmed.

Jed appeared behind her. "Did you call the plumber?"

"I think we need more than a plumber. Both bathrooms are going to have to be completely remodeled. And there is the ceiling in the kitchen—and who knows what's happening to the floor down there. There's even muck dripping down the basement stairs, Jed!"

"A plumber is the place to start. He'll be able to assure us that we can use the water in the rest of the house without causing any more damage."

"I'll call Kathleen back—"

"No, I'll call Jerry. If they weren't happy with their plumber, we should find someone else. This is going to be a big job. Why don't you find the Polaroid camera and start taking pictures of this stuff? Then we can start cleaning up. I should call the insurance company right away, too. . . ."

Susan left her husband to make his calls and started back downstairs. She knew that the cameras were in the closet in Jed's study. And unlike much of the other equipment in the house, she knew how to work them all. She trotted down the stairs, averted her eyes from the mess in her kitchen, and hurried to the study. She was opening the closet door when she noticed the light flashing on the answering machine. Maybe someone other than Kathleen had called; she might as well listen to the messages while putting film in the camera. She pressed the correct button.

The first three calls were from Kathleen. But the next message was very interesting.

"Hello, Susan. Jed. It's Brett Fortesque. Susan, could you please give me a call as soon as possible? Call the police station. Whoever answers will know how to get hold of me."

And did, she wondered a minute later, the next message hold a clue to the reason why the chief of Hancock, Connecticut's, police department seemed so anxious to speak with her?

"Hello, Susan. This is Margo Kellerman. Did you hear? If you start investigating this one, Susan, you're going to have to consider me as a major suspect. I would have enjoyed shooting that man myself. Of course, everyone who's had a house worked on in this town had more than a few good reasons to murder Simon Fairweather."

The irritatingly loud beep at the end of the tape startled Susan. She was wondering how she was going to get three bathrooms and a kitchen repaired when the town's building inspector had just been killed.

TWO

"SUSAN? DID YOU FIND THE CAMERA?" JED APPEARED IN the doorway behind her. "I got hold of a plumber—he's not the one Jerry recommended, but at least he's willing to come over immediately. And Kathleen says it's important that you call her back—she just heard something about Simon Fairway—"

"Simon Fairweather," Susan corrected her husband. "You met him when we wanted to build the workshop over the garage. He's the building inspector."

"That ass—"

"You might not want to insult him," Susan interrupted. "Apparently he's been murdered."

That stopped him. "Hon, we've only been home fifteen minutes. How did you end up in the middle of a murder investigation so quickly?"

"I'm not in the middle of anything! I just happened to get some interesting messages on the machine." She reached for the phone. "I guess I should call Brett back first."

Jed sighed and left her to it. When the chief of police called, his wife usually answered.

Susan was about to dial Brett's number when the phone rang. Kathleen was on the other end of the line.

"Hi. Did Jed tell you about Simon Fairweather?"

"No, but Margo left a message that he had been murdered. What happened?"

"I don't know that much," Kathleen admitted. "Margo just called me, too. She said that Simon's body was discov-

ered in his office down at the municipal center this morning."

"Who found him?"

"Brett."

"You're kidding!"

"No. The police department's open all night, of course,
and I guess Brett was wandering around early this
morning—"

A loud click interrupted Kathleen.

"Kath, we had call waiting added to the line because we
were worried about the kids not being able to get through,"
Susan explained.

"Fine."

Susan pressed the correct button and found herself listening to Brett.

"Susan, I'm glad you're home. Simon Fairweather was
found dead in his office this morning."

"How was he killed?" Susan asked. She had heard this
part of the story already.

There was a short pause before Brett answered. "Do you
know anything about nail guns?"

"You mean . . ."

"They're very effective weapons," Brett said succinctly.

"I understand you found him," Susan said, not wanting
to think more than was necessary about what she had just
been told.

"You have good sources."

"Do you think he was murdered last night?"

"Absolutely. He was at work yesterday. A lot of people
saw him here as well as around town. We don't know who
the last person was to see him alive yet, but we'll be finding out."

"His family . . ." Susan began.

"His wife is on a cruise up the inland passage from Van-
couver to Anchorage. We put in a call to her ship, but she
hasn't gotten back to us yet. I don't know if they had any
kids. If they did, they must be grown up and living away
from home."

"They didn't have children. There may be other relatives

around here. I think Simon's aunt lives on the other side of town in the house that both she and Simon were brought up in," Susan began.

"Then you know a lot about the family."

Susan thought that Brett sounded relieved. "A little. But it's not like we're close friends," she admitted, remembering her husband's comment about their planned garage expansion. "In fact, Jed is still angry about a proposal that was turned down by the building inspector's office."

"Recently?"

"Last year. I was just telling Kathleen about— Oh, my goodness, I left Kathleen on the other line. Hold on a sec, Brett." She pressed the button and returned to her friend. "Kath, are you still there?"

A dial tone answered her question. "Damn." She punched the button that she thought would return her to Brett but got an identical response. "Damn, damn, damn." She dialed the police station again. "Brett? I'm sorry I cut you off," she apologized.

"No problem. I'm used to it. Just one of the minor irritations of life in our electronic age. Right now I'm more interested in knowing about your relationship with Simon Fairweather."

"I don't have a relationship with Simon Fairweather." Susan was aware of noises indicating that someone had let Clue into the house. "I mean, I didn't. I know his wife because I've taken classes with her at the Art Center downtown. But I didn't have any sort of relationship with Simon Fairweather—not more than anyone else in town. He was our building inspector, that's all. Why? Why are you calling me rather than someone else?"

She thought she heard Brett sigh before he answered. "Would you mind if I stopped over for a few minutes? I'd like to show you something."

Susan remembered that the plans she and Jed had made for a romantic evening had already been turned over to plumbers and repairmen. She wanted this month alone to be free of interruptions, but what the hell. "Of course. We'll be here."

"Great."

Susan barely heard the final consonant of Brett's reply. She didn't have any idea what the loud noise was; it sounded like someone was holding a demolition derby in her driveway. She muttered a few words, hung up, grabbed the Polaroid camera, and dashed to the front of the house.

Her guess had been a good one. Years spent on the demolition derby circuit was the only possible explanation for the state of the two vans in her driveway. On closer inspection she realized that only one and a half vans were actually on the macadam. The rear wheels of one of the vehicles were firmly planted on a much-prized rhododendron. Apparently the driver was aware of this. He got out of his van, pulled his MEET THE REAL KING OF BEERS hat off his head, and grinned. "Looks like the thing coulda used a little pruning, huh? Helps 'em grow. It's a puny thing, ain't it?"

"It's a rare miniature variety," Susan stated as calmly as possible.

He frowned. "Ain't got no thorns, does it? Them's new tires."

Susan chose to ignore this particular concern. She was trying to make out the painted letters under the layers of dirt on the sides of the identical vehicles. " 'Plumbers R Us'?" she read aloud slowly.

"That's what we are—plumbers!"

" 'We fix pains in your drains'?"

"Yup!"

" 'Let us flush away all your problems—except your in-laws'?"

"The wife made me add that. You know how women are." He frowned again and thoroughly scratched the few inches of exposed flesh between his greasy jeans and stained red cotton muscle shirt.

Susan had no trouble deciding that this man was not going to enter her house under any circumstances—even before meeting the driver of the second van.

The other guy was tall and thin and wore a crew cut that would have made any marine proud. The military look, however, stopped at his eyebrows. From the nose down he was furry. His beard spread out between a handlebar mustache and an unpolished brass belt buckle. The hair on his arms extended from knuckle to shoulder and then peeked out of the drooping neck of a tie-dyed T-shirt that declared eternal allegiance to the Grateful Dead. Matching hair sprang up from his toes and around the rubber thongs on his feet. "You the lady with the problem?" he asked directly.

"Oh, yes, I have a problem," Susan agreed, not admitting that he and his partner were not the solution. "That is, I had a problem. It's been fixed," she lied. "You're not needed anymore."

"Lady, Harry and me ain't here for nothing," the hirsute deadhead insisted.

"And it costs a lot more than nothing to get us here," the other man reminded her.

"Naturally, you have a fee for house calls," Susan said quickly. "I'll just go get my checkbook."

"We prefer cash . . ."

"Course you can write a check to cash . . ."

"Now, look," Susan said, irritated at the assumption that she would help this dreadful duo avoid paying taxes. "I don't see why I should write a check to cash—and I'm not actually sure why I should pay you to drive in my driveway and run over a very rare shrub."

"You called us, lady." The heavyset man turned to his thinner partner for confirmation. "She called us."

"We didn't get no call from heaven to come here, that's for sure."

Susan had no idea why they were enjoying the situation so much—until she looked down at the piece of paper that the "beer king" handed her. "One hundred and forty dollars! For what?"

"For coming right over to help you with your emergency. What else?"

"You think we're here because we ain't got nothing better to do?"

"Can I mail you a check?" Susan asked.

"See what it says at the top of the paper? 'Please Pay Promptly.' We means what it says."

"I'll go get my checkbook," Susan said flatly.

"Me and him—we'll be right here."

"We ain't leaving 'til we get paid."

Susan wanted them off her rhododendron and out of her driveway and her life as fast as possible. She was back outside in record time. "Shall I write this out to Plumbers R Us?" she asked, ignoring their previous request. "My husband insists," she lied, hoping to add conviction to her statement.

"Yeah, well . . ."

Susan got the impression that as long as she paid the outrageous bill immediately, these two men would be happy to leave. She wrote quickly, then ripped the check from the book and handed it over without a smile. "Thank you for coming," she said through gritted teeth.

"Yeah. Well, we'll be seeing you, lady."

"Yeah. We'll see ya."

There wasn't a lot of time for those threats to do any ringing in Susan's ears. The vans sounded worse than they looked as the engines roared to life and, squashing only a couple more plants, Plumbers R Us headed off into the sunset.

"Why are they leaving?" Jed appeared beside his wife.

"You wouldn't believe what they charged us—"

"Charged us for what? They didn't even come into the house! Susan, what's going on?"

"I sent them away."

"You sent . . ." Jed's face turned an interesting shade of red. "You did what?"

"You don't usually act like this," Susan protested.

"I don't usually have a cracked main drain . . . smashed walls . . . a kitchen ceiling in the middle of the room . . ." He took a deep breath. "Susan, why did you send them away?"

"Jed, you didn't meet them. They were disgusting. You should have seen their clothing—they were dirty and . . .

and they ran over your rhododendron. Look!" She pointed dramatically to the crushed bush.

"Susan. They're plumbers. Their work is dirty and messy. What did you expect them to be wearing? And I don't care about the landscaping right now," he added quickly before she could explain further. "I would just like to have some running water."

"There must be other plumbers, Jed. Believe me, you wouldn't have wanted them to work on our house."

"Susan, I called seven numbers in the phonebook and left messages on six answering machines. Plumbers R Us has a woman who answers the phone and who relayed a message to their vans. They came here immediately. No one else has even returned my call. Don't you want to have running water?"

"I . . ."

"That's the phone. I certainly hope it's a plumber!"

Susan hoped so, too.

"Did you take those photos?" Jed called back over his shoulder as he jogged to the phone.

"Right away." She waved the camera in the air to display her good intentions, but he was gone. "Well, onward and upward," she muttered to herself. "May as well begin at the top."

Susan spent the next fifteen minutes recording the damage. Two packs of instant film later, she was very depressed. She must have been out of her mind to send those men away. Anything was preferable to living with this mess for one second more than was actually necessary. For one wild moment she considered calling back Plumbers R Us. But reason prevailed. Besides, Jed was coming down the hall with a smile on his face. He must have good news.

"The company that Jerry recommended is on the way. I'll wait for them outside. Maybe you should put Clue in the backyard."

"She really hates being out there when things are going on in the house."

"Susan, do you have any idea what that dog-run cost? Why did we have it put up if we weren't going to use it?"

"I—"

"There goes the phone again. Why don't you get it, and if it's the insurance company, tell them what's going on. I've got to get outside."

"I'll answer the phone," Susan assured him, hurrying off to the kitchen. All this tension was making her hungry and she might as well get a snack. A leisurely meal out sure didn't appear to be looming in the immediate future.

The refrigerator bore signs of her children's food preferences. Chrissy, the eternal dieter, had stocked up on peach-flavored mineral water and fat-free strawberry yogurt while Chad had filled the bottom shelf with high-calorie ingredients for the pepperoni pizza he concocted daily. Susan, ever an adaptable mother, grabbed a yogurt and a few slices of whole-milk mozzarella. At least she'd be getting enough calcium today, she thought, maneuvering around the water to answer the phone. As she picked up the receiver, a drip of rusty water fell on her shoulder.

"Damn!"

"Excuse me?"

"Oh, I'm sorry. I wasn't talking to you," Susan apologized to the unknown caller. "There's water dripping on my new white linen shirt."

"That's why I'm calling."

"What? Oh, you must be a plumber."

"Got it in one, lady. Your husband left a message on my machine."

"Oh, he'll be so thrilled that you called back. Let me tell you about our problem," she added, and then explained. After extracting a promise of immediate attention, she hung up, pleased with her own competence. She did, however, wonder if it was essential for all plumbers to address her as "lady."

Clue was drooling on her foot and Susan tossed the dog a piece of cheese and then led her outside to the dog-run. One of her neighbors, one she didn't particularly like, was always saying things like "When you're stuck with lemons, make lemonade." It was beginning to occur to Susan that maybe that was her best approach to this situation. She'd always wanted to remodel the bathrooms; she'd read articles guaranteeing that the money spent on remodeling was almost always recouped when a house was sold; somewhere around the house she had stashed a bunch of magazines with titles like *Kitchen and Bath* and *Remodel*. And she had just seen a wonderful article about ceramic tiles in Martha Stewart's *Living*—or was it *House & Garden*? She pushed Clue through the metal gate and returned to the house.

When Jed found her, she was sitting in his den, magazines piled on the desk before her. "Hon, why did you tell another plumber to come over? We don't need two plumbers—"

"What we need, Jed, is a contractor," Susan interrupted. "I've been thinking. This is the perfect opportunity to remodel both bathrooms . . . and maybe the little one on the third floor, too. We should—"

"We should get our pipes fixed and then worry about everything else later. Susan, we have to get our priorities straight here—"

"And I hate to tell you folks, but no matter what else is going on here, this murder investigation is going to go right to the top of the list."

Chief Fortesque had joined them.

THREE

"W_{HY}?"

Her marriage was right on track, Susan decided. She and Jed had asked the question simultaneously. "Hi, Brett," she began again.

"What exactly do we have to do with this murder investigation?" Jed asked, leaping directly to the point.

"I'm not sure."

A tall young man with a mohawk appeared behind Brett. "I need someone up on the top floor. Gonna have to take up the rest of those floorboards, and I sure don't want to run into any surprises."

"I'll come," Jed said quickly.

"And I'll explain why I'm here," Brett added, sitting down on the edge of the desk.

"I really don't think I can tell you very much about Simon Fairweather." Susan repeated what she had said on the phone less than an hour before.

"I came over hoping you could explain this," Brett said, handing her a sheet of slick paper. "You don't have to be careful with it, it's a copy of the original document."

Susan sat back and read through the paper without asking any questions. "I don't understand."

"It was found crumpled up in Simon Fairweather's fist."

"Well, that explains all the tiny lines, but I still don't understand," Susan repeated. She studied the document carefully before asking another question. "Do you know if it's his handwriting?"

"We believe so. The secretary in the building department

says that it is, but we'll have to call in a handwriting expert to be sure."

"So you think he was writing it right before he was killed."

"It seems likely. It's also possible that the murderer found it someplace and put it into his hand after killing him."

"Why would anyone do that?"

"I have no idea, but it's still a possibility."

"Do you know what this other name means?"

"Only because I looked in the phonebook. They're listed as a contracting company. The address is down by the water."

"In Hancock?"

"Yes."

"I don't understand it," Susan said, then paused. "Why would Simon Fairweather write my name over and over and then Cory Construction? There are even arrows connecting the two."

"It looks to me like he was just scribbling," Brett said. "And it may mean nothing."

"But why would he scribble my name at all? I don't think I ever actually met Simon Fairweather. When he came out to the house to approve—or, as it turned out, disapprove—of our garage extension, I wasn't even here. Jed handled it all."

"And I gather Cory Construction doesn't mean anything to you?"

"No. Although the name is familiar. I may have seen their trucks on the street or heard them mentioned by someone. You know how many people have their houses worked on around here."

Brett nodded. He had noticed. Couples living in five-bedroom houses with two children felt urgent needs to add on family rooms, dens, guest suites, etc. He didn't understand, but he had noticed.

Susan grinned at the expression on his face. "I know. A lot of people are more than a little house-proud. And there are plenty of old houses in town, too. And, believe me, old houses need constant maintenance." She grimaced, thinking about the mess her not-so-old house had just become. "Is it getting warm in here?"

"Hmm," Brett agreed without interest. "Maybe you should open the windows."

"I'll turn down the thermostat," Susan said, doing just that. "That's funny," she commented. "In this room you can usually hear the air-conditioning come on immediately."

Brett reached out and flicked the switch on the desk light. Nothing happened. "No power."

"Oh, fine! We don't have water. And now we don't have power. What else is going to happen today?" Susan asked rhetorically.

"I wonder if it's just your house or the entire grid," Brett said, reaching for the two-way radio that hung from his belt.

"Jed's yelling something," Susan said, moving toward the doorway to hear him better. "Something about electricity, in fact."

"They must have turned off the main circuit breaker," Brett exclaimed, putting his radio back in place. "I should have known. Professionals have too much sense to break through walls without making sure they don't cut a live wire."

"Which leads us back to death and Simon Fairweather." The mystery of the power crisis solved, Susan was busy opening windows as she spoke. "I suppose I'd be a bigger help to you if Cory Construction had worked for me—"

"This paper may not mean anything," Brett interrupted. "You know how people scribble ... Are you listening to me?"

"Yes," she lied. Actually, she was trying to remember the details of an article she had scanned in the dentist's office a few months ago. Something about how unconscious thoughts or needs or desires are revealed in small everyday activities. There had been more than one mention of doodling. She cringed as the sounds coming from above increased in volume. "Maybe I should ask Jed about Cory Construction. The name may mean something to him."

"Good idea." Brett nodded approval as he motioned for her to precede him from the room. "This sure is a mess," he added, glancing in at the kitchen.

"Wait till you see the upstairs," Susan promised, heading to the bathroom at the top of the stairs from which she thought the loudest sounds were emanating.

"Good lord!"

Susan nodded. "We're going to need more than a couple of plumbers to fix this, aren't we?"

"An entire army of plumbers is going to be kept busy for weeks cleaning up this."

"Months," Jed suggested, joining them. He held a piece of paper in his hand. "These are the names of contracting companies that these guys have worked with. Maybe we'd better start making calls as soon as possible."

"I'll do it," Susan volunteered, taking the paper and glancing at it. "Looks like Cory Construction isn't here," she added to Brett.

"Cory Construction?" Jed repeated. "No, they didn't mention that company, but if you've heard something good about them, go ahead and call. We've got to get going here."

"Shouldn't the insurance company come over first?"

"There'll be lots of time for that. It's not likely that we'll get a major job like this one started immediately."

"I'll start calling then."

"Yes. But maybe you should check around first and see who your friends suggest. A big job like this is going to take a lot of time and cost a lot of money. We want to get the right crew for the job."

Susan nodded.

"I'd better get going," Brett said, now that he was sure Cory Construction meant nothing to Jed. "If you think of anything that might add to the investigation, you'll let me know?"

"Of course," Susan said.

"Investigation?" Jed repeated, looking at his wife. "Hon, you're going to be pretty busy if we're to get this house back in order."

"I know. Don't worry," Susan insisted as Jed returned to the third floor. She walked Brett to the front door. "It sounds as if I'm going to be talking with a lot of contractors. I may as well check out Cory Construction at the same time, don't you think?"

Brett gave her a stern look. "I suppose this is my own fault. I should never have come over here today. There's probably a perfectly reasonable explanation for that piece of paper—and it may have nothing to do with the murder."

Susan didn't say anything. Brett assumed that she was going to leap into all this. But actually she was torn. For the first time in recent years she didn't want to get involved in a murder investigation. This was her only month not being a mother in years and she deserved a vacation. On the other hand, since she was going to be calling half the contractors in Connecticut, she might as well check Cory Construction. "I'll let you know if I find out anything" was all she said.

And, she reminded herself, watching the police car back out of the driveway, I didn't actually promise anything. She was heading into the house to make her calls when Jerry Gordon's car pulled up. Three doors opened and Jerry and his son got out. Kathleen struggled more slowly to slide her large stomach through the space a designer in Detroit had assumed was more than adequate for exiting an automobile.

Susan smiled and waved. "Hi. What's that you've got in your hand, Ba—Alex?" Susan had almost called the child by his nickname. In preparation for his entrance into kindergarten in only a few more weeks, Bananas was insisting on being called by his given name.

"It's a book," he explained solemnly. "I'm learning to read. Babies," he continued, "can't read."

"That's true," Susan agreed, equally serious. "You know what else they can't do? They can't play with big dogs like Clue."

"But I can!" The boy beamed.

"I wish you would. She's been penned in the backyard for a long time. She'll be thrilled to see you."

"Why don't you and I visit the golden monster?" Jerry

suggested to his son. "And then we'll go see what Jed was talking about on the phone."

Alex turned to his mother and handed her his book. "You better keep this for me. Sometimes Clue likes to chew on paper."

"I'd be happy to," Kathleen said, taking the book and putting it in her purse. "And then I think I'd better sit down. We'll be in the kitchen if you—"

"No, we'll be in the study," Susan interrupted.

Kathleen raised her eyebrows.

"You'll understand when you see the kitchen," Susan explained.

"You're going to give me the grand tour, aren't you?"

"Follow me."

Fifteen minutes later the women were splitting a bottle of seltzer around Jed's desk. It had taken a few minutes longer than Susan would have expected to show Kathleen around. The plumber, who had done a small job for the Gordons last year, remembered Kathleen well and the two of them had exchanged greetings and family news while Jed glowered in the background. "Jed seems to be having trouble with all this," Kathleen commented, taking a swig of water.

"He doesn't like crisis . . ."

"Who does? You know," Kathleen continued, "maybe the two of you should move to a hotel for a few days. You could stay in my guest room, but you'll have to move out as soon as I go into labor."

"Your mom is coming right away?"

"She has her bags packed and waiting by the door—as she calls and tells me every single morning. Actually, she keeps offering to come up right away. I know Ban—Alex would love it, but I'm afraid she would drive me crazy."

"The last couple of weeks are the hardest part of being pregnant."

"And my last two weeks are now the last four weeks," Kathleen said ruefully, getting up awkwardly and stretching out her back. "I'll be back in a second."

"Where are you going?"

"The bathroom. Where else?"

"There's no running water. Don't flush."

"You know," Kathleen said, walking out the door, "you really should consider moving to a hotel for a day or two."

Susan nodded, pulled the Yellow Pages toward her, and started looking up the numbers of the companies Jed had given her. Kathleen was back almost immediately. "You don't have any power either," she announced.

"The electricity was turned off by the plumbers— Hello, is this Connecticut Contracting?" she interrupted herself and spoke into the phone.

Kathleen picked up a magazine and skimmed through it while Susan explained the situation to the person on the other end of the line. "I have an idea," she announced when Susan was finished.

"What?"

"Since you're obviously going to have to pretty much start from scratch on the bathrooms, why don't you remodel? Maybe something like this would be nice." She held up a two-page spread displaying an elaborately decorated bath.

Susan took the publication and studied it. "This looks more like your house than mine, but, you know, I've always wanted an all-white bathroom. And I've been thinking the same thing: Since we're going to have to replace the tubs in both rooms and the toilet—"

"Commode," Kathleen corrected her. "That's what plumbers call it. Or w.c. for water closet. For some reason they don't like using the *t* word."

"Okay. The commode is cracked in one bathroom and more than half of the tiles on the walls and floors are going to have to be replaced in both rooms." The lights over the desk flickered on. "Hey, look at that. We have power. Can water be far behind?"

"Maybe sooner than you think," Jerry said, entering the room and sitting down next to his wife. "It may not get above the first floor, but you'll have running water in the kitchen and the half-bath on the first floor—and in the basement. At least that's what they're working on up there." He pointed to the ceiling.

Susan looked up from a photograph of a bathroom that was mirrored on the ceiling as well as on all four walls. "Do you think anyone ever brushes their teeth in a room like this?"

"Only if they have live-in help," Kathleen answered. "Soap scum isn't an integral part of the designer look."

"I have an idea," Jed said, joining the group. "Why don't we just copy that design for both baths on the second floor—and we won't connect the water so no one can use them. They'll always look perfect. And if we don't have water, maybe we can claim that we're just redecorating, not remodeling."

"What difference would that make?"

"Then we wouldn't have to worry about applying for permits and inspections," Jed explained.

"And you wouldn't have to worry about who replaces Simon Fairweather," Jerry added. "You should have heard what they were saying upstairs."

"What?" Susan asked.

"You know how people talk. . . ." Jed began.

"They were saying that someone from a contracting company in town was threatening to murder Simon Fairweather," Jerry added.

"Something called Cory Construction. Were they on the list that I gave you?" Jed said to his wife.

"Not yet," she muttered, more to herself than to anyone in the room. "Are you going to close that window now that the air-conditioning is back on?" she added to her husband, who had turned his back to the rest of the room.

"Sure, but that isn't what I was doing. I was wondering why there's another plumbing truck pulling into the driveway."

FOUR

"PROMISE ME THAT MORE PLUMBERS AREN'T GOING TO TURN up on the doorstep."

Susan rubbed her eyes. "If they are, they're going to be waiting outside until tomorrow morning. I'm taking Clue for a quick trip around the block and then locking up for the night. . . . You're sure it's okay if we turn on the water in the bath down here? It won't back up the pipes and leak out of the ceiling—or anything horrible like that?" she asked her husband as she sorted through the magazines and sheets of paper on the desk in front of her.

"Positive. The men explained everything to me before they left just now." Susan wondered exactly how much this day's work was going to cost them, but she decided now wasn't the time to ask. "You don't have a thing to worry about. They said we can even use the dishwasher and the washing machine in the basement."

"I didn't know that 'we' did the laundry," Susan said. She was feeling a little cranky. Their month alone certainly wasn't beginning the way she had imagined it would. Now, instead of showering à deux, she could do the laundry alone. So much for change. "Do you want to walk around the block with me?"

"Sure. And you can tell me what you've been doing for the past few hours."

"The same thing I'm going to be doing for a few more hours."

"You're kidding! It's been a long day. Aren't you going to bed?"

"I want to make sure that everything's ready for the contractor tomorrow."

"You found someone? Susan, that's great! Of course, I don't suppose he can start right away."

"It's possible," she said quietly. "He had a job planned that was recently canceled or something."

"Well, anything you can do to speed it along would be great. It's going to be difficult living here with just the two of us, but think what it'll be like if we don't get everything fixed by the time the kids get home."

Susan didn't want to consider that thought for even a moment. As she got up from the desk, the phone rang.

"Who could be calling this late?" Jed asked irritably.

"It's probably Kathleen. I don't suppose you could walk the dog. . . ."

Jed smiled. "Sure. It's a beautiful night. We'll both enjoy it—unless we meet that monster from over on Chestnut."

"Jed! How can you call him a monster?"

"He's a menace. The neighborhood Lothario. And I feel like an idiot being followed around by a horny poodle."

Susan just laughed and answered the phone. As she had expected it was Kathleen, who wasted no time in coming to the point.

"Did you get them?"

"Yes. I couldn't believe it," Susan answered.

"Do you have time to tell me what happened?"

"Wait a sec. Jed's just walking out the door with Clue." Susan paused for a moment after the door had been slammed by her husband. "I'm not sure he'd be thrilled if he knew why I called Cory Construction almost immediately."

"Probably not."

"If they're awful, I'll pay them off and find someone else. It won't be the first time I've done it," Susan explained, remembering the two plumbers that afternoon.

"But you do know something about them, don't you?"

"Not much. Just what they told me, in fact."

"What did they tell you?"

"Well, it took a while to get hold of them. Jed and I have

both spent a lot of the day leaving messages on various answering machines and voice mails. Cory Construction has a particularly short tape or their machine isn't working properly or something. It took three calls to leave the entire message. But they called back promptly—maybe because I said we were looking for a company to work on a major renovation project."

"Good idea."

"I've done this before, remember? And it doesn't take a genius to realize that the bigger the job, the more profit there is for the contractor."

"So what did Cory Construction say?"

"The man who returned my calls is named Ken Cory. It's his company and he's also a carpenter. I think that's a good sign, don't you? I mean, hands-on experience is awfully important."

"What did he say?" Kathleen persisted.

"Well, I explained what had happened here. At least the damage I can see. I'm a little unclear about the main drain-pipe breaking—or cracking or leaking or whatever—that caused all this. So I told him about the walls and the toilets and the third-floor half-bath, and that I was thinking that we should go ahead and remodel all the bathrooms while we're at it."

"Could you hear the drooling over the phone?"

"I know. It does sound a bit like I'm trying to eliminate our life's savings, doesn't it? But it's the truth. And then Ken—he asked me to call him Ken—said that the job they had been about to begin had just been canceled. The couple decided they wanted a divorce more than a gourmet kitchen, apparently. So it's possible that he could start immediately. He said he'd be here first thing in the morning to talk about it."

"Fast work."

"Do you think it could be ... whatchamacallit ... kismet? You know, something that was meant to be."

"That's one way of looking at it."

"What do you mean?"

"Susan, if I know you, you're sitting someplace surrounded by magazines and floor plans."

"Sure, but—"

"And you're probably thinking just as much about Simon Fairweather's murder and what sort of connection it has to Cory Construction. What happened to that nice, selfish month you've been planning for Jed and yourself? And which you deserve after over twenty years of parenting, I might add."

"I'm not giving it up."

"So you're not planning to hire Cory Construction to fix your house and beginning investigating the murder at the same time."

"Not at all. I only called Cory Construction because Brett asked me to." Susan heard how defensive she sounded. "Kath, I know you're only thinking of me ..."

"And of your house and of your marriage. Susan, does Jed know about the note found on Simon Fairweather's desk?"

"No, but that note isn't why Ken Cory is coming over tomorrow morning. It's because he's free to start work immediately. And Ken Cory is a carpenter as well as the owner of the business," Susan reminded her.

"Is this the way you hired the company that remodeled your kitchen? Or the company that added the laundry room to your basement?"

"No, but neither of those jobs was an emergency," Susan reminded her, feeling she had the upper hand here. "Kath, there's no way to shower in this house now. We only have a half-bathroom working. Even if Simon Fairweather hadn't been murdered, I wouldn't have the luxury of waiting to choose the perfect company. I may not even have the chance to pick out the perfect tiles and bathtubs. Although I was thinking of a whirlpool and a separate shower in the master bath like you have. Do you use the whirlpool a lot?"

"Not recently. I can't get in and out of the tub without risking a fall. I'm sticking to showers until little what's-her-name is born."

"No wonder my decision to hire Cory Construction is

bugging you. After all, I took almost twelve hours to hire a contractor—you haven't managed to find a name for your daughter and you've had six months."

"Almost seven since the amniocentesis, actually," Kathleen said. "But I don't want the poor thing to end up with some sort of silly nickname like Bananas. Do you know, I'm not even sure why we started calling him that!"

"Well, it's a mistake that he seems to be having no trouble correcting. That's one determined kid you've got there," Susan said.

"True. I hate to rub it in, but I have to go to the bathroom—and it's getting late for us pregnant people. Why don't I stop over early tomorrow to see what you're thinking about doing to the bathrooms?"

"Great. Sleep well."

"Ha!"

It was Kathleen's final word for the day. Susan hung up and got back to her planning. She wanted to have at least a general idea of what she was aiming for to show Ken Cory tomorrow morning. The third-floor bathroom, tucked under the attic eaves, was a piece of cake. A new floor, possibly of nice, neat white tiles, and then the old white porcelain sink and toilet could be replaced with new white porcelain fixtures. Over the years she had thought of making the entire attic into a guest room, but first things first. She had to get the two baths on the second floor in working order.

Pleased with her own sense of order, Susan looked down at the neat drawing lying on the table in front of her. It represented the two bathrooms on the second floor and proved beyond a reasonable doubt that Chrissy's artistic talent hadn't been inherited from her mother. She was so involved in her work that she didn't hear the return of her husband and their dog.

"What are you doing?"

She looked up to find her husband leaning over her shoulder. Clue had flung herself in a corner of the room in a canine imitation of Camille. "Long walk," she commented casually.

"That damn poodle," Jed responded before returning to his question. "What are you doing?" he repeated.

"Trying to figure out exactly what we want in the new bathrooms. We really should take this as the opportunity to get the bathrooms we've always wanted, don't you think?"

"I thought we had the bathrooms we always wanted—except for the color schemes," he added quickly, remembering their conversation earlier in the day.

"Sort of," Susan said slowly. "But think of it this way, Jed. We have to buy new tiles, bathtubs, and toilets for both rooms, so why not get something interesting."

"Like a separate tub and shower in the master bath? Does that say whirlpool?" He pointed at her drawing. "And is that a bidet?"

"Of course not. A bidet would be an affectation," Susan said indignantly, taking off her glasses and looking closely at the drawing. "That's a built-in laundry hamper and there are recessed shelves for storing towels and things."

"How about a heater built into the wall while we're at it?"

"Good idea! I'm really being practical about this, Jed. And I was thinking about recessed lighting in the ceiling and over the shelves—and also in the tub. It's so difficult to see properly to shave my legs. Do you think lights in the ceiling over the tub are safe?"

"If they're not, the building inspector will let you know, I'm sure. That type of thing must be in the code."

"What code?"

"The building code. This town follows the U.B.C.—the Universal Building Code. You must remember that from the problems we had venting the laundry room through the garage."

"Oh, yes," Susan lied. She did know that there had been extensive conversations on the subject, but she had tuned them out, preferring to put an intelligent (she hoped) look on her face and think of more interesting things. Her excuse was that her husband enjoyed the technical aspects of any remodeling job. She hoped it was true. "Maybe things will be different now that Simon Fairweather is dead."

"The law is the law. Someone else will just have to enforce it, that's all. But why don't you explain these drawings to me?" he requested.

"First, I have some questions for you." Susan grabbed a pile of pages obviously ripped from glossy shelter magazines. She chose two sheets and held them out to her husband. "Which do you like better?"

"I don't really like pink or . . . what is that color? Maroon?"

"I'm not talking about the color. I'm talking about the floor plans, although I like the pattern in the tile floor here in this one." She pointed. "And it's really peach, not pink."

Jed was more interested in her diagrams than in the photographs. "You're planning on turning this into a big project, aren't you?" he asked slowly.

"It is a big project—and as long as we're going to have to do it anyway, we might as well do it right. Don't you think?"

"I think those may turn out to be famous last words. But you're the one with great taste in the family. I'm sure you know best. Just add a radiant heater in the bathroom we use and choose anything but pink, please. Or apricot. Or peach. Or mango—"

"Mangoes are orange."

"Whatever. I'm going to go upstairs now. I'm exhausted. But you can wake me up when you come to bed if you'd like. I'm not that tired."

Susan smiled. "I'm just going to spend a few more minutes here. Then I'll shower . . . Oh. Well, I guess I'll just wash my face. I'll be up soon."

She was back to her drawings before her husband had left the room. The bathroom that her kids and guests used wasn't going to be much of a problem, she decided. She knew the fixtures she wanted: reproductions of English porcelain that she had admired in the home of a friend. And brass and porcelain faucets. Probably white and black tiles on the floor in a traditional pattern that would go with the rest of the house. Maybe pinstripe wallpaper. She could add color with towels and accessories. Although it would be nice to replace that ugly jalousie window that someone had put in years ago. She looked down at her drawings. One Andersen double-hung window couldn't add that much to the cost. . . .

Truthfully, it wasn't the cost of that bathroom that worried her. She looked down at the drawings she had made of the master bathroom of her dreams. For the next few hours Susan was involved in plans for watery iridescent tiles, extra-large bathtubs, shimmering mirrors, and everything else she had ever wanted in a bathroom. She drew lines on her diagrams, erased and redrew them, happy to be planning before the reality of finance and workmen got in her way. It wasn't until she was washing her face in the tiny half-bath next to the kitchen that she remembered her conversation with Kathleen.

She returned to the desk and pulled a new notebook from the desk drawer, placing it on top of the pile. She'd just spend a few minutes, she decided, making some notes about Simon Fairweather's murder.

FIVE

Susan heard the knocking in her sleep. She thought it was a dream although it seemed a little odd that Jed was having the same dream.

"The door," he muttered, pulling a pillow over his head. "Smmm at dur."

Susan correctly interpreted his statement. "I'll go find out who it is," she said, trying to reach the floor with her feet. They had managed to have a small personal celebration after all, late last night, and she wanted nothing more than to stay in bed. "I'm coming," she called out, and headed for the bathroom. And then she remembered. "Damn."

Jed sat up in bed. "The bathrooms. That must be the investigator from our insurance company. I thought he wasn't coming until just before noon."

"Probably Cory Construction," Susan said, grabbing yesterday's jeans off the floor and yanking them on. The T-shirt on top of the pile in her dresser drawer and plastic sandals from the closet completed her hastily assembled ensemble and then she ran down the stairs.

The man standing on her doorstep didn't look like any of the carpenters Susan had hired before. In fact, he looked a lot like the professor in the abnormal psychology class she had taken during her sophomore year of college. But that was just prejudice, she reminded herself, thinking of the charming and well-dressed young men who leaped around roofs and crawled under beams on one of her favorite PBS shows. And Ken Cory probably didn't wear chinos, loafers, and a madras sports jacket while he worked. He brushed his slightly long sandy hair off his forehead, straightened his horn-rimmed glasses, and smiled. "You must be Mrs. Henshaw. I'm Ken Cory."

"Of course. Won't you come in?" Susan offered, opening the door wider. She could hear Clue scratching, apparently trapped behind a closed door nearby. "Could you wait a minute while I get my dog? You do like dogs, don't you? I mean, you don't mind working in a house with a dog around?"

"I love dogs." The answer was accompanied by a bright smile. "What kind do you have?"

Susan didn't have to answer, as Clue had discovered an escape route and was leaping around with joy at the sight of a friendly face.

"Hey! A golden. I grew up with a golden retriever." Ken Cory knelt down and allowed Clue to taste his face.

"Why don't I walk the dog while you make some coffee and then we can all talk?" Jed appeared at the top of the stairs, tucking his chambray shirt into the waist of his jeans.

Susan introduced the two men, thinking that they should exchange clothing; Jed looked more like a workman than Ken Cory did. "I'm spread out in the study. Why don't I show you the stuff and then you can look it over while I make the coffee," she suggested to Ken as the dog pulled Jed out the door.

"Great. Back there?"

"Yes. How did you know?" Susan asked, leading the way.

"This is a fairly common house plan in this part of Connecticut. Although yours has some unusual features. I particularly like the chestnut wainscotting here in the hallway."

"We added that ourselves," Susan said.

"Who did the stenciling around the ceiling?"

"My daughter."

"Good job." He looked more closely. "In fact, it's an excellent job for an amateur."

"She's an art student."

"Nothing like having talent in the family," Ken Cory said, sitting down where Susan indicated.

"Too bad one of us didn't take up plumbing," Susan said, handing him the sheets of paper she had spent hours poring over the night before. "We could use something more practical around here right now."

"Cory Construction can take care of the practical things—"

"I'll go make some coffee," Susan interrupted, resisting the urge to hire him on the spot. She knew that Jed would object if she hired the company without his approval. And so would she. If she took all the responsibility, she would end up taking all the blame if something went wrong. She hurried off to the kitchen.

It wasn't easy to make coffee, but Susan managed, getting water from the bathroom and moving her grinder and coffeemaker to the table instead of the counter to avoid treading through the mess on the floor. She'd be glad when the insurance person had finished looking around and they could clean up. It took longer than usual and she was carrying a heavy tray (she'd pulled some small Danish pastries from the freezer and heated them in the microwave) back to the study when Jed and Clue returned.

"I filled her food dish and put it in her dog-run. I don't think she should be left alone in the kitchen until it's cleaned up. And there's coffee and Danish for the rest of us," she said.

"Looks good. I'll take her out and join you. What did he think of the damage?"

"I . . . I decided you should show him around. I just gave him the plans I made last night." She hurried off, not wanting to hear any criticism of her priorities. Besides, she was anxious to know what a professional thought of her ideas for the master bathroom.

Ken Cory was sitting at the desk, apparently too engrossed in her drawings to notice her entrance.

"What do you think?" Susan asked, setting the tray on a corner of the desk.

"Looks wonderful." He eyed the tray.

"Actually, I was asking about the plans I made," Susan admitted, pouring coffee into a cup and handing it to him. "There's milk and sugar. And please have some Danish."

"Thanks." He helped himself. "I'm impressed with this," he added, motioning to her plans. "Did your daughter draw them?"

"No, she's in Europe for a month. I'm afraid that's just my own inept scribbling. But you probably want to see exactly what happened. My husband can show you around. He's just feeding Clue."

"Clue? That's the dog's name?"

Susan nodded. She didn't want to explain that her family had named the puppy Susan Hasn't Got a Clue in honor of some of her more difficult moments during a murder investigation. "You know, I was wondering if we could replace the window in the master bathroom with something more interesting."

"Like a round window or a hexagon?"

"Exactly!" Susan felt she had found a kindred soul.

"Sure can. But you have to remember that most of them don't open and the ones that do are pretty expensive."

"Everything is going to be pretty expensive." Jed had joined them.

Ken put down his food and stood quickly. "I haven't seen the damage yet."

"Maybe we should start there," Jed suggested.

"The house is a mess . . ." Susan began, and then realized how stupid she sounded.

"Don't worry. I'm used to it." The two men left her alone.

Susan absently ate a couple of poppyseed Danish while trying to decide whether or not it was necessary for the only window in the master bath to open. She had moved on to wondering if maybe a black and white color scheme was slightly . . . well, slightly colorless . . . by the time the men returned. They were laughing. Susan suspected some male bonding had taken place over the cracked pipes.

Ken broke off as soon as he saw her. (Jed didn't.) "You

sure weren't exaggerating when we spoke on the phone yesterday. You have a true mess on your hands here."

"Luckily, Cory Construction can start on the job as soon as the insurance inspector leaves," Jed surprised Susan by saying.

"Even sooner, if you include planning and ordering all the fixtures," Ken added.

"Are you sure enough about what you want for us to go ahead now?" Jed checked with his wife. "It usually takes you longer than this to make decorating decisions. And the color of tile and the position of a window isn't easily changed."

"Actually, I've been thinking about the second-floor bathrooms for a while," Susan admitted.

"I suspected that all those magazines didn't just appear overnight," Jed said, glancing at the pile of reading material covering his desk. "But you really know what you want?"

"I don't have all the specifics. Like I know I want the sink that the Kenneys have in their guest bathroom, but I don't know who manufactures it—"

"I have dozens of catalogs in the truck," Ken interrupted. "If you're really anxious to get started, you two'd better spend some time figuring out exactly what you want. The sooner you decide, the sooner I can order. And I can't give you a final price until all the specs are in place."

"Sounds like we're going to have a busy morning," Jed said, pulling up a chair and sitting down next to his wife.

"I'll go get the catalogs from the truck and then I'd better head back to my office and start getting your job organized."

"You'll bring back the preliminary figures?" Jed looked up to ask.

"Absolutely."

Susan waited until Ken Cory had returned with a foot-high pile of catalogs and then left again before she asked Jed if he was completely satisfied with the decision to hire Cory Construction.

"Do you think it's a mistake?" he asked anxiously. "I

thought you were hot on this company. Did you hear something against them?"

"No, nothing," Susan lied. As she was thinking about that, the doorbell rang and someone opened the door without waiting for an answer. "Susan? Jed? It's me. Kathleen."

"Come on in, Kath. We're in the study," Susan yelled back.

"I'll be there as soon as I visit your bathroom," Kathleen called as she passed the doorway. "Is there water?"

"Just on the first floor," Jed called out, frowning over the Kohler price list. "Black bathtubs?" He flipped to the back of the pamphlet. "Good lord! What are they making these faucets out of? Solid gold?"

Susan didn't respond. She knew it would take a while for Jed to adjust to the prices of things he had taken for granted all these years.

"And look at the difference in price between an ordinary cast-iron bathtub and a whirlpool."

Susan started to scratch out the rectangle on her plans for the master bath.

"Of course, you could get a whirlpool that's made from acrylic for a lot less," he continued.

She retraced her original.

"But I'll bet no one uses it after the first few months."

She just shook her head and reached for the catalog of Andersen windows. "Did you know that you can buy both hexagon and octagon windows?" she asked casually.

"Do they open? A window should open," Jed said.

Susan made another mark on her design and then returned to the catalog. "There are also parallelograms and diamonds and trapezoids. . . ."

Jed stopped writing numbers down on the edge of a used envelope and looked up at his wife. "Sue, why are we talking about windows? The windows in the bathroom are fine. It's the inside wall that we have to worry about."

"As long as we're doing this, I thought we could get rid of that ugly window in our bathroom. You know how we've always said we hated it."

"Okay, but I don't think we need to worry about parallelograms and other exotic shapes."

"I was just commenting," she assured him. She wasn't even sure what a parallelogram was.

"You two look busy," Kathleen said, coming into the room with an empty mug in her hand. "I hope that's still hot." She nodded at the coffeepot.

"I thought you were giving up coffee during your pregnancy," Susan said.

"I don't think I have to worry about damaging this little sweetie's development so late in the pregnancy," Kathleen said, choosing a Danish pastry from the plate. "Have you chosen a contractor yet?"

"Cory Construction," Jed said, while Susan frowned at her friend. Kathleen had asked that question just a little too casually.

"That's right. Ken Cory was due over here this morning, wasn't he?" Kathleen asked.

"Yes. Susan explained her plans and I showed him around the disaster area. He's a nice guy, and due to a last-minute change of plans, his company is free to start right away, and you know how Susan always checks out everyone on the town hotline. So we hired him. He left all these catalogs and he'll be back to finalize things this afternoon. That reminds me, I want to get our insurance policy out of the safe-deposit box before that inspector shows up."

Susan glanced at her watch. "You better hurry up and do it then."

"If the inspector appears, just show him around. Don't sign anything until we have a second chance to look it over."

"Fine with me." Susan wondered why Kathleen was kicking her under the table. And she asked her why as soon as they were alone together.

"I just wondered if Jed knew that you hired Cory Construction just because you were investigating the murder."

"No, and I'd appreciate it if you didn't mention it. I don't want to worry him."

SIX

THERE WAS LOUD MUSIC FALLING DOWN THE STAIRWAY AS Susan led Clue into the house. For a moment she thought one of the children was home. Then she realized that neither teen ever listened to country-and-western ballads. She optimistically ordered the dog to stay and climbed the stairs.

"Hello? Jed? Is that you?"

It wasn't Jed. The music was emanating from a gray boom box liberally covered with black fingerprints. Susan assumed the fingerprints would match the fingers of the heavyset man peering into the hole in her bathroom wall. He wore a greasy T-shirt with green Sears, Roebuck work pants. He had graying hair, tan skin, and what looked like a dozen gold chains around his grimy neck. Susan could see three crosses and at least four other religious medals tangled in the hair on his chest. Seeing her, he reached over and turned down the volume on his radio . . . slightly.

"YOU MUST BE THE LADY OF THE HOUSE," he announced loudly.

Susan nodded, trying to put an appropriate smile on her face.

"I'M BUNS," he added.

"What?" He had said it loudly, but she still thought she must have misheard.

"BUNS," he repeated a little more loudly. "DON'T ASK WHY, BUT IT'S WHAT THE GUYS ALL CALL ME."

"But who are you?"

"PLUMBER. I'M ONE OF YOUR PLUMBERS. YOU

GOT TWO. THIS HERE'S GONNA BE A REAL BIG PLUMBING JOB."

She had spent over a hundred dollars to get rid of those men yesterday and look who had replaced them. Susan felt a headache gathering behind her temples. "Do you think you could turn down that . . . the radio?" she requested loudly.

"YOU DON'T HAVE TO WORRY ABOUT MY MUSIC," he insisted, doing as she requested. "I DON'T LISTEN TO NO HEAVY METAL. NONE OF THAT SATANIC SHIT FOR ME, IF YOU'LL PARDON THE EXPRESSION. YOU KNOW WHAT THOSE CULTS DO TO PEOPLE?"

"I think I hear the phone ringing," Susan told him, backing away. Actually, she was fairly sure the ringing was coming from inside her head, but an hour or two alone might cure it.

"YOU THE LADY THAT INVESTIGATES MURDERS, AIN'T YOU?"

"I have in the past," she admitted reluctantly.

"YOU GOING TO FIND OUT WHO KILLED SIMON FAIRWEATHER?"

"No, I—"

"YOU FIND HIM, I'LL GIVE HIM AN AWARD. THAT SLIMY BASTARD REALLY SCREWED ME. I'LL TELL YOU ABOUT IT SOMETIME."

"I'm not investigating," Susan repeated. "And I'm pretty busy now."

"WE'LL BE SEEING A LOT OF EACH OTHER IN THE NEXT FEW WEEKS—OR MONTHS," he added, chuckling, as he reached out to turn up his radio. And he turned back to his examination of the hole in the wall, giving Susan the opportunity to see for herself the reason for his nickname.

She frowned and decided to continue up to the third floor. She wanted to check out the clearance under the eaves and contrast it with some measurements in the Kohler catalog. It might just be possible, she thought, to add a tiny tub in the far corner of the room. As long as they were going to be doing so much work, surely one extra bathtub would add little to the cost. And it would be nice to have a third-floor guest room in case there were grandchildren in her future. . . .

This time, she thought, stopping on the third-floor landing, it was certainly the ghost of Chad who was playing the local college station she was hearing. She gingerly opened the door. Warm, musty air from under the eaves wrapped itself about her, and a good-looking young man standing in the middle of her attic turned around and smiled. "Hi."

"Hi." Susan felt herself begin to slip into giggly adolescent girl mode and made an effort to pull herself together. "I heard your radio downstairs. I'm Mrs. Henshaw," she explained, offering her hand.

He jumped over and turned off the radio. "I'm sorry. I didn't know there was anyone else at home, and Art never hears anything." He nodded toward the bathroom and his blond hair swept his broad shoulders. Susan could see an older man bending over the largest toolbox Susan had ever seen. A bright yellow Sony Walkman was plugged into his ears.

"That's Art Young. He's the head carpenter on this project and my boss. He can't hear anything," he added as Susan started to speak. "He has a headset on. He's listening to his tapes."

"He doesn't like your music?" Susan asked politely.

"He's boning up on general information this week. He wants to be a *Jeopardy!* contestant. And you wouldn't believe how much information those guys have to know just to get chosen to go on the show!"

"So I've heard," Susan commented. "I don't think I know your name. . . ."

"Wow. I'm sorry. I'm Kyle Barnes." He offered her a large callused hand.

"Hi, Kyle. Can I ask what you're both doing up here?"

"Measuring. We have to get the lumber order into the yard before it closes in a few hours if we're going to accept delivery tomorrow."

"So you're a carpenter?" Susan asked, staring at his LIVE

TO SKI—SKI TO LIVE AT BRECKENRIDGE T-shirt. He didn't appear to be much older than her son.

"I am these days," Kyle answered cheerfully. "This was supposed to be just a summer job—I finished my freshman year of college last June—but now I'm thinking about taking a year or so off. I can work at this until Christmas and then I'll have enough money to bum around Europe for a while. I may even find a job at a resort in Switzerland, you know?"

"Sounds like fun."

"The highest mountain in Switzerland is the Dufourspitze. It's 15,203 feet." Art Young had removed his headset. "Most people think it's Mont Blanc, but that's actually in France."

"Really?" Susan feigned polite interest, then introduced herself. What she was most interested in was the clearance between her eaves and the floorboards, not the mountains of Europe.

"Yup. I'm past that geography stuff though. Going on to jewels and minerals of the world now." Art Young was slightly chubby and boyish-looking. His hair was cut in a style that had been popular in the fifties and his nose was dusted with freckles. In his jeans and plaid shirt, he made Susan think of Jerry Mathers, the Beaver, blown up rather than grown up.

"I understand you're interested in being a *Jeopardy!* contestant."

"I'm going to be one, ma'am. All it takes is determination and concentration. Last time I screwed up the geography part. But I didn't care as much back then. This time I'll be more prepared for my audition. I'm also growing bonsai—they're ugly little trees, never make much in the way of lumber, but it will look good on my bio, don't you think? They like people with interesting hobbies."

"Really?" She was trying hard not to stare at the note hanging from the toolbox. After all, she was there to check out the bathroom, not to investigate a murder.

"Yo, Artie, man." A young man with blond dreadlocks had joined them.

"Frankie, you might want to talk like a high school graduate. This here's Mrs. Henshaw. The lady of the house." Art Young introduced Susan. "This here Frankie is one of your plumbers. You have any leaks after this project, you blame him."

Susan smiled weakly. This was all getting to be a bit much. Maybe they could learn to live without water in the bathrooms. . . .

Frankie took the time to nod to Susan before returning to the reason for his visit. "I need to see one of you downstairs. If there's going to be any changes in the venting system of those bathrooms, someone better figure it out now—before the window order gets picked up."

"I hadn't decided on the window shape," Susan protested.

"All I know is that there's an opening hexagon in the diagram I was given," Frankie replied. "If you have a problem with that, you better give Ken Cory a call."

"Yes, I will. Right away," Susan agreed, heading down the stairs to her bedroom and the phone.

Clue was nestled in the middle of the quilt on the bed, a look of extreme contentment on her face. Susan knew that she was doing nothing for the discipline in the house by allowing the animal to stay, but how many times had she heard the expression "let sleeping dogs lie"? Why fight the wisdom of the ages, especially when she had more important things to deal with, she thought, flipping through the Cs in the phonebook. Impatiently, she dialed.

And got an answering machine.

She hadn't remembered the number, but she remembered the answering machine with its skimpy time allowance. Her message was short and to the point. "This is Susan Henshaw. Please call me immediately."

Susan hung up and stretched out across the bed in the space Clue had generously left. Maybe she should have left her home phone number. She found the number again and called back, adding "It's important" to the message before lying down again.

Clue nudged Susan's arm.

"You know what I need, Clue? A snack."

Apparently Clue felt the same way. The two of them were in the kitchen staring into the refrigerator in record time. Susan was juggling low-fat cheese spread, crackers, and a dish of leftover tomato, basil, and mozzarella salad when someone knocked on the back door. Susan called out a greeting and a strange man appeared.

Susan was becoming accustomed to seeing strangers within her territory, but this man was different. He was wearing a suit. She had a moment or two of confusion until he explained that he was from their insurance company.

"Your husband called the office and asked that we do our inspection as soon as possible," he explained. "And I can see that you wouldn't want to live with this mess for any longer than necessary," he added, looking around the room. "Have you found a contractor yet?" He put his black briefcase on the countertop.

Susan, remembering her husband's admonition about offering extra information to this man, didn't answer immediately, and he continued to talk while removing a Polaroid camera from the case and proceeding to take three pictures of the room. "The rest of the damage is on the floor above this?" he asked, knowing the answer.

"And on the floor above that," Susan answered. "Do you want me to show you the way?"

"Please."

"Just let me put the dog in the yard first."

"Take your time. I need to get the rest of my materials together."

He was rummaging in his briefcase as Susan pulled Clue out the door.

And he still hadn't found what he was looking for when she returned to the kitchen. Susan sighed and picked up the broom that was waiting in the corner. She might as well begin to clean up this mess. After all, the photographs of this room had been taken.

"Why are you doing that?"

"Excuse me?" Susan looked down at the substantial pile

of plaster and slop that she had accumulated by taking three swipes at the floor with the broom.

"Don't all those trucks in front of your house belong to the contractor's crew?"

Susan nodded.

"They're going to tear down before they start building up. I wouldn't bother to clean if I were you—you'll be doing enough of that in the next few months." He chuckled ominously and followed Susan from the room.

It turned out it wasn't actually necessary for Susan to direct the insurance investigator from damage location to damage location. He could have merely followed the filthy footprints up the stairs and through the hallway. "I can't believe how messy all this is," she muttered at one point.

"You think this is messy? Wait until these people start to work" came the reply. "I guess you haven't had a lot of work done on your house," he added, snapping a photo of the gaping hole in the bathroom wall.

"We had the kitchen remodeled and a laundry room added in the basement," Susan protested.

"But both of those jobs were next to outside entrances, right?"

Susan agreed that he had hit the nail on the head.

"But this job—first, second, and third floors—is going to be different," he suggested. "This job is taking place all over the house."

Susan, who remembered how the plaster dust had invaded every corner of the living room when her kitchen had been remodeled, began to understand what he was talking about.

"Of course," he continued. "That's not going to be your biggest problem. Your biggest problem is going to be Simon Fairweather. In Hancock the biggest problem in any remodeling job is always Simon Fairweather."

"Simon Fairweather? I don't understand," Susan protested. "How could he be a problem now that he's dead?"

"Dead?" The man seemed taken aback. "Well, what do you know. So who murdered the son of a gun?"

"Exactly how did you know that Simon Fairweather was murdered?"

Susan turned and found that they had been followed up the stairs by her husband and Brett. "I don't believe Mrs. Henshaw told you that Simon Fairweather was murdered. I'd like to know how you heard about it," Brett repeated, a serious look on his face.

Jed, standing at the police chief's side, was wearing a similar expression.

SEVEN

By THE TIME THE INSURANCE INVESTIGATOR HAD EXPLAINED that he had only heard negative things about Simon Fairweather and that he had never actually met the man and was continuing his inspection accompanied by a grim-looking Jed, Susan was more confused than ever.

"Why are you back here?" she asked Brett when they were alone together.

"We have a problem—nothing serious, but I need to speak with you. And Patricia Fairweather is back in town. I was wondering if you would come along when I meet her. It might make her more comfortable and we could chat on the drive."

"Fine."

"But this has to be done right away."

Susan decided to ignore her grubby clothes and go. A recent widow probably wouldn't notice what anyone was wearing. Besides, she wasn't going to resist Brett's offer. Usually she had to plead and connive to go along on a police questioning. She followed him to his patrol car.

"You said something about Patricia Fairweather living in Hancock for a long time," Brett began as he steered the car onto the parkway.

"A native. At least that's what I've heard," Susan answered, scowling at her shoes. They were scuffed brown suede, old and dirty. Well, she'd just keep her feet tucked underneath her.

"Anything wrong?" Brett asked, noticing her expression.

"Nothing important. Let me see. Patricia Fairweather.

Well, she was born a Storm, and she and Simon moved into the Storm family home shortly after they were married. I don't know the exact address. It's that gigantic dark green Victorian with the cream and burnt-orange trim up on the hill—you probably know it. It's been expanded and remodeled over the years, of course. That's one of the things people get angry about when Simon Fairweather is mentioned—"

"Excuse me for interrupting. You're telling me that Patricia Storm married Simon Fairweather and became—"

"Patricia Fairweather. I know. And I'm sure she's gotten tired of hearing cute comments about it over the years."

"Understandably so. I wasn't going to mention it. I just wanted to get everything straight. I gather they weren't married recently."

"Probably twenty or thirty years ago. But that's just a guess."

"Any children?"

"None. I'm sure about that. People have mentioned it to me more than once in relation to Simon's position."

"How does having or not having children relate to being a building inspector?" Brett asked.

"His job was to approve or disapprove of any building project that fell outside of the town's standards and he frequently rejected plans that called for major expansion."

"So?"

"So he lived in a huge house that his wife inherited and they had no children. The general feeling was that he lacked a personal understanding of the fact that no house is big enough when you have a couple of preschoolers—or a teenager."

"And did the Storms need such a large house? Was it a large family?"

"There were four girls. Patricia is the youngest. She's also the only one who still lives here in town."

"Which is why she moved into the house?"

"I don't know about that, but by the time she got married, her older sisters had moved out and established their own homes. In fact, I think that her father died fairly close to the time of her marriage and her mother moved in with one of the other sisters—in North Carolina, I believe. I know it was someplace warmer than Connecticut."

"So this recently married couple moved into a large house in the best part of town?"

"Yes. I suppose they expected to fill it with children, but then none came. On the other hand, Simon was exactly the type of man to live in a large, old Victorian. Everyone says that he had worked wonders with the house—and that he'd done all the work himself."

"Do you know what he used for cash?"

"Not really. I do know that he created an apartment above a carriage house on the property and they rented that out for years and years. Also he ran a contracting business and I imagine it was profitable. And he subdivided the property behind his house and built two houses there. And then he bought some land down near the creek and built a few houses on that."

Brett nodded. "Those fake Victorians that look like they belong in Disney World."

"They're very popular," Susan said, although she agreed with him.

"But he didn't build them anymore," Brett said, not bothering to argue about questions of taste.

"Not for years and years. He became the building inspector and stopped contracting. I suppose there must be laws about that type of thing—conflict of interest and all."

"Let's get back to Patricia Fairweather. What do you know about her beside the fact that she's a native and she takes classes like you do at the Art Center?"

"Don't think that everyone who takes classes there is like me, just a housewife looking for some sort of creative outlet."

"I don't—" Brett began.

"Patricia is a serious craftsperson—an artist, really. She was a weaver and she does fabulous watercolors. She only began to work in clay in the last few years and she's not just competent, she's developed her own style. And it's wonderful to take a class with her—she's willing to help out the most incompetent student, which in our class was me," Susan admitted.

Brett chuckled. "Sounds like we wouldn't have any suspects if anyone had murdered Patricia Fairweather."

"Except for Simon Fairweather."

"Exactly what do you mean by that?"

"It's just a thought. . . ."

"What is just a thought?" Brett insisted on knowing.

"Well, it's possible that Simon Fairweather hit his wife."

"Simon Fairweather was a wife beater?"

"Not necessarily a wife beater, it's just that he hit her once that I heard about."

"A man who hits his wife is a wife beater. Even if it only happens once. And it usually happens more—much more—than that." Brett's tone of voice didn't allow for argument, not that Susan disagreed with him.

She was silent for a moment, looking out the window as they drove down the quiet, tree-lined street. Susan knew, better than many, the pain that lay behind some of those elegant, brass-trimmed doors. But imagining Patricia Fairweather in the role of subservient, abused wife was difficult.

"She doesn't seem like that," she began.

"Like what?"

"Like someone who would let that happen to her. You know, let someone else hurt her—especially not more than once. She's always struck me as a very strong woman."

"You know how I respect your intuition about people," Brett said, not taking his eyes off the road, "but there are some women in this town who have been abused by members of their family, husbands in particular, whose identity would shock you. Believe me."

Susan knew Brett was too professional and discreet to mention names. "Have you heard anything about the Fairweathers' marriage?"

"No, nothing. So why don't you tell me exactly what you know?"

"I don't actually know anything, but I can tell you what happened in my class one night." She continued when Brett nodded his agreement. "Well, it was one of the nights that I was working at the wheel and it wasn't going very well. I had to concentrate very hard to get the clay centered, and forming a small vase or pot was impossible at that point. Mainly I made a few passes and screwed up the entire thing— And I am getting to the point," she interrupted herself to add.

"I never suggested that you weren't. I'm just slowing down so we don't get to the house too soon. I'd like to hear the story before I meet her."

"Well, the point I'm trying to make is that I didn't pay attention to anything for the first half-hour or forty-five minutes of the class. And then when I got up to stretch my back or maybe to wedge more clay ... That's what happened, I remember now. I was going to wedge some fresh clay because I went over to the table and was kneading away when I looked up at Patricia Fairweather. Her back was to me and she was leaning over her wheel. She was wearing a pretty short T-shirt and it had come untucked from her jeans."

"And?" Brett encouraged her to go on.

"And there were huge bruises all across her back. It looked like she had been in some sort of terrible accident. Like falling backward." She paused, remembering the sight. "I was shocked, of course, and I started to say something, but the teacher stopped me."

"I don't understand."

"She had been standing behind me and she just reached out and put a hand on my arm to attract my attention. And then she put her finger to her lips—you know, warning me not to say anything."

"And you didn't."

"No. The teacher asked me to help her do something in another room and I followed her there. And that's when she told me that Patricia Fairweather would be very upset if I mentioned those bruises.

"I didn't understand what she was talking about, of course, so I asked her what she meant. And she said that she thought Patricia Fairweather's husband sometimes hit her."

"What exactly did she mean when she said that she thought Patricia Fairweather's husband hit her?"

"Of course that's what I asked, but another student came into the room and my teacher said that we could talk after class—and that I shouldn't mention it to anyone. I could tell that she didn't want me to say anything to Patricia, so I didn't. When I returned to the room, I noticed that she—"

"Patricia Fairweather?"

"Right. Well, she had put on a long sweatshirt that covered her back. I thought that was significant since the room was very hot. She must have been trying to cover those awful bruises."

"And what happened when you met with your teacher after class? What did she tell you?"

"Well, by the time class was over she seemed to have reconsidered her impulse to be open with me." Susan paused, remembering that evening. "We weren't alone together for a while. Some of the better students stayed after class to talk about formulas for some new glazes—Patricia Fairweather was one of them," she added quickly. "By the time everyone else left, I was feeling very uncomfortable about being there. And I was wondering just how much Patricia Fairweather had noticed. I felt like I was prying."

"You said that your teacher's attitude seemed to have changed," Brett reminded her.

"Yes. Definitely. She had stopped me from saying anything to Patricia Fairweather earlier and maybe she would have been more forthright if we had been alone longer. But then she shut down. I actually had to bring up the subject and explain why I was still hanging around."

"And did you remind her that she had suggested you stay after the others?"

"That's exactly how I began. And then I said that I was worried about Patricia Fairweather and she interrupted me and asked in a rather snotty way if I had any reason to believe that Patricia wasn't capable of taking care of herself. I was a little taken aback by her attitude and I said that I had seen the bruises and I was worried. And then my teacher lied to me."

"What did she say?"

"She said that Patricia had fallen down her basement stairs carrying a full basket of laundry.

"I was stunned, of course. It was so different from what she had told me originally. I started to mumble something about that—I think I mentioned Patricia's husband—and she rather abruptly told me that I was meddling in things that weren't my business.

"I was shocked, of course, and I'm sure she could tell by the expression on my face. She backed down immediately and added that I didn't have to worry about Patricia. That she had a lot of friends who were taking care of her."

"And that was that?" Brett asked after a moment of silence.

"Yes. I thought about it all the way home and just about half the night. I even considered going over to the Fairweathers' home and confronting whoever came to the door. The idea of him hitting her just got to me. I really felt I should do something. But I didn't," she added sadly. "I finally just decided that there was nothing I could do, that Patricia Fairweather undoubtedly did have friends who were aware of the problem and helping her out."

"And since then you've been feeling guilty whenever you think about it." It was a statement, not a question.

"Of course. I tried to make myself feel better by thinking that Patricia had realized what I had seen and spoken to the teacher and asked for privacy."

"Which might be true."

"Even if it was, it didn't make things better. I should have done something, said something. And look what I've done now. The first person I talk to about it is you—right after Simon Fairweather's murder," Susan added, feeling guilty. "It's a good thing she was on that cruise ship when he was killed."

"She wasn't," Brett said quietly. He steered the police car through the heavy stone pillars that marked either side of the wide driveway that led to the Fairweathers' home.

"I thought—"

"So did we. But when we got hold of the ship, we discovered that Patricia Fairweather was a no-show."

"But everyone thought she was there. Where was she?"

"That's one of the things that we're here to find out," Brett answered.

EIGHT

"YOU'LL LIKE HER," SUSAN SAID AS SHE AND BRETT STOOD on the porch waiting for someone to answer their ring. "Everyone does," she added.

The door opened before Brett had a chance to reply.

Susan looked at his face and realized that she had forgotten to mention Patricia Fairweather's appearance. He'd probably assumed she was as old and folksy as her husband had been. But Patricia was close to Susan in age and closer to the sixties in style. Her long, straight hair was graying. She wore no makeup and tiny gold granny glasses sat on her sunburned nose. Still slender enough to look fine in the jeans and T-shirts that she habitually wore, Patricia appeared comfortable and relaxed. Not, Susan suddenly realized, like a recently bereaved widow.

"Patricia, I was so sorry to hear about your husband," Susan started, hoping to remind the other woman of her expected demeanor. Surely this was no way for a possible murder suspect to be acting.

"Thank you, Susan." Patricia looked at Brett. "Are you also here to offer your condolences, Chief Fortesque?" she asked him in a steady voice.

Susan, a little shocked by this unexpected attitude, remained silent while Brett expressed polite sorrow at Simon's death. "But we'd like to come in and speak with you, if this isn't a bad time," he added quickly.

"By all means." Patricia stepped aside and motioned for them to enter the large home.

Susan started in and then, startled by the sight that met her, trod backward on Brett's toes.

Patricia smiled at Susan's confusion. "The house always surprises people—especially if they've seen the outside for years. It isn't what most people expect, of course."

"Of course," Brett muttered, closing the door behind them.

They all gazed at the dramatic interior. No Victorian had ever lived like this. Pale, bleached woodwork accented the white enameled walls on which dozens of tiny spotlights caused glassy reflections. Stairs seemed to float up to the second floor without proper suspension. But the most amazing sight, to Susan, was the tiny niches that were cut into the walls, each one the exact size, shape, and depth to encompass a carefully chosen work of art.

The threesome stood on a pale handwoven rug centered on the pickled-oak floor. It blended in beautifully. Susan tried not to imagine what it would look like after Chad's friends made a few post-soccer game trips across it.

Brett was the first to speak. "This is truly remarkable, but you must hear that all the time."

Patricia just nodded.

Susan walked slowly around the entry foyer. "Some of these pots are your work, aren't they?"

"The two with the Raku glaze to your left, yes. But I've been a collector for years. Most of this was done by other artists.

"But you wanted to speak to me about Simon's murder, not art. Why don't we go into the living room and I'll get us some lemonade—unless either of you would prefer beer or wine? If we have it. I've been away for a few days, and I'm not really sure what's chilling in the refrigerator."

"Lemonade will be fine with me. And now that you mention it, that was one of the things we're here to speak to you about," Brett said, following the two women into a large room as light and modern as the entryway. "Where have you been for the last few days?"

"When I was supposed to be on a cruise in Alaska?" There was a smile on Patricia Fairweather's face. "I'll get you that lemonade and then explain. But I think you'll be disappointed. That is," she added, turning and beaming at them as she left the room, "if you want to see me as a suspect in my husband's murder."

Brett sat down on a couch covered with a contemporary quilt and frowned. Susan wandered around the room, peering at the artwork. "I wonder if this is one of Patricia's weavings," she muttered, looking up at the large tapestry of children playing that hung over the mantel.

"Nice marble fireplace," Brett muttered.

"It's not marble. It's a faux finish," Susan corrected him, leaning closer to the wall. She had always wanted to try something like this. "I think they use feathers."

She heard Brett's impatient sigh but decided to ignore it. They would get around to asking their questions, but this room was fascinating. She continued to examine the art. The work represented there covered a broad spectrum of crafts as well as, in some ways, tastes. Abstract acrylics shared walls with tiny golden icons. Appliquéd pillows were tossed on woven throws. Collector's glass was displayed on furniture hand-formed from rare fruitwoods. Susan had about a dozen questions to ask that had nothing to do with Simon Fairweather's death, but Brett insisted on getting to the point when the widow returned carrying a large tray.

"You were going to tell us where you were when your husband was killed," he reminded her abruptly.

Patricia set the tray down on an end table near the couch and unloaded it onto the large glass coffee table as she answered slowly. "I was at my sister's. She has a house out in Montauk—on Long Island." She put a piece of cork shaped like a star in the middle of the table and placed a tall, crystal pitcher of lemonade on it. Thinly sliced lemons and fresh raspberries floated among the ice cubes.

"It's on a hill overlooking the town and you can even see the water in the distance." Three tall glasses of translucent green were placed near the pitcher and a brass sculpture of a snail beneath a trillium was moved to make room for a plate of sugared gingersnaps.

"So you decided at the last minute to go there instead of on the cruise?" Brett asked, accepting a full glass.

"Yes." She offered him a cookie.

"Why?"

Patricia looked at him curiously. "Why not? I was planning to go on a tour, but frankly I had my doubts from the beginning. I just don't think I'm the tour type. Too independent or something." She sat down and sipped from the glass she had poured for herself. "I had some last-minute doubts about the trip I'd planned and at about the same time my sister called me and suggested a visit. I canceled my plans and took her up on her offer."

"Did you usually vacation without your husband?" Brett asked.

"Sometimes. But never alone—with one of my sisters or a friend. I have traveled for other reasons without Simon. I've taken a lot of courses at various craft schools around the country—and in foreign countries, too, for that matter." She looked up from her hostessing and stared seriously at Brett. "I'm not an artist, but I do consider myself a serious craftsperson and I have been lucky enough to study with some extraordinary artists over the years."

"So Susan told me," Brett assured her.

Patricia gave Susan a grateful look before continuing. "My husband has always worked very hard and he is, of course, a fine craftsman himself—he is an excellent finish carpenter and he has done a lot of woodworking as a hobby—but he has no interest in taking classes or in being around people who consider themselves artistic. He is—or was—a very down-to-earth man."

"How much of this house is his work?"

"All of it. We moved in soon after our wedding. My father died almost immediately and my mother moved out a few months later. Simon was just beginning to build his company back then—he started his own remodeling business the month before we were married—and we didn't have extra money. He did almost all of the first floor at night after a day of hard work. It took years, of course."

"You designed it?" Susan asked.

"We designed it together. And it has changed over the years, mainly to accommodate our collection as it grew."

"Like the niches in the walls in the entryway."

"Exactly." Patricia smiled at Susan.

"I wish I could get some designing help from you. Cory Construction is tearing apart my bathrooms and I have very little idea what I want to have done," Susan began.

"Could we get back to where you were when Simon died?" Brett reminded them all why they were together.

"But I told you where I was—at my sister's house out on Long Island."

"When we tried to find you to notify you of your husband's death, we were told that you were on a cruise. Your cleaning woman answered the phone when we called your home, and she said that you were away and gave us the emergency number that you left behind. You changed your plans without telling anyone?"

"No. I told family members—my other two sisters as well as Simon, of course. What my cleaning woman read from was the sheet that the cruise line sent with emergency numbers. It went up on the bulletin board by the back door almost a month ago—the day it arrived in the mail, in fact. I was afraid of losing it. When I changed my plans, it didn't get removed. That's all there was to it."

"But what about your friends and neighbors? Did they know that your plans had changed?"

Patricia seemed to mull this over carefully before answering. "I don't think so. I may have mentioned it to someone in passing, like at the grocery store or the dry cleaner's, you know. But I don't specifically remember telling anyone about it."

"Then your plans changed very close to the time you left."

"The day before. I was standing in my bedroom trying to decide if cotton sweaters would do for Alaska in August or if I needed to pack wool ones when the phone rang and it was my sister. We're very close and for the last few weeks I had been telling her that I was beginning to regret signing up for this cruise. She called to see how I was feeling and when I explained that I was less enthusiastic the closer the time came to leave, she suggested that I cancel the trip and come visit her in Montauk." She paused to take a bite out of a gingersnap and then continued the story.

"Lillian, my sister, had been expecting her in-laws to come for two weeks, but there was an emergency and they canceled at the last minute. She has a large house with a pool and suddenly spending time with a person I love in a warm, relaxing place sounded a lot better than being chilly with strangers. So I said yes, dumped out my suitcase, re-packed it with the few things I knew I'd need on the island, and I went."

"Surely you called your husband first?" Brett asked.

"Of course I did. He was busy that night, as he was on so many nights. There was a meeting of some sort down at the municipal center that he had to attend. So there was little reason for me to wait until morning as I had originally planned. I left right after dinner."

"Which is why you didn't bother to let anyone know," Susan suggested.

"I had already arranged everything that needed to be done while I was gone," Patricia said.

"Like what?" Brett asked.

Susan didn't have to ask since she knew better than he what was needed to keep a home running while the person primarily responsible for its care was away. Patricia explained about frozen meals in the freezer; appointments with lawn men, tree men, the chimney sweep; and the weekly cleaning woman who would have to come at least twice as often to take care of one man rather than a man and a woman.

"What about the cruise line?" was Brett's next question once he had a firmer grasp on the logistics of running a house this large.

"What about them?"

"Did you contact them and let them know that you weren't going to arrive on schedule?"

"No, I didn't. But I'm sure Simon did. I doubt if he was

thinking of being considerate. He was probably hoping to convince them that a refund was appropriate."

"And it wasn't?"

"Well, the contract says that some of the money can be refunded if the cancellation is due to illness or death, but no one was ill."

Or dead yet, Susan added to herself when Patricia didn't continue.

The phone rang in another room and Patricia excused herself, suggesting that they might like more refreshments while she was busy.

They took her up on her offer. Susan poured out more lemonade and munched on cookies while Brett wrote in the tiny notebook that he carried in his pocket. Patricia returned in less than ten minutes, writing on a notepad of her own.

"Calls about funeral arrangements," she explained, sitting and jotting down a few more words. "I understand my husband's body"—she paused and it was the first time Susan had seen her act like most recently created widows—"is going to the mortuary this afternoon. So plans need to be made."

Brett surprised Susan by standing up almost immediately. "We're imposing. I'm sorry. There will, of course, be more questions. I need to know further details about your husband's personal life as well as his professional affairs, but if you'll just give us your sister's phone number, this will do for now. You will be available later?"

"Naturally."

"But I do have one request. . . ." Brett struck Susan as unusually reluctant.

"Yes?"

"Would you give us a tour of the house?" Brett asked.

NINE

"I WAS SO GLAD YOU ASKED . . . I MEAN, I CERTAINLY WAS wondering what the rest of the house looked like, but still it was a surprise. And what do you think about Patricia's last-minute trip to her sister's house? Do you think . . . Why are you stopping the car? Is something wrong?"

"I just need to make a few notes before I forget anything."

Susan suspected that Brett's brisk answer was his way of telling her to shut up, so she did, sitting quietly in her seat and thinking over the extraordinary home she had just toured.

The second floor, not surprisingly, continued the theme set up on the first: a unique collection of crafts incorporated into a spectacularly attractive setting. Two large guest rooms were decorated in ways that indicated to Susan that children never stayed in them. (Especially the one that contained the collection of delicate glass goblets. Susan had found herself clutching her hands behind her back in there.) She had even checked out the bathrooms for ideas that might be appropriate in her own home. The master bedroom suite had surprised her by being very old-English-leather-smoking-room masculine with traditional furnishings until she discovered that Patricia was sleeping in what had once been a small sewing room or nursery tucked between a bathroom and a large linen closet. Unlike the voluptuous visual appeal of the rest of the house, that room was almost monastic. Its twin bed was fashioned from rough twigs; the mattress was covered with white cotton sheets and an elegant silk paisley shawl. But the hardwood floor was uncovered, the lone window was hung with a paper shade, and a tiny, white night table with a modern halogen lamp was the only other piece of furniture. Nothing was displayed on the rough white walls, and Susan assumed a large walnut-burl dresser that stood on the landing in the hallway contained Patricia's casual wardrobe. Two paperbacks were sitting on the bed and Susan had been intrigued to see *Zen and the Art of Motorcycle Maintenance* keeping company with a cozy mystery novel.

It was the third floor Susan kept thinking about. A more competitive craftsperson might have been tempted to explain Patricia Fairweather's superior products on the multiple studios that filled the large space. Susan, a humble class-taker, wasn't deceived, but she was momentarily jealous and permanently impressed. Two Swedish looms as well as a large American tapestry frame stood beneath a pair of skylights. A table covered with watercoloring supplies was against the far wall. And close to the stairs an electric wheel, a small drying kiln and shelves of unfinished work, jars of glazes, and potter's implements were handy. Without prompting, Patricia explained that she had recently installed an outside kiln under an overhang near the carriage house. Susan had left that floor reluctantly.

Brett had asked for a drink of water, so they stopped in the kitchen on their way to the car. In the name of good taste, Susan had resisted reading the personal messages and notes on the bulletin board and had discussed the relative merits of gas versus electric stoves until a phone call from the director of the town's interfaith mortuary interrupted them.

"Okay, I think I've recorded all the pertinent facts," Brett said, tucking the notebook back in his jacket and starting the car. "So what do you have to say about that?" he continued.

"Amazing. I wish we'd had a chance to look at the kiln, though. I understand it's got some unique features—"

"Susan, what are you talking about?"

"The Fairweathers' home. What else?"

He chuckled and gave her a sidelong glance. "You're not going to tell me that you missed the note on that bulletin board, are you?"

"What note?" So much for being polite.

"I suppose I shouldn't have called it a note. It was a full page, after all. It was from the cruise line, outlining various details about the trip."

"I didn't see it. I guess I was thinking about something else." She was unwilling to admit that she had been so intrigued by the hand-thrown canisters that she had—only momentarily—forgotten that she had been invited on this trip to help investigate a murder.

"Susan, that note was the reason that I suggested a tour of the house. Why else did you think I would ask to look around, for heaven's sake?"

"I thought perhaps you were interested in getting some idea of the Fairweathers' lifestyle," she answered, somewhat miffed. Exactly what gave this man the right to act like they'd been married to each other for twenty years?

"Such as?"

"Well, didn't you think it was interesting that Simon and Patricia didn't share a bedroom?"

"You think it has something to do with his death?"

"If they didn't share a bedroom, were taking separate vacations," Susan began, and then stopped.

"You think that's a sign she killed him?" Brett asked.

"Or that they had developed parallel but separate lives, which would eliminate the tension that might be necessary to get mad enough to kill someone, don't you think?" Susan suggested a different interpretation.

Brett gave his passenger a skeptical glance. "Possibly."

"And, in fact, Patricia has a very happy and productive life in that house. Why would she kill her husband and risk it all?"

"Well, let's think about that. Her life is very independent. Apparently she didn't need her husband in her life at all. He turned her parents' home into a showcase for the work she loves to collect and the work she loves to do. She produces excellent crafts and presumably could make a living selling them. If not, she has family members with enough money to own large homes on Montauk—they might help her if she had trouble supporting herself. Added to that let's assume the story your pottery teacher told you is correct and Simon Fairweather was beating his wife before he died. She might have an excellent incentive to kill him and reason to believe that she could create a good life for herself after his death."

"You think . . ."

"I think it is too early to think anything. I didn't even begin to ask all the questions that I wanted to, but I was afraid that Patricia Fairweather would realize what she had said, figure out a reason to return to the kitchen and tear that notice off the wall before I got a chance to read it."

Susan shook her head. "I hate to admit it, but I have no idea what you're talking about."

"The notice from the cruise line. I wanted to be sure it said what she said it did, that it was a list of emergency numbers."

"And was it?"

"It was the complete itinerary for her trip. Where it started, where it stopped and when, as well as numbers to call in case there was an emergency. It's not like the old days when liners crossed the Atlantic; a cruise ship going up the Inland Passage between Seattle and Anchorage, Alaska, has little trouble staying in almost constant phone contact—some of the cabins have their own phones, in fact."

"That's interesting," Susan said, not really understanding why he thought it was.

"It very well could be, in this case."

"Why?"

"Because, according to the details from the cruise company, Patricia Fairweather had her own phone line. In fact, someone had circled it."

"So?"

"So that wasn't the number that the cleaning woman gave us. She gave us the number that the cruise line has for emergencies." He frowned. "It could, of course, mean nothing. But it's possible that she had some inkling that Patricia Fairweather wasn't on board."

"I suppose it's worth checking out. I assume you'll speak with her." Susan doubted if he would find any answers. So many of the women who cleaned in Hancock were recent immigrants, trying to earn a living while getting their green cards, frequently unable to understand all but the simplest English phrases.

"I don't understand why you're so serious about this," Susan continued. "Isn't it just routine? After all, we know that Patricia was out in Montauk at the time of her husband's murder. Her sister will be able to verify it."

"Her sister, whom she admits to being very close to, remember," Brett reminded her. "A sister who just might lie to keep her from being convicted of murder, don't you think?"

"I suppose it's possible."

"Look at it this way, Susan. Assume Patricia Fairweather is the murderer. She plans to go on a cruise, tells her family and her friends that she'll be gone for two weeks. Makes preparations, chats about it around town at the dry cleaner's and the grocery store, just like she says she probably did, and then when she leaves the house everyone naturally assumes that she is where she said she was."

"Except that she's a smart woman and she knew the police would check her whereabouts when her husband was murdered. What was she going to do? Make a dummy with the pillows and keep it on the bed on the ship and claim that she slept through the cruise? Besides, the police called the cruise line to notify her of Simon's death. Surely she never thought that anyone would wait until a murder victim's spouse returned from a vacation to tell them that someone had died!"

"But she didn't do that," Brett reminded her. "She claims to have gone off to her sister's house at the last minute, conveniently forgetting to tell anyone but her husband—who is now dead and can verify nothing—about her change in plans. So she had accomplished something. She not only has an alibi for the time of her husband's murder, but she managed to keep us from finding her immediately after his death."

"And what advantage is that to her?" Susan asked, genuinely perplexed.

"She could have come to Hancock, killed him, and returned to Montauk without us knowing."

Susan didn't argue.

"Do you think I'm wrong?" Brett asked.

"Actually, I was just thinking. . . ."

"Did you say anything about Simon Fairweather hitting Patricia to anyone else?"

Susan thought for a moment before answering. "When I was worrying that I should do something—speak to Patricia Fairweather or someone—about Simon hitting her, I probably talked to Kathleen about it. I usually tell her what's worrying me. But she's been so busy with Banan—her son and her pregnancy that it was probably just mentioned in passing."

"Jed?"

Susan shook her head. "I guess so. I don't actually remember."

They had turned on to Susan's street. A gigantic truck was unloading the biggest Dumpster she had ever seen at the foot of the driveway.

"Oh, no!" Susan cried out. "Hurry up. We've got to stop them!"

"What's wrong?" Brett asked as he accelerated the car.

"They're going to trap my car in the garage!"

TEN

"LADY, BELIEVE ME, WE DO THIS EVERY DAY. WE AIN'T never trapped a car in a garage—not since that lawyer sued us, at least . . . course that wasn't his car. Wasn't even his wife's car. Belonged to his secretary; he claimed she fell asleep working late."

Susan spied her husband over the shoulder of the man who was speaking to her. "I didn't mean to imply that you didn't know your business. I think I'd better go see what's happening in the house," she muttered, smiling weakly and starting up the walk. She noticed that the small rhododendron had once again gotten in someone's path; the poor thing had lost a few more branches.

"Jed," she breathed. "Why is that Dumpster so huge? And how long is it going to sit in the driveway?"

"As long as it's needed. And it's not so big. Ken says they're expecting to fill and dump it more than once." Jed shook his head. "Susan, that's not our most immediate problem. What are you doing investigating a murder at a time like this? We have to get this house in shape before the kids come home. Let someone else worry about who killed Simon Fairweather. Please."

"Hey, you trying to find out who killed Simon Fairweather?" Buns appeared behind Jed and stuck out a greasy paw. "Let me shake your hand. And I'd like to shake the hand of the person who did it when you find out." A large grin appeared on his face. "Just kidding, Mrs. Henshaw. Just kidding," he repeated, chuckling, as he left the house.

Susan looked at her husband. "I'll tell you about that. Everything's fine. There's not a chance in the world of having a nice, quiet glass of iced tea in the kitchen, is there?"

"None. The house is an oven because the air-conditioning is off again. We shouldn't open the freezer if we don't want things to start melting."

"Maybe I could change and we could go to the inn." Susan began envisioning a cool, intimate lunch.

"At least one of us should be here to answer questions, hon. And we have more than a few decisions to make. Once the construction begins, every change is going to cost money. Why don't you go around back to the patio, I'll bring you something to drink, and we can talk. You look tired."

Tired, Susan knew, was her husband's code word for dreadful. "I could use a shower," she muttered, pulling her hair off her forehead. "But I'd like to see what's happening in the house. Then I'll tell you everything Brett told me. I promise."

"Okay. But, remember, things look worse before they look better."

Susan understood his warning as soon as she stepped through the door. A heavy, black plastic runner snaked its way down the hall and up the stairs. Woven batting of the type movers use to wrap furniture had been hung over the wood paneling on the walls. Transparent plastic was attached to the molding around open doorways, sealing off the rooms. Through one Susan spied Clue lying on the living room couch, chewing on one of Susan's favorite leather sandals.

The second floor was worse than the first. The carpet was covered and the doors to her children's bedrooms were sealed with large sheets of the same plastic.

"We talked it over and decided that it was the best way to localize the dirt and dust," Jed explained.

"Well, I was thinking about straightening out the kids' rooms while they're out of town, but that can wait. And we're certainly not going to have guests with all this going on. Why didn't they seal off the guest room?"

"We might want to sleep in there," Jed said, opening their bedroom door.

"We definitely don't want to sleep in here," Susan agreed, looking around. Plastic covered everything: the floor, each piece of furniture, the shutters on the windows, the doors to the closets. On the bed, towels, tissues, makeup, a full wastebasket, and the entire contents of the medicine cabinet formed a large pile.

"Nothing is sealed tightly. I knew we would want to get things out of the closets and the dresser."

Susan, staring through the plastic over her nightstand at the paperback she was reading, only nodded.

Kyle Barnes appeared in the bathroom doorway, a red bandanna wound jauntily around his head, a toilet bowl in his hands. "Hi. Want to look around?" He tossed his head to indicate the room behind him.

"You were going to tell me what Brett said," Jed reminded her before she followed Kyle.

"It will only take a second. There's not much left in there to look at." Kyle laughed, then headed out into the hallway.

There wasn't.

The tall young man with blond dreadlocks, Frankie, was kneeling on the floor cradling the rest of the toilet in his arms.

Susan stood in the middle of the room with her mouth open. Pieces of the bathtub were shoved up against the walls, the light fixtures were dangling in place, falling wallpaper hung across the window.

"Susan? Are you okay?"

"I think . . ." she started slowly, ". . . I think there's room for a large bathtub in here. Like the one at that hotel in Lucca, remember?"

Jed grinned. "I sure do. And we need one, definitely," he added with a matinee-idol leer.

"And maybe a shower in that corner," Susan added, kicking aside some rubble and peering down the hole in the floor. "Why is there newspaper in here?"

"It's where the toilet was installed. It keeps sewer gas

from escaping. Sue, you were going to tell me about your conversation with Brett," Jed reminded her again when she didn't respond to his teasing.

"Yeah, let's go downstairs. He just wanted me to go with him to Patricia Fairweather's house because I knew her from the class we took together."

"I remember that. Didn't you tell me some sort of dreadful story about them last spring?" her husband asked, following her down the stairs. "Wife beating or something?"

"Do you think this plastic is strong enough to take much traffic?" Susan asked, ignoring his question and looking down at the steps.

"Susan!"

"Okay. I just don't like to remember that. It makes me feel like killing Simon Fairweather myself."

"Did you kill that son of a bitch? Far out, lady," Frankie cheered her as he started back up the steps.

"Maybe we should sit in the backyard and get some fresh air," Susan suggested, ignoring the comment.

"Good idea. Let's take Clue with us before she consumes the entire living room."

They hurried through various barriers of plastic to collect the dog and leave the house. The brick patio, shaded by trees, was perceptibly cooler than inside the house and Susan threw herself down on the teak reproduction of a Victorian lounge and wondered for the millionth time if they had known what the word *lounge* actually meant. Jed sat at her feet and listened as Susan told him what she and Brett had discussed.

"I remember you telling me about the bruises and the man who hit his wife, but I didn't remember that the woman was Patricia Fairweather until today," he said when she was finished, scratching Clue behind the ears as he spoke.

"Simon Fairweather was that tall, distinguished man with gray hair who checked out our garage plans, right?"

"Yes. Brett says that we'd be surprised at the people who hit their wives," she added when he didn't respond immediately.

Jed merely nodded. "So you think you can help solve this murder even though you didn't know the murdered man and you know his wife only slightly?"

Susan decided to ignore any implied insult. At least he wasn't objecting to her involvement.

"But you know you're going to be very busy around here. If you wanted to just duplicate the old bathrooms, this would be a piece of cake. Messy, of course, but easy. But if you want to remodel . . ."

Susan got the message. Of course, she reminded herself, Jed didn't know that Cory Construction was, at least in a small way, connected with Simon Fairweather's death. Although the members of the crew weren't doing a very good job of keeping their hostile feelings about him a secret, she thought as Clue leaped up to greet Kathleen and her son.

Kathleen chose the least comfortable chair and eased herself down onto it as her son ran about the backyard with Clue at his heels. "Hot, isn't it?"

"Our electricity isn't on," Susan admitted. "Want some seltzer or something? There may be some lemonade in the refrigerator, but everything is going to be warm."

"Anything is fine. I'm dying of thirst. Nothing has made me as dry as this pregnancy."

"I'll get it," Jed offered, jumping up.

Susan waited until they were alone before leaning toward Kathleen, an intense expression on her face. "I'm glad you're here. You and Jerry used to visit some friends out on the island, didn't you? Do you know how long it takes to drive from here to Montauk? Could you get there and back in one day?"

"Round trip? I don't see why not." Kathleen thought for a moment before answering. "There are probably a lot of options. You could drive like a maniac and you might make it if the Long Island Expressway wasn't jammed up—but in the summer that's taking a huge chance. I suppose you could drive to Hartford and then get a commuter flight to the end of the island. Or maybe drive to Westchester airport and go that way."

"So you think . . ."

"Most people would just take the ferry in Bridgeport if they wanted mass transportation. Why? Are you thinking about taking a vacation while the work is going on here?"

"No, although that's beginning to sound like a good idea. I was wondering if Patricia Fairweather could have gone to Montauk, returned here and killed her husband late in the evening, and then been back at her sister's house in Montauk by the time his body was found."

Kathleen raised her eyebrows. "That's what Brett is thinking?"

Susan nodded.

"You don't believe she did it."

"No, but she has a motive and I told Brett about it."

"What?" Kathleen asked seriously.

Susan explained about the bruises on Patricia's back for the third time that day.

"I remember you telling me about it. You're right. It sounds like she's got a motive," Kathleen said.

"Yes. I sure wish I hadn't mentioned it to Brett," Susan admitted. "You know, Kath, there's really only one thing to do."

"What?"

"Go back to her house and ask some more questions. Don't you think?"

"Well, she might not answer you. And I wouldn't blame her. After all, Brett has every right in the world to question her after her husband's death. You don't."

"True, but I could point out to her that I'm trying to help her."

"What about Cory Construction? I thought you were going to look into the possibility that someone on the crew murdered Simon Fairweather. Anyone here who might have a motive for murder?"

"You wouldn't believe it!" Susan exclaimed. "Everyone that hears his name is almost anxious to talk about how much they hated him, how glad they are that he's dead."

"Really? I wonder why," Kathleen said as Jed rejoined them.

"Why what?" he asked, putting a tray containing three

mismatched tumblers on a nearby table. "I brought Kool-Aid for Alex. Cherry," he added.

"He'll love it," Kathleen assured him.

"You forgot a lemon for the seltzer. Kathleen might need it," Susan said.

"That's okay. I don't use—"

"Well, I'd like some," Susan interrupted. "Jed . . ."

"Okay. I'll go back. I can tell when you two want to speak in private."

"Susan, what is it?" Kathleen asked as soon as the door slammed behind Jed.

"He still doesn't know why I hired Cory Construction! And I don't want him to!"

"Good idea."

"You think he would object to choosing a contractor that way?"

"Do you know anyone who wouldn't object to having a possible murderer working in his home?"

ELEVEN

The only answer, Susan had decided after Kathleen and Alex had gone home to nap, was to go down to the Hancock Field Club and take a long shower. Maybe it would help her think. Certainly it would make her smell better. Now she stood under the sharp spray, letting the warm water rinse the shampoo from her hair, and tried to figure out what to do next.

The field club had recently remodeled its locker rooms to make them more "spalike." Rows of utilitarian white shower stalls with muslin curtains had been replaced by a crescent of tiny Mexican-tiled shower rooms each with its own bench, hooks for clothing, and spray bottles of shampoo, conditioner, and liquid soap. Susan had never before appreciated these amenities; of course, she could usually find her own soap without crawling through a couple of inches of rubble. She was tempted to lean back against the wall until the water turned her into a human prune. But it wasn't going to be easy to shave her legs in the small first-floor bathroom sink, so she lathered up and got to work.

Around her, women who had completed an afternoon of tennis or paddleball were cleaning up before heading home and starting dinner. Other women, having left work early, were changing into aerobic togs or swimsuits and were preparing for evening exercise. At least they knew where they were going, Susan told herself, reaching for the pink plastic razor she'd just dropped on the floor. That's when she heard her name.

". . . Susan Henshaw. I'm sure I saw her Jeep in the lot.

There's that dent in the bumper where she ran into that metal post trying to back out of the driveway after the Jamisons' Memorial Day barbecue. . . ."

"Someone should tell Jack that people don't appreciate punch so loaded with sugar and lumps of fruit that you can't tell how much rum is in it," someone else suggested.

"I wasn't drunk. It was dark. I just didn't see the post." Susan stuck her head out between the swinging wooden doors and defended her reputation.

"Hey, Susan!" a neighbor called out. "Edie's looking for you. Evidently your husband called her husband yesterday. Something about a plumber."

"Is that Susan Henshaw?" a familiar voice called out. "I heard rumors of a disaster at her house. A flood in the kitchen or bathroom or something like that."

Susan, never surprised by the extent and efficiency of the grapevine in the town, turned off the water and reached for a towel while explaining. Her audience was wowed by her story and quick to offer names of favorite plumbers, contractors, and the like. Susan explained that she had hired Cory Construction and demolition work had already begun.

Cries of appreciation for her efficiency were followed by harrowing stories of remodeling disasters and near disasters, each woman topping the tale of the person before her. Susan just towel-dried her hair and pulled on clean shorts and T-shirt. Even a friend's story of an intermittent and apparently untraceable leak in the ceiling over her kitchen sink sounded better than living with the mess that her home had become in the last forty-eight hours. She slipped on her Keds and slipped Simon Fairweather's name into the conversation at the same time.

"That bastard!" A voice from the shower stall next to hers summed up the general response. Tales of variances rejected, bedroom windows that had to be enlarged to meet new safety standards, long lists of requirements that had added time and expense to numerous building projects over the years bounced among the tile walls. Susan frowned and wondered if everyone in town had had a reason to dislike the building inspector. And perhaps even a reason to kill him?

"Of course, sometimes, it's merely a matter of hiring the right contractor. Everyone knows that Simon Fairweather played favorites. Some companies could do no wrong and some couldn't do anything right," someone called out from the locker area.

There was general agreement to that statement and more stories to support everyone's opinions. But Susan, picking up her towels and depositing them in the laundry bin, was pulled aside by a blond woman she knew by sight but couldn't quite place.

"Do you have a few minutes? I need to talk with you privately," the woman asked. "It's important. It's about Cory Construction."

"Of course." Susan looked around the crowded room. "We could meet in the bar in a few minutes. I just have to get some stuff from my locker."

"I'll be there."

It took Susan slightly longer than fifteen minutes to gather her stuff together and say goodbye to friends, but the other woman was waiting patiently at a table near the window overlooking the golf course. She stood up and waved as Susan entered the wood-paneled room. Susan hurried over to the table.

"You don't remember me, do you?" the other woman said after they were seated and had ordered iced coffee from the college-age woman waiting on their table.

"I know I've seen you around, but I just can't place you," Susan admitted.

"I'm Natalie McPherson. I was in a class you took at the art center—beginning ceramics—only I had—"

"You were a brunette then!" Susan exclaimed. "And you wore glasses," she said, not adding that the woman before her had lost at least twenty pounds and grown long red nails in the intervening year.

"I got a divorce."

They nodded at each other. It was fairly well known that women whose husbands left them for younger, more glamorous women frequently became more glamorous themselves as a result. "You look wonderful," Susan said honestly. "Are you still taking classes?"

"Yes. But I decided that pottery was not my thing. Not at all. I took a class in silversmithing and fell in love with it. I've even sold some of my work at a gallery up in the Berkshires."

"That's impressive." Susan made a mental note. Maybe a class change was a good idea. Maybe she had an undiscovered talent for a different craft.

"But that's not what I wanted to tell you about. I think you should know that there was some very bad blood between Cory Construction and Simon Fairweather."

"Really?" Susan decided there was no reason to say anything more.

"Yes. He—"

"Simon Fairweather?"

"Yes. Well, he tried to get Ken Cory's license taken away from him."

"What?" Susan accepted the coffee the waitress brought but was too involved in Natalie's revelation to sample it.

"I don't know all the details, but I can tell you what I do know. Of course, if you've signed a contract with Cory Construction . . ."

"Did they work for you?" Susan asked, not answering the implied question.

For some reason the question seemed to embarrass Natalie. "Yes, they did," she admitted. "Right before my divorce went through, actually. I decided that my ex might as well be the one to pay for having a bathroom added to the first floor of the house. He was anxious to be free—for the usual reason—and I thought I could get something out of it."

"And they didn't do good work?" Susan asked, thinking of the rubble in her house.

"Well, the tub doesn't drain properly and it all took a lot longer than it was supposed to. . . . But that's pretty much the same with everyone, isn't it? No job is ever perfect."

"I suppose so. But you were going to tell me something about Ken Cory and Simon Fairweather."

"Simon Fairweather hated Ken Cory."

"Really? How do you know that?"

Natalie paused and then the story came out in a rush. "It would never have happened if my husband hadn't had a midlife crisis. Or, actually, if he hadn't decided that a blonde half his age was going to be his midlife crisis. I was crazy for a while—for a long while, actually. I lost weight, took enough aerobics classes to fill the hours, bleached my hair, and had an affair with the best-looking, available young man I could find: Ken Cory."

"You're kidding!"

"Well, that's tactful," Natalie commented, a wry look on her face.

"I'm sorry."

"Don't worry. My feelings aren't that easily hurt. It was a stupid thing to do—and I'd do it again," she added a little defensively. "You can't imagine how wonderful it is to go to bed with a fabulous-looking young man unless you've done it yourself." She looked at Susan, who didn't respond. "Anyway, I felt like twenty years had dropped from my life. And a lot of the damage my husband's philandering had done vanished." Natalie picked up a packet of artificial sweetener, ripped off the top, and poured it into her coffee, then added a splash of cream before stirring slowly. When she was finished, she sipped her drink, then continued. "That's really the reason I hate to tell you this. I owe a lot to Ken Cory."

"But . . . ?" Susan asked gently.

"But he once told me that he'd like to kill Simon Fairweather." Natalie bit her lip and then looked up at Susan. "You're looking into the murder, aren't you?"

"Not really."

"Then why did you hire Cory Construction?"

Susan was surprised. "Why not?"

"Well, Susan, they're not exactly known as the best contracting company in town."

"You're kidding."

"Susan, everyone knows who the best contractors are."

"Yeah, the ones that are busy when you need a job done in a hurry," Susan muttered. "I waited almost a year to get a laundry room added in the basement. But Cory Construction isn't incompetent, is it?"

Natalie gave Susan a shrewd look. "You already hired them, didn't you?"

"Yes. Should I figure out a way to fire them?"

"No, just keep an eye on their work every step of the way. They need a lot of guidance. If any of that crew is left to make a decision on his own, they'll surely make the wrong one."

"I was going to do that anyway," Susan admitted. "We're sort of planning this as we go. But what about what Ken Cory told you, about how he wanted to murder Simon Fairweather. I can see that you don't like talking about it, but better I know than the police. . . ." Susan didn't finish the statement. She wasn't even sure that it was true.

Natalie began slowly. "It was after I'd known him for a while."

"After you'd been sleeping together for a while?" Susan tried to clarify the situation.

"Yes. In fact, we were in bed when he told me. I had noticed that they didn't get along almost from the very first time I met him, when we were planning the project."

"Simon Fairweather was there then?"

"No, of course not, but he was mentioned." She sipped her drink and thought for a moment. "We were planning the project: talking about the bathroom's design and how much space we were going to need if we butted out into the backyard. The architect who drew up the plans before the divorce had included a huge extension for my ex-husband's exercise equipment. I see that now as the beginning of his midlife crisis. The man I married filled his required team-sports time by managing the soccer team for four years at his prep school. I should have known something was up when he began talking about pumping iron here at the club and when he filled our basement with expensive instruments of torture.

"Well, I wasn't interested in that, so I eliminated the area and asked Ken for something a little less elaborate."

"And Simon had to approve the new plans?" Susan guessed.

"Of course, but we ... I have a few acres of property and the house is small. Ken just said something like 'that so-and-so Simon Fairweather won't be able to turn this one down.' I didn't know him very well at that point, but it was obvious that he was pleased."

"So pleased that you got the feeling that there was a certain amount of bad feelings between the two men?"

"Definitely. Ken didn't even try to hide it. Nor did any of his workers. The carpenters—Art and George—used to talk about it all the time. And the rest of the guys on the crew were always making comments about how much they didn't like Simon."

"They're not exactly reticent on the subject these days either," Susan admitted, wondering if she had missed a carpenter named George working in her home.

"Well, then you know what I mean. But our bathroom was planned by one of the best architects in the state and all we did was make the extension smaller. There was nothing for anyone to object to and we didn't need a variance or anything like that."

"So there weren't any problems with the inspector's office during the work?"

"Well, he did some pretty irritating things."

"Like?"

"Well, you know how work has to stop periodically for inspections—like electrical inspections—that have to take place before the next step can begin. So that walls can be closed up and things like that."

"Sure."

"Well, he never showed up on time or there was always some sort of complication. It really held up the work. I was sure glad that there were two other functioning bathrooms in the house."

Susan grimaced but didn't speak.

"But those things weren't that big a deal and they irritated me more than Ken. At least there didn't seem to be enough to make Ken so mad—or that's the way it seemed to me."

"And he was really mad?"

"Furious."

"What did he say exactly?"

"Well, we . . . we were in bed together, just like I told you. Ken had been antsy all day."

"You were together at your house?"

"Yes. Ken would just come over to check out the day's work and hang around after his crew left."

"Then the men working on your house didn't know that you and Ken were involved?"

"I'm not sure. The young plumber with the crinkled blond hair—"

"Frankie?"

"That may have been his name. Well, he walked in on Ken and me kissing once, but I don't know if he said anything to anyone else.

"Anyway, it had been a bad day for Ken and I had opened a bottle of champagne, hoping it would calm him down, but the more he drank, the madder he became. I don't remember everything exactly. I guess he wasn't the only one who drank a lot that evening. But he kept talking about how Simon Fairweather hated him, that Simon Fairweather had always hated him, and that now, if he wasn't careful, Simon Fairweather would take away his business. I said something like, Oh, surely that isn't so. And he answered that he . . . he would kill Simon Fairweather if he thought he could get away with it."

" 'If he thought he could get away with it.' You're sure that's what he said?"

"Pretty sure. It sounded creepy to me. You know, people say things like 'I sure would like to kill so-and-so' and it doesn't mean too much. But saying that about getting away with it struck me as very strange. Like he had thought about it or something."

"He didn't happen to say just how he would kill him, did he?" Susan asked.

Natalie opened her eyes wide, giving Susan a chance to admire her new sapphire-blue contact lenses. "That's the other thing that's so creepy. He said he would nail him. And the paper said that Simon Fairweather was ... was shot with a nail gun, wasn't he?"

Susan nodded grimly. It sounded more and more like she had hired a murderer.

TWELVE

In fact, her husband had just given Ken Cory a check for seventeen thousand dollars.

"And there are a lot of decisions that have to be made as quickly as possible," Jed reminded her before she had a chance to drop her purse on the hall table—assuming she could have found the hall table.

"Where . . . ?" she began, looking around.

"Everything has been moved out of the hallway. They've been carrying stuff up and down the stairs for hours. Both bathrooms are pretty much cleaned out—even the third floor is almost back to the eaves. Susan, we need to figure out exactly what you want in each room."

"I . . ." She reminded herself that they were talking about decorating, nothing life-threatening, nothing to panic over.

"It's going to cost more if we have to make changes. And orders for appliances have to go in, hon."

"I thought there was time. Which room do we have to decide about first? The third floor is going to be pretty easy. I already know which sink and toilet. I even marked them in the American Standard catalog."

"I think Ken was planning on doing all the bathrooms at once."

"Jed, I can't do that."

"It doesn't have to be that big a deal. And I don't see what was wrong with the bathrooms before. Why don't we just replace everything and you can paint the walls the colors that you were talking about on the way home from the airport," Jed suggested again.

"Jed, those bathrooms were decorated in the fifties. You can't even get the same bathtubs and toilets anymore! And why would anyone want to reproduce those hideous cabinets under the sinks?"

"I always liked them."

The phone rang as Susan began to wonder if a divorce decree was going to precede new toilets to her house. Jed answered and then handed the receiver to Susan. "I'm going to go upstairs and check things out with Ken. Maybe they can work on the third floor first. That would give you time to make your selections, right?"

Susan just nodded and took the receiver from him. "Hi."

It was Kathleen, and after being assured that the baby was content to remain in utero, Susan explained what she had learned talking with Patricia Fairweather and the women down at the field club.

"You didn't mention the fact that Ken Cory was young and good-looking" was Kathleen's first comment.

"Yes. Sort of an intellectual-looking hunk—like the guys in the Bloomingdale's catalog. But that's not relevant here," Susan insisted. "After all, he could also be a murderer."

"So maybe you should find another contractor," Kathleen suggested. "Unless you're looking for an affair?"

"Just as soon as I pick out three new toilets," Susan answered rather sarcastically.

"But, Susan . . ."

"Look. Jed is so happy with them that he gave them a deposit and they've already started to work. Besides, I don't know where I would find another company."

"But, Susan, what if one of them actually is a murderer? And what if that person discovers that you're looking into Fairweather's death? You could be putting yourself in danger."

"I'll be safe enough. You have to be alone with someone for them to kill you. You can't believe how many people have walked in and out of this house over the last two days."

"Well, just be careful."

"I will." Susan continued to chat until her husband

stepped into the room, a large bathroom-fixtures catalog under his arm. "You'll call me if you begin labor?" she asked before saying goodbye.

"It's a small town. You'll hear the cheering without a phone," Kathleen assured her, and hung up.

"Good news," Jed announced. "Ken agreed that there was no reason not to do the third floor first. And he marked the toilets and sinks that are in stock at his supplier's in this catalog. If you can agree on one of them and if we can pick out tiles for the floor up there tonight, he'll start rebuilding as soon as the permits are approved."

"That will be easy," Susan enthused. "There's a wonderful tile store over in Stamford and I'll bet it's open tonight. They have the most beautiful hand-painted tiles."

"Ken said he has a good working relationship with Tile City—it's out on the highway. He said Tile City has most of the standard tiles in stock." He gave his wife a stern look. "Susan, we're talking about the attic. I can understand if you want to add some charm to the second-floor bathrooms. That might even add substantially to the value of the house. But there isn't even a bedroom in the attic. Let's try to keep it simple."

"Of course," Susan agreed, taking the catalog from his hand. "Just give me a few minutes and I'll look at the sinks."

"Ken said nothing acrylic. Only cast iron. Or maybe he was talking about bathtubs," Jed muttered.

Susan just kept looking through the glossy pages, wondering how they had managed to photograph so many naked men and women in tubs and showers without displaying any sexual attitudes. Even the couple sharing the bubble bath in a large square tub looked as though they were casual acquaintances who just happened to be in the same place at the same time. "What do you think about these?" she asked finally, showing him a page.

"Nice. Plain, white. Did Ken mark this page?"

Susan pointed to the check mark in the right-hand corner.

"Great! Why don't I show him right now and he can call

in an order. He was up in the attic doing some last-minute measuring."

"I'll do it," Susan said, leaping to her feet. "Could you take Clue on a walk? Then we can leave immediately for Tile City. I think plain tiles would be nice on the floor up there, but it should be a color. White is too difficult to keep clean."

"Okay," Jed agreed, and they headed off in opposite directions.

Fifteen minutes later they were in the car following Ken's directions to the store he had recommended. "Tomorrow is Sunday," Susan muttered, leafing through the Andersen windows catalog. "They won't be working in the house."

"Actually they will be. Ken's already spoken to me about it," Jed said. "The town frowns on working Sundays—in fact, there's an ordinance against all but emergency work being done. But he thought that the fact that we're living without water qualified as an emergency. And besides—"

"Simon Fairweather isn't around to check up on him anymore," Susan finished his sentence.

"Exactly."

"No one on the crew—or Ken—seems to be distraught about Simon's death," Susan said, trying to keep her voice casual. "They must have known him fairly well."

"That's true." Jed chuckled. "That carpenter . . . What's his name? The one who wants to be on *Jeopardy!*?"

"George?"

"No, that doesn't sound right."

"Art Something."

"Art Young. That's it. Well, the only time he takes off his headset is to ask for a measuring tape or some other tool—or to tell anti–Simon Fairweather stories."

"Like what?" Susan asked as casually as possible.

"Oh, I don't know. I don't see much point in listening to that type of thing. People bitching are just blowing off steam; I don't like to get involved."

Susan knew what he meant. She'd listened to friends complain for hours and ended up feeling used. But, on the other hand, she sure would like to know what Art Young was saying about the building inspector. She'd have to get that headset off the man and get him talking. If Jed could do it, she could. People were always sharing their life histories with her whether she wanted to hear them or not.

"Jed, you are happy with Cory Construction, aren't you?" Susan asked the question that was nagging at her.

"Ken seems very well organized and his crew seems to be nice people. Is something about them worrying you?"

"No."

"Because I'll be in the city working and you're going to be the person that they're going to be driving crazy at home."

"How much time do you think I'll actually have to spend here?" Susan remembered what Natalie McPherson had said down at the club.

"Well, at first you might want to be home most of the time. There are going to be a lot of questions until everything is planned completely."

"Of course. The planning doesn't worry me a lot. I'd rather have more time, but I can do it. I just wondered how much you think I should check out the technical aspects of the job."

"You mean because Simon Fairweather is dead? I wouldn't worry about that. The town will appoint another building inspector as soon as possible and his work will be taken over by someone in the office right away."

Susan hadn't been talking about that, but it gave her something to think about. "So it was the man that everyone hated, not the job. I mean, someone is going to do all the inspections and everything like that whether Simon is around or not."

"True."

"So killing him would make no difference to anyone with any of the contracting companies at all," Susan said.

"Oh, that's not true. Everyone brings their own personality to a job. One man is more particular, more likely to follow the letter of the law rather than the spirit of the law. One person is prompt and friendly; another is always late and abrupt. Whoever replaces Simon Fairweather might well be liked better than he was. But, you know, that might be a problem here."

"What?"

"Well, Simon Fairweather was known to be tough, but that also means that the projects he inspected were done to the letter of the law, and that means they were safe. I was pretty mad when we got turned down for the workshop over the garage because he could have granted a variance if he'd wanted to. But, on the other hand, you didn't have to worry about an incompetent electrician doing something that might catch on fire when Simon Fairweather was around."

"Do we have to worry about it now?"

"No, I'm sure the town council will appoint someone who's competent. They must have had someone doing the work while Simon was on vacation or when he was ill. Don't worry about it."

Susan ignored her husband and worried all the way to Tile City.

And Tile City gave her more to worry about.

"This is it? This is where Ken sent us?" Susan asked, peering through the windshield at a small, square building made of concrete blocks that had last been painted many, many years before by someone who liked the color of Pepto-Bismol.

"We shouldn't judge by the outside." But Jed didn't sound all that sure of his statement.

"There couldn't be a very big selection," Susan said, getting out of the car.

"We're here for something basic, remember? And if we can't find something you like, we can always go somewhere else."

But Tile City, though not a very large metropolis, was crammed full of tiles, and Susan had no trouble choosing the type she wanted. The color, however, was a different story.

"Didn't you say something about apricot?" Jed asked tentatively after Susan had spent over twenty minutes arranging and rearranging various shades of green and blue tiles on the floor.

Susan glanced at the box of tiles her husband's hand rested on. "When have you ever seen an apricot that color? That's hot pink, Jed. What do you think about this pattern?"

"Wonderful."

"Not that one, this one over here next to the shelf," Susan directed him.

"You folks need any help?" A cheerful middle-aged man appeared behind them.

"Well, we—" Jed began.

"Are these blue tiles appropriate for use on floors?"

"In an entryway, bathroom, or kitchen?"

"What's the difference?" Jed asked, feeling that asking an intelligent question was one step up from being a complete moron.

"Well, they're all graded and numbered, see . . ."

What followed was one of the longest, most complicated systems of grading that Susan had ever heard. After listening for a few minutes she began to understand that the store didn't want to discourage any purchase. So instead of a system that divided tiles into those hard enough to be walked on and those that would scratch easily, tiles had been divided into a series of grades that implied that some floors were not walked on, or at least walked on rarely and then presumably only by barefoot children incapable of dragging their tiny feet.

Jed listened, nodding sagely. Susan felt a headache coming on. "But these tiles . . . the green and blue ones." Susan insisted on returning the salesman's attention to her original question.

"Oh, they're the hardest finish there is. Fine for anything. But that pattern . . ."

"Yes?" Susan was feeling proud for choosing the diagonal design.

"It's going to look a little strange unless the walls are exactly plumb. I don't want to discourage you, but we've had customers complain that we didn't tell them things before they'd ordered."

"Oh."

"Why not just the standard tile pattern?" Jed suggested. "You know," he responded to his wife's curious look, "with the little diamonds at the corners of the larger ones."

"Sure. One of my favorites," the salesman agreed with what Susan assumed was false heartiness. How could anyone be so enthusiastic about such an unoriginal idea?

"Well . . ." Susan began.

"Or look at this," the salesman urged, rearranging the design Susan had worked over for so long. She was about to protest when the pattern emerged.

"That's wonderful!"

"And it will work in any room, no matter how many corners or whether or not they're square."

"You like it?" Jed asked.

"Yes!"

"Let's figure out how many we need then. I have Ken's measurements here." Jed fumbled in the pockets of his chinos.

"I'll look around. I may get some ideas for the other two rooms," Susan muttered, moving toward the rear of the store.

Fifteen minutes later the Henshaws were back in Jed's Mercedes, a box of sample tiles tucked in the trunk.

"That place was better than you thought it was going to be, wasn't it?" Jed said, frowning at a Jeep full of teenagers that was swerving into their lane.

"Um. Can't judge a book by its cover," Susan muttered.

"You like the ones we picked out, don't you?" Jed asked, sensing her mood. "We can go back and change the order if you want to. Ken won't pick those up until tomorrow morning at the earliest."

"No. I think they'll be just fine," Susan said. "I was thinking of something else."

"Anything I can help with?"

"I just happened to look back in the stockroom," Susan began slowly.

"You've just happened to look in stranger places than that," Jed kidded her. "What did you see?"

"Well, they have this bulletin board with schedules for employees and OSHA notices—that type of normal stuff. And in the middle of it all was one of those fake wanted-dead-or-alive posters that you can have made on the board-walk or in some stores, you know?"

"I think so."

"Well, this poster was being used as a dartboard and guess whose face was in the center of it?"

"Whose?"

"Simon Fairweather's."

THIRTEEN

SUSAN WOKE UP THE NEXT MORNING IN THE MIDDLE OF A
dream in which the entire town of Hancock was lining up
outside the municipal center to vote for "the most hated
man in the world." Naturally, Simon Fairweather was coming in first. The other candidates included a well-known se-
rial killer and a fascist dictator.

Susan rolled over, trying to get back to sleep. And she
might have succeeded if Jed hadn't asked her a question.

"Do you hear that?"

"What?"

"Sounds like music. Coming from above."

Susan giggled. "Heavenly choirs? An angelic chorus? It
is Sunday, you know."

"Aretha Franklin," Jed insisted, swinging his legs over
the side of the bed. "I think I'd better check it out."

Susan reached down toward the end of the bed for a cotton blanket before remembering that they had spent the
night in the guest room, their own room being covered in
plastic and a thick layer of plaster dust. "Damn." She was
cold and it occurred to her that the sounds Jed had heard
were coming from the attic. The second day of work on the
house had begun. She might as well go downstairs and start
the coffeemaker so that there would be a cup waiting when
she returned from walking Clue. All she had to do now was
sneak into her bedroom and get her bathrobe.

Susan was wearing a bright purple nightshirt; it had been
a Christmas gift to her daughter from a friend at college.
Chrissy had refused to have anything to do with the gift

and it had ended up in the bottom drawer of the guest room dresser. Until the lights had gone off the night before, neither she nor Jed had realized there was a suggestive glow-in-the-dark message printed on the shirt. Susan had been slightly shocked; her husband had thought it was a good suggestion.

Jed reappeared with a paper cup of steaming coffee in each hand.

"Hey, where did you get that?" Susan asked, taking a cup and starting to remove the plastic lid.

"The worker with the weird hair brought it for us."

"They're called dreadlocks and his name is Frankie. And bless him; I needed this," Susan said, taking a long sip of the potent brew. "Did you know they were going to start work this early?"

"Actually, Ken told me yesterday. I guess I forgot to mention it to you."

"I guess."

"Maybe you'd like me to walk Clue?"

Susan accepted the offer. "Do you think I could get into the bedroom and find some clean clothes without being seen?"

"Definitely. They're working on the third floor putting in the new piping up there. See you in a while. Maybe we should go out today—to the park or something—and spend some time lying under the trees and thinking these bathrooms out."

"Good idea. But don't you want breakfast first?"

"Sure. Why don't I walk Clue, then drive down to the bakery and pick up some breakfast. It was nice of those guys to get coffee for us and I think we should return the favor. Then we can leave after we eat and glance at the *Times*."

"Fine." Susan hopped out of bed and trotted across the hall to her own bedroom as soon as Jed was gone. Promising herself that she would spend some time today moving essentials to the guest room, she lifted up the sheet of plastic, dumping filth down the front of her nightshirt before succeeding in retrieving fresh underwear, shorts, and a knit shirt. The angry words of Bob Marley alerted her to

Frankie's whereabouts and she glanced at the gaping hole in the bathroom ceiling before fleeing back to the guest room to dress. She had good reason to hurry. She wanted to talk to Frankie before Jed returned from the bakery.

In an orderly world Frankie wouldn't have been the person she started her investigation with, but life right now was anything but orderly. She tossed the nightshirt on the bed, pulled her clothing on, and ran downstairs to brush her teeth and wash her face.

Art Young was sitting at her kitchen table, drinking coffee and reading a 1993 *Information Please Almanac*. He looked up when Susan entered. "Hello. Your husband just left with the dog. Did you know that all golden retrievers are descended from a pair of Russian circus dogs that visited London ... Ah, I don't know how long ago. Damn. Better look that up." He pulled a tiny black notebook from the pocket in his plaid shirt and after shuffling through it to find an empty page wrote himself a note.

"Actually," Susan began, feeling a little awkward about socializing with someone she barely knew before she had brushed her teeth or her hair. "I think that story about retrievers is just a romantic tale. Clue's breeder said they were descended from Newfoundlands."

"Interesting," Art Young said, making another note. "Better check that out, too. You never know when 'Perky Pets' will appear as a topic on the show."

"I ... uh, I have to use the bathroom," Susan said honestly.

"Don't flush until you check with those guys upstairs. They've pulled out that cracked drain."

Susan knew it was too early to knock on a neighbor's door and ask to use the john. She hurried off to do what she had to do, deciding that she should find out what time the field club opened. Then maybe she would ask Art Young about the letter to Simon Fairweather that she had spied hanging out of his tool chest.

But opportunity wasn't going to wait for her to brush her teeth, and the carpenter had vanished from her kitchen when she had finally managed to make herself presentable. She headed toward the reggae beat.

"Hi!" Frankie, ever cheerful, rubbed a filthy hand across his forehead and turned off the radio propped on a window-sill. "We're making too much noise, aren't we?"

"I told him that shit was too loud," Buns said, turning off the flame on the torch. "Can't understand a word myself. But I like the beat. Reminds me of the music in the bar at the hotel where the wife and I spent our honeymoon."

"You went to Jamaica for your honeymoon?" Susan asked, to be polite.

"Nah. Who do you think we are, Rockefellers? We went to Atlantic City. Sprung for the honeymoon suite at the Polynesian Princess Palace. It was torn down to make way for one of them skyscraper casinos."

"Oh, really?" Susan said, noticing that Frankie had turned around so that his co-worker wouldn't see his grin.

"Yeah, nice, simple beat," Buns said, returning to his work.

Susan, who understood enough of the lyrics to know that this nice, simple beat accompanied a plea for the world to unite through the use of an illegal drug, couldn't think of anything to say this early in the morning.

"Damn!" Buns put his torch down on a sheet of metal and stood up. "Back to the truck. Ran out of flux again."

"I'll . . ."

"Nah. I could use some coffee, too. You stay here and explain to Mrs. Henshaw what we're doing. The house-holder always likes to know what we're doing—leastways at first." Buns threw this last cryptic remark over his shoulder as he vanished down the stairs.

Frankie waited until they were alone before speaking. "He's a nice guy."

"Have you two worked together for a long time?" Susan asked, leaning against the wall and looking around.

"Couple of years. Buns gave me my first on-the-job training. He's the only plumber I've ever worked with—although maybe I shouldn't tell you that. Might not build your confidence."

"You seem to know what you're doing."

"Yeah, well, the first few months I worked with Buns he threatened to fire me if I screwed anything up. I was scared to death of ending up on the street, so I learned real quickly. I'm a good plumber and I like my work. You don't have to worry about your pipes leaking."

"You work for ... Buns." Susan had trouble saying that name. "Or do you work for Ken Cory?"

"We both work for Cory Construction, but Buns is the senior plumber. Ken actually hired me. A little over two years ago."

"You like working for Cory Construction?" Susan asked casually, ducking under one of the eaves as she walked around.

"Yeah. They're all right. Ken's a real nice guy and everyone on his crew gets along okay."

"Just okay?"

"Well, we work together every day all day long. Sometimes we get on each other's nerves."

"Do you work on more than one project at a time?"

"Sometimes. Not this one though." Frankie chuckled and his dreadlocks bounced. "This job is bigger than most. After all, it's really three jobs in one location, isn't it?"

"I suppose so," Susan agreed. "Does that mean that the men working on this job are all the men who work for Cory Construction?"

"Pretty much. Buns and I are the only plumbers. Art Young has been Ken's main finish carpenter for years. Kyle just hired on this summer. He's replacing a carpenter who was with Ken forever—maybe even before Art. And Ken works along with the crew a lot of the time. Then there's Angelo. I don't know if you've met him yet."

"I don't think so." Susan was feeling a little confused, trying to connect the names with the faces.

"He's the electrician and that's about it, except for the Joes. They're the tile men we usually use. They work for other contractors, of course. Tiling a bathroom rarely takes more than a day or two—of course, on this job, that's six

days, so you'll get to see more of the Joes than most homeowners do."

"Why do you call them the Joes?"

"That's what everyone calls them. They're all named
Joe. There's Uncle Joe and his two nephews, Joe and
Joel—both named after their uncle. They are an experience.
Uncle Joe believes two things: First that he knows everything about the world that is worth knowing, and second
that his nephews know nothing. He spends all his time in-
structing them in the ways of life while the three of them
do the best job of laying tile of anyone in Connecticut." He
looked up at Susan. "Pick out interesting tiles. Those three
are truly masters of their trade. Uncle Joe's uncle came
over here from a little town in Tuscany and brought not just
the skills but an eye that can't be beat—and it's been
passed down in the family."

"That's good to know," Susan said, regretting the dull
pattern she'd chosen for this floor. Maybe there was time to
change it.

"The Joes picked up the materials you selected at Tile
City last night," Buns announced, appearing at the top of
the stairs. "That is what you were talking about, isn't it?"

"Well . . ." Susan began.

"Actually, I was just trying to help Mrs. Henshaw figure
out who was who on the crew," Frankie explained.

"Not a bad idea. Not a bad idea at all. Lots of homeowners never figure out who's who and then phone messages
and all get real mixed up."

"Phone messages?"

"Don't you worry, Mrs. Henshaw, Ken Cory's not like
other contractors. We'd be in big trouble if we started using
the homeowners' phone for personal calls. We don't do
things like that. No way. But you'll be getting calls for us.
Sometimes Ken will call with an important message—
work-related, mind you. And sometimes the companies we
do business with will call. Like to see if there's someone
here to accept a delivery. Or to check out information about
an order. Course, they're told to call Cory Construction first

and Ken carries one of them new cellular phones, but still you'll get calls."

Susan remembered how difficult it had been to leave a message for Cory Construction and resigned herself to more calls than usual—or maybe not, she decided, remembering that her children's friends wouldn't be tying up the line.

"Frankie was just telling me that you've been with Cory Construction for quite a while," she said as casually as she could.

"Yup. Almost from the beginning, and that was almost six years ago. Before that I worked with different crews, lots of different ones. That was in the eighties. No reason for any competent carpenter to sit on his butt during the eighties. And plenty of incompetent ones worked then, too."

Susan wondered how long ago it had been since Simon Fairweather had had his own business. "Did you work for many of the companies in town?" she asked.

"Nah. I worked down at the Jersey shore. Just came up to Connecticut five years ago. The wife's father died and she wanted to be near her mother. The old lady lives up in Hartford. The wife sees her on weekends. Me, I like working on Sunday, so I don't have to go along."

Susan smiled at this display of family devotion.

"Course, George and Art have worked in this town all their lives. They were working with Ken before I was."

Susan was glad that he had brought up the name of the other carpenter so that she could ask some questions about him. "George? I think someone mentioned him before," she said.

"George Porter. The original finish carpenter for Cory Construction. He's the guy that Kyle replaced a few months ago. Yup, George was a real original. I sure miss him."

"He retired?"

"Died. One of those accidents. Touched a live wire with his metal wrench. Burned him to a crisp in less time than it takes to say Kentucky Fried Chicken."

Susan gagged as Jed appeared at the top of the stairs, a bulging white bakery box in his hand.

"Doughnuts, anyone?" he offered.

Just the scent, usually delicious, made her nauseous and it was with relief that she rushed past her husband and fled down the stairway to answer the phone.

"Hello?" She fell on the bed, gasping for breath and only managing to fill her lungs with plaster dust. She had assumed it was for one of the crew, so the message surprised her.

"I'll be right there," she assured the caller before hanging up and running from the room.

"Jed! I'm on my way to the Gordons' house. Kathleen's labor has begun!"

FOURTEEN

"YOU'RE CERTAINLY BACK QUICKLY. I THOUGHT YOU WERE going to be there until Kathleen's mother came up from Philly. No one can make that drive in less than three hours," Jed said, looking up from the newspaper he'd been reading when Susan appeared on the patio.

"True, but the woman had some sort of premonition and left home before five A.M. She got there about an hour after I arrived. Actually, I would have been home quite a while ago if Mrs. Somerville hadn't insisted on a critique of the bathroom plans I was working on when she walked in the door."

"Any word about Kathleen or the baby?"

"Nothing yet. I'm sure they'll call as soon as there's any news." She sat down on the lounge next to her husband. "Do you want to see what I accomplished while Ba—Alex built a spaceship with Legos? You'll be thrilled; I think I've finally got everything figured out," she added, handing him a large sheet of paper.

"What the . . . ?"

"Ignore the marks made in red pencil. They're Kathleen's mother's—she wanted to be sure I'd recognize the improvements she was making. What sort of woman has a red pencil conveniently tucked into her purse?"

Jed stared at the plans she had handed him. "I don't understand."

"I've moved the wall! It came to me on the drive over. Look, all you have to do is shift the linen closet in the hall-way and the bathroom off our bedroom becomes a rectangle instead of a square. We can put in a truly long bathtub and an extra-large separate shower."

"A double shower."

"Yes, with a seat at one end. It will be so much easier to shave my legs."

"You could practically swim in the bathtub you've planned here. Does anyone actually make a tub that long?"

"Yes, it's right here in this catalog of European tubs and sinks."

"How much?"

"The other bathroom is very simple, Jed," Susan said earnestly. "All the fixtures are Kohler. Inexpensive. White. Standard. Good, but inexpensive," she repeated, to drive home her point, and placed the Kohler catalog on top.

Jed looked at the one underneath. "You're planning one very luxurious bathroom here."

"But I . . ."

"But I know how you like to relax in the tub with a glass of white wine."

"And it's cheaper than years with a psychiatrist."

"Well, maybe," Jed answered, flipping to the price list in the back of the catalog. "Or maybe not! Susan . . ." He glanced at his wife's face. "Okay. If anyone deserves the best bathroom in the world, you do." He looked back at the plan. "What is this?" He pointed to a corner of the room.

"Laundry chute to the basement. It was Kathleen's mother's idea."

"It's a good one."

"Only if you like your filthy clothes landing on the middle of the dining room table. There's no direct route to the basement from the master bath," Susan explained.

"Oh. Well, shall we go upstairs and show Ken?"

"He's here?" Susan had been hoping to ask Buns some more questions about Simon Fairweather and felt that he was more likely to answer extensively—and perhaps truthfully—if his employer wasn't around.

"Upstairs introducing a new carpenter to the rest of his

crew. He's worried about finishing this project in only six weeks, so he's taken on another employee."

"That's good, isn't it?" Susan asked, not understanding the expression on her husband's face.

"You would have thought so, but ever since Josie came, the men have done very little work. Mainly they're huddled together up in the attic or out in the truck making suspiciously angry sounds. My guess would be that they don't like working with a woman," he added, knowing exactly how Susan was going to react to his statement.

"You're kidding. What a bunch of—"

"Chauvinist pigs." Jed finished the sentence for her.

"What century do they—"

"Think they're living in."

"Jed, this is serious!"

"I wouldn't argue with you. But I do think you're going to have to let these guys solve this one by themselves. They have to work together. And they're not children. Their boss brought in a new worker and they know they're going to have to make their peace with the situation."

"Sure. And their peace may be bought at this woman's ... What did you say her name was?"

"Josie."

"At Josie's expense."

"I appreciate the thought. I really do. But I can handle this myself."

The Henshaws turned and looked at the woman standing in their kitchen doorway.

"Hi. I'm Josie Pigeon." A bright smile appeared amid the freckles on her face. Burnished red curly hair was struggling to free itself from an elastic band, and her clothing, a white T-shirt and denim overalls, barely contained her chubby but curvaceous body. She had such bright green eyes that Susan felt they could only be the result of colored contact lenses. She didn't seem to mind Clue drooling on her work boot.

"You're a carpenter?" Jed blurted out. "You look so young," he added quickly before his wife could accuse him of an attitude similar to that of the men upstairs.

"You've never seen a thirty-two-year-old carpenter before? You've got men upstairs younger than I am!" But Josie's remarkable eyes were sparkling and her smile became a grin. "I am," she added, "a very good carpenter. And I'm much more likely to realize that you're hanging your towel racks in an inconvenient place than a male carpenter. Men don't notice those things." She grinned again. "See, we're all a little sexist, so I have to accept the shit that I get. Until it gets out of hand."

"Then this is going to work out?" Jed asked quietly.

"Don't worry about it. Every business has its own conventions. In mine the men have to make a big stink, complain and complain and complain, and force me to prove that I'm competent. Then we all work together and get the job done. And sometime during the last week on the job, the men begin making cracks about how they're sure glad I didn't live up to their worst expectations." She shrugged. "I like what I do, so I deal with it."

"Well, it's nice to meet you," Jed said politely.

"Nice meeting you, too. I know that most of these guys just wander into your house and get down to work and an entire job can be finished without the owners connecting the faces and the names. I like to introduce myself. It will make us all feel more comfortable when we run into each other and one of us isn't dressed."

Susan glanced over at her husband and smiled at the foolish grin on his face. She had a feeling that Josie Pigeon was going to be a great addition to the crew. And the comment about towel racks reminded her that she hadn't included such details in her diagrams. "I suppose towel racks won't matter until the job is almost finished," she muttered.

"We'll want to know where they're going to go before the wallboard is put up," Josie corrected her. "That way we can build in support. Otherwise they're going to pull right out of the walls when you drape a pile of wet terrycloth over them."

"I think I have some work to do," Susan muttered, picking up the diagrams.

"I've got to get back upstairs, but if you need any help

with those towel racks—or anything else—just give me a yell." Josie gave Clue's head one last scratch, grinned, and hurried back into the house.

"Well, isn't she charming?" Jed commented.

"Hmm. How many towel racks do you think we need in the bathroom?" Susan asked, shuffling through the papers.

"How many did we have?" he asked.

"Jed, you've been using that room for almost twenty years! How could you ask a question like that?"

"Susan, this is your specialty. You plan the bathroom you've always wanted and I'll be thrilled with it—whatever it is."

"Are you going out?"

"I was thinking about going over to the club for lunch and seeing if I can pick up a game of tennis this afternoon. Want to come?"

"I think I'll stay here and work on all of this. I can find something to munch on in the refrigerator."

"You're sure?"

"Definitely." As if to demonstrate her point, she shook the sheets of paper on her lap, shifting a few of them to the ground. "I'll get them," she insisted as her husband stooped down. "I need to do some sorting."

And she really did, she realized as she heard Jed's car start up. Her notes about Simon Fairweather's murder were mixed in with lighting options. She knelt on the patio and made two piles on the lounge on which she had been sitting. The larger one was bathroom plans. The other listed the suspects in Simon Fairweather's murder. Right now that included Patricia Fairweather and Cory Construction. But, of course, that didn't make sense. If the motive was professional rather than personal, it was just as likely to be someone on another construction crew, after all.

She got up, then sat down and closed her eyes. She really liked to sleep late on Sunday. . . .

A while later she opened her eyes and found Brett Fortesque sitting on a chair at the edge of the patio.

"Oh, wow, how long have I been asleep?" she asked, brushing the hair from her eyes and sitting up straight.

"I don't know. I've just been here for a few minutes. I was looking at your diagrams. Are you sure you've got this right?" he asked, pointing to a sheet of paper. "It looks like you have your perspective wrong. This bathtub is awfully long."

"It's made in Europe," Susan answered as if that explained everything.

Brett raised an eyebrow but didn't comment. "Actually, I was interested in this list more than plumbing plans." He held up her notes on the murder.

"I was thinking about that before I drifted off," Susan said, grabbing an American Standard catalog from Clue's mouth and replacing it with a dog biscuit from her pocket. "But I don't believe Patricia murdered him, I really don't. And I don't understand why I should accept the fact that someone from Cory Construction is more likely to be a murderer than someone from a different company."

"Actually, there are a couple of reasons," Brett said, looking at her seriously.

"Something's happened."

"A few things," Brett admitted, glancing around. "Could we go someplace where we won't be overheard?"

"Sure, we could go for a drive. Or take Clue for a walk."

The dog leaped to her feet, tail wagging energetically.

Brett glanced down at the animal. "It's hard to deny such enthusiasm. Besides, maybe her name will inspire us."

"There's a leash on the gatepost," Susan muttered, getting up and stretching. "I'd better get a plastic bag."

"A plastic bag?" Brett looked confused.

"Surely the chief of police knows that there's a pooper-scooper law in Hancock."

"So why don't you bring a pooper-scooper?"

"A plastic bag's easier. I have them right inside the back door. It just takes a second to get one." Susan ran in and was back out five minutes later, returning to Brett's side as she tucked a bag that bore the Pepperidge Farm trademark into her shorts pocket.

"That took a while. Are you ready?" Brett had the leash attached to Clue's collar.

"I stopped to call Kathleen's mom to see if there was any news from the hospital—there wasn't," she added. "But I'm ready now." She opened the gate and slid back out of the way as the dog pulled Brett through. They were down to the street in record time.

"Does she always pull like this?"

"Until we get off the property. She loves her walks. You can just give the collar a good jerk and she'll slow down."

Hancock was a town of lovely tree-lined streets that wrapped around houses with large yards. The bluestone sidewalks, which were easy to trip over at night, were set far enough away from the homes that Susan and Brett had relative privacy. As Clue sniffed a towering Norway maple, Brett got right to the point.

"The preliminary report came from the coroner's office."

"I didn't think there was any doubt about the method of death. I mean, a nail gun . . ." Susan bit her lip and tried not to think about it too closely.

"It's where the gun came from," Brett added quickly.

Susan looked at him questioningly.

"It was marked with heavy black ink. The mark was C.C."

"Cory Construction?"

"It's very likely. I actually was on the way over here to check that out when a strange phone call came through."

"What sort of phone call?"

"It had to do with the murder and the caller claimed to be a member of Cory Construction's crew. The call was made from your house."

FIFTEEN

"You're kidding!"

"No, we checked our caller ID. It was your number. The call came from your house."

Susan thought about that for a moment.

"When?"

"About fifteen minutes before I arrived there. I left right away. And Jed said—"

"You saw Jed?"

"He was backing out of the driveway as I got here."

"Then I must have been asleep for only a few minutes," Susan said.

"He said that, as far as he knew, the entire crew was working this morning. As well as some new female carpenter."

"And Ken Cory is here, too," Susan mused. "But if the call was made from the house fifteen minutes before you arrived, it probably wouldn't have been Josie Pigeon."

"That's the woman carpenter?"

"Yes, but she was talking to Jed and myself around that time. Besides, she just got here. She probably wouldn't even know about the murder."

"Well, that might eliminate her. How many does it leave?" Brett asked, stopping for the dog to do what dogs do.

Susan knelt down with the plastic bag covering her hand and picked up the resulting mess. "Let me think," she said, slightly embarrassed by her part in this natural occurrence. "There's Ken, of course. And Art Young and Kyle—he's a carpenter, too, but I can't remember his last name. And there's Frankie. He's a plumber; he has dreadlocks and I don't think I've even heard his last name. And there's Buns, the other plumber." She started to giggle. "I don't even know his real name. And also the electrician. I don't remember his name." She tied a knot in the open end of the bag.

"What about the tile men?"

"The Joes? That's what everyone calls them, apparently," she added, seeing the surprised look on Brett's face. "I've never met them and I didn't know they were here. Surely no one is even thinking of laying tile. There aren't any walls or floors anywhere yet."

"There's a tile company truck parked in your driveway," Brett said.

Susan sighed. "I hadn't noticed. People come and go, and there's so much noise and mess. It's difficult to keep track of everyone. If their truck is here, I suppose one or all of them could have been in the house when the call was made."

"How many phone extensions do you have?"

Susan thought for a moment. "An absurd number, really. There's one in the kitchen. One in the study. One in our bedroom. And one in the laundry room in the basement as well as one on the wall hanging near the pool table down there. There's also a cellular in the upstairs hallway that can be removed from its base and carried around. The kids have their own phones and their own lines, too."

"Then they don't count. This call was made on the number listed for you and Jed. For heaven's sake, why do you have so many phones?"

Susan shook her head. "I have no idea. Each one seemed like a necessity when it was bought, but I really don't know. I suppose that's one of the reasons Jed plays all these sports and I started to run—to get the exercise we used to get dashing to answer the phone. But it's not going to be easy to find out who called the station, is it?"

"No."

"You didn't tell me what he said. It was a man, wasn't it?"

"Sounds like you and this Pigeon person were the only

women in the house and you don't think she did it. So it was probably a man," Brett conceded.

"What did he say?"

"He said that we had better keep an eye on Cory Construction. That someone on the crew killed Simon Fairweather."

Susan stopped dead. "You're kidding."

"No. I don't kid about murder. What we need to do right now is see if anyone knows who made that call from your house."

"Are you going to question everyone?" Susan asked, wondering if she would be allowed to watch.

"I was hoping you would do that."

"What?" Susan shrieked so loudly that a neighbor, setting out on a power walk and busily adjusting ankleweights, jumped up and asked if anyone needed help.

"We're fine!" Brett called out, waving genially at the other man.

"No, I'm not!" Susan muttered. "I'm not a policeman. I can't just walk up to people and interrogate them about phone calls that they may or may not have made."

"But you're the homeowner and you have a right to ask questions about who is using your phone. Just make up some story and ask questions. And it would be best if you could do it in a way so that no one knows why you're asking."

"Brett . . ."

"Susan, I don't want anyone to know that we're investigating this. It's obviously what the caller wants us to do and I don't like anyone thinking they can manipulate the police department with anonymous calls. And you are good at this," he said.

"Flattery will get you everywhere. Okay, I'll do it." Actually, she had already thought up an excuse to ask the men working in her home some questions.

Brett tugged on the dog's leash and turned back toward the house.

"You want me to call you right away with anything I find out?" Susan asked, trotting behind.

"Good idea. But, Susan," he added, becoming even more

serious, "there could be a murderer in your house. There is no reason in the world to believe that you're at risk. But if you get too close to the truth . . ."

"I know. A person who kills once finds it easier to kill a second time."

"Sounds like you've been reading old English mystery novels," Brett said with a chuckle. "I don't actually know if that is true. In my experience, murderers are as varied as most groups. But if you put a murderer at risk, you very well could be risking your own life. That's one of the reasons I decided to talk to you in person."

"I don't get it."

"Your family's connection to the police department could help protect you. Everyone in town knows that you've been involved in murder investigations. I just thought that my presence at your house might send a message, an important message, to someone."

Susan frowned. "It's hard to imagine that anyone on that crew is a murderer. Of course, I really don't know them that well."

"Then this is your opportunity to get to know them better," Brett answered, turning up her driveway.

Clue felt a compulsion to sniff the tires of each van and pickup truck parked there so Susan had plenty of time to read all of the logos after Brett had driven off. As he had said, the tile layers' van was parked at the end of the line. Peeking inside, Susan saw a few boxes of beige tiles.

"Pretty color, aren't they?"

People always seemed to be sneaking up behind her these days. Susan turned and found herself looking up at a large middle-aged man with deeply tanned skin and thick, wavy salt-and-pepper hair.

"Uh, yes," she said, although she didn't actually think so. "You must be . . . uh, Joe."

"Sure am. Always like to meet the missus at the beginning of a job. And those are certainly nice tiles you picked out for that upstairs room."

Susan glanced into the back of the van. "Those aren't the tiles I ordered."

"They just look different through the window." Joe grabbed the door with a large, hairy arm and swung it open. "Take a closer look."

She did. "They're not the tiles I picked out. They may be the same design, although I don't think so, but I know that I ordered white."

"They're not white?"

"They're beige. Maybe off-white. Maybe cream. But the tiles I picked out are perfectly white. With little diamond-shaped tiles in green and blue between them. I'm absolutely sure of that."

"Junior!"

Susan jumped as the man beside her shouted in her ear.

"Junior, get down here this minute. Ya picked up the wrong tiles again. Them kids. Can't trust them for a minute," he groused, smacking down a meaty hand on one of the cardboard boxes.

Susan turned as she heard someone running up behind her. She had expected a teenager, but the man who appeared around the side of the van was in his mid-twenties at the very least.

"You called me, Uncle Joe?" he asked politely.

"Look at them tiles. Do they look white?"

"Definitely not. I think the company calls them 'Peach Breath.' They're for the job over on Cedar Lane. That tiny little half-bath off the dining room. Should they be white?" he asked politely.

"What happened to the white tiles for the Henshaw job? You and your brother were sent out to pick up white tiles for the Henshaw job."

"We did. They're stashed in the corner of the attic. Out of the way until needed."

That didn't stop Uncle Joe for a moment. "How many times have I told you and that brother of yours that nothing should go into the house until I've checked it over? You guys never listen. Now I'm going to have to go all the way back up those stairs and look at those tiles myself." He slammed the van's door and turned to Susan. "Pardon me, ma'am. You want a job done right, you do it yourself."

"Of course. It was nice meeting you. I guess I'll be see-ing you around."

"That you will. And you want something real nice for those other two bathrooms you go see Giuseppe over in Norwich. He does tiles himself. Tell him I sent you. He'll give you a good price." He started back to the house. "Ju-nior, give the lady Giuseppe's card!" he yelled back over his shoulder.

"Here." Junior held out a small white rectangle of card-board. "Giuseppe really is the best in the business if you're looking for something special."

Susan took the card and a deep breath. She might as well start now. "How long have you and your uncle been here? I keep finding all these different people in my house," she added quickly lest he think it was an odd question.

"About an hour. Uncle Joe likes to see what a job looks like—and yell at the carpenters to make sure they get the corners square and the walls plumb. Makes it easier to lay tile that way."

"I heard that your brother worked with you," Susan be-gan tentatively. "I wonder if he was the tall man that I saw using the phone in the hallway upstairs," she improvised.

"I doubt that. Uncle Joe is real big on not getting in the homeowners' way. His rule is, we don't use anything of yours. Even if you offer us coffee or something, we're sup-posed to turn it down. What we need, we bring in. And if we need to phone someone we go to a pay phone nearby. Besides, I was with my brother until I came out here. Must've been someone else."

"Probably was," Susan agreed.

"I better get back upstairs. Uncle Joe needs to yell at me every fifteen minutes or so or he gets nervous. But he is re-ally the best tile man in the business." He paused and looked seriously at Susan. "You pick out good tiles and we'll make great bathrooms for you."

As he entered the house, Kyle Barnes and Josie Pigeon came out.

SIXTEEN

THEY WERE LAUGHING TOGETHER AND SUSAN WAS RELIEVED to see that Josie had apparently found an ally on the crew. She walked up to them with a smile on her face.

"How's everything going?" she asked casually. "Looks like you've found a friend," she added to Josie.

"Some of the guys are a little chauvinistic, but a female carpenter isn't all that unusual these days. They'll come around," Kyle said, brushing blond hair off his forehead.

Josie smiled but didn't say anything about that. "Ken sent me to look for you. He wants to check out some last-minute details before he begins framing in the far wall of the third-floor bath. Something about the possibility of a tub under the eaves."

"I was thinking about that. I'd better go see him," Susan muttered. "Say," she added to Kyle, throwing caution to the winds, "were you talking on the phone this morning?"

He didn't seem particularly surprised by the question. "No. Were you expecting a call?"

Susan realized that he assumed she was talking about answering the phone, but there was no reason to elaborate. If he hadn't been on the phone, he hadn't been on the phone. "Did you see anyone else on the phone?" she asked.

"Nope. This is the first time I've been off the third floor since I got here this morning—no one's been working anyplace else. But I'll ask around, if you'd like me to."

"Don't bother. I'll check it out," Susan said. "But first it sounds like I'd better go talk with Ken."

"That's a good idea," Josie approved, nodding her head.

"Sometimes if you wait you'll find that things have been done that need changing. Better to do things right the first time. Saves money. Saves a lot of wear and tear on your nerves. And the crew usually doesn't like repeating the same work."

"Let's go on up," Susan said, taking the not-too-subtle hint.

"And I'd better go find that nail gun," Kyle said, heading off toward a Cory Construction truck.

Susan followed Josie into her house, determined to get a look at that particular tool as soon as possible. On her way up the stairs she noticed that the plastic had shifted in the hallway and there were grungy footprints on her light-colored wool carpet.

Josie noticed her attention. "You might want to get some gaffer's tape and fasten down the plastic. It's going to get worse, much worse, before it gets better."

"Good idea," Susan agreed. "What do you think about the design of the third-floor bath?" she asked as they started up the stairs.

"Not bad. I think I'd add a wraparound vanity. Extend the vanity under the sink across the far wall and under the window. It will unify the room and add countertop space. You're going to build a master-bedroom suite up there?"

"Maybe a guest room. Someday," Susan added.

"Then that small tub under the eaves would be a nice addition—or maybe a shower stall?"

"A shower stall. That's an idea. Maybe one of those all-one-piece things."

"Talk it over with Ken Cory. It's not too late to decide on something like that," Josie suggested, speeding up slightly.

"How are you getting along?" Susan asked, matching her pace.

"I do my work. Don't worry, they'll accept me in time." She chuckled. "Of course, when they do, I'll have to live with a bunch of old, stale jokes about working women." She moved aside so that Frankie, carrying a large acetylene torch under his arm, could pass by without smashing it against the wall.

"Oh, Frankie," Susan said quickly, feeling that she might as well get it over with, "were you talking on the phone about half an hour or maybe an hour ago?"

He looked startled. "No, of course not—" he began to protest.

"We don't use the phones in the house for personal calls," Buns interrupted, coming around the corner right behind his assistant. "You don't have to worry about that. Frankie and I don't tie up the lines."

Frankie smiled and hurried on down the stairs as Buns continued. "Mr. Cory is looking for you. We've got the copper laid. Time for you to figure out whether we go up for a shower or down for a tub—or skip it altogether."

Susan, completely mystified by this, followed Josie into her attic. "I . . ." she began, before looking around. "Wow!"

All of the Henshaws' personal possessions had been piled up along the far wall and the partition that formed the original half-bath had been removed. The space looked huge. And there was no longer a gaping hole in the floor.

Ken Cory looked up from where he was kneeling on the floor, slamming nails into a large sheet of plywood. "Susan! I'm glad you're here. We need a final decision about whether or not you want a tub. And what about adding a skylight or two up here while we're at it?"

"A skylight?" Susan took a step back. "I hadn't even thought of it," she protested. "But maybe it's a good idea—"

"How old's your roof?" Josie interrupted to ask.

"My roof?" Susan looked at Josie as though she was surprised to discover herself in possession of such an object.

"Has the house been reshingled since you moved in?" Josie asked patiently.

"Yes. Right after we moved in, actually. We had almost no money after the closing, but we realized that it had to be done after the first big storm. It meant that we had to put off decorating the living room."

"When was that?" Josie interrupted.

"Sixteen . . . no, seventeen years ago." Susan had trouble with numbers that exceeded the number of her fingers.

"Then you'll probably have to shingle sometime in the next five years. You could add a skylight then. There's no real reason to make that decision now if you don't want to."

"But if you want that tub you've mentioned," Ken prompted.

"Or maybe a shower?" Susan suggested quietly.

"That won't fit under the eaves where we talked about putting one," Ken said. "And we have some of the copper pipe laid."

Susan looked at the line of shiny piping he was indicating. "That's where the tub would be?"

Ken nodded.

"Did you see the square tub that I marked in the American Standard catalog?" Susan asked slowly.

"It will fit right in there. We could even ask the Joes about adding a tile border around the edge in the same pattern as the floor. That would make it blend right in," Ken added earnestly.

"How much would it cost?"

"Not all that much. Depending on the extra cost of the tiling and the amount for the tub itself. Maybe a couple of thousand. A fairly small percentage of the entire job."

Susan took a deep breath. "Okay. Let's go with it." She glanced at the frown on Josie's face. "And how about extending the vanity top across that wall while we're at it." She waved to indicate the direction.

"Great idea!" Ken enthused. "Now if only Kyle would get back here with that nail gun, we could get on with this job."

"Where is Art Young today?" Susan asked, looking around.

"Downstairs. He's checking on some of our orders at the suppliers who are open on Sunday."

"On the phone!" Susan realized immediately that she had said this a little too enthusiastically to make sense.

But Ken was apparently too busy to notice. "Yup." His next words disappointed Susan. "He's got the cellular."

"You brought your own phone?"

"Don't want to tie up your line," Ken said, not paying much attention.

"Was the electrician—Angelo or whatever—here today?" Susan asked.

"Angelo Ferraro. Nope. Not today. No reason for him to be hanging around billing me for his time unless there's something for him to do."

Susan thought for a moment. "I was expecting a phone call," she improvised. "I just thought that someone else might have answered the phone."

"Or possibly been talking on the line when the call came through," Josie suggested, kneeling down to examine a heavy pencil mark on the newly laid underflooring.

"Well, I doubt it. I haven't used the phone today, but if you want to ask any of the crew, feel free," Ken offered casually.

Susan didn't admit that she had already done so. Josie had pulled a tape measure from the pocket of her overalls and was busy with something else. Susan wondered if she should give Brett a call. Her investigations there had certainly turned up nothing of importance. "What about towel racks up here?" she asked, remembering her other current concern.

"They were supposed to hang on the sides of the vanity. At least, that's what I remember of our original discussion," Ken said. "But if you want a ledge to extend from the sink under the window and across that wall, we could hang the racks from underneath."

"Would look nice," Josie said quietly, flipping the tape back onto its reel.

"Let's do that," Susan agreed quickly. For some reason she had come to trust this young woman.

"They could be made from pine dowels and holders. They'd blend in and be less expensive than the ones you buy," Josie added.

"Great idea," Ken jumped in. "And every little bit of saving helps."

"Good," Susan agreed, having little idea of what was actually being decided. Had this project escaped her control so soon? Had she ever been in control? "I'd like to show you the diagrams I've been working on," she announced. "I think I should review them with somebody."

"I'd be happy to do it," Josie offered. "Then you'll be free to explain to Buns and Frankie where to put the pipes for the tub," she added to Ken.

"Fine. Why don't you do it downstairs? It's going to get pretty noisy up here real soon. Do me a favor and see what's happened to Kyle. And find Art and tell him I need him."

"Sure will." Josie stood up and followed Susan from the room.

"I think I left my notes on the patio," Susan muttered.

"Why don't you go get them and I'll deliver Ken's messages to Art and Kyle and meet you . . ."

"In the kitchen?" Susan suggested. "I could use a cup of coffee. How about you?"

"Sounds great."

"You know the way?"

"I'll figure it out." The charming grin reappeared on Josie's face. "See you in a few minutes. We have some talking to do."

Susan rearranged the plastic runner as she went, remembering Josie's suggestion about gaffer's tape. She'd have to get busy with that tonight after the crew left. Right now she just hoped she would find that she'd left her diagram in a place where Clue hadn't mistaken it for a snack.

Happily, the diagram was still tucked under the stack of catalogs on her garden bench. She grabbed the entire pile and headed back into the house for coffee.

The dust from the attic had somehow found a way into her kitchen and she reached for the sponge by the sink to wipe off the English pine table in her kitchen before sitting down.

But it's difficult to clean anything without water. She

was still wiping away when Josie entered the room. "How do you take your coffee?" she asked, tossing the sponge in the parched sink and reaching for the coffeepot.

"Black, but I really should be getting mine from the thermos in my truck."

"You drive a truck?" Susan asked, momentarily diverted.

"Notice the cherry-red '66 Chevy at the end of your driveway? The sweetest truck in the world and it's all mine," Josie bragged. "And I'd love a cup of coffee. But we should talk quickly while we're still alone."

"Really?" Susan asked, surprised by this statement. "Is something wrong?"

"Well, first, and believe me this is completely unprofessional, you're going to end up spending a fortune on bathrooms that you may not particularly like if you don't get busy and figure out what you do and don't want."

"What do you mean?"

"Well, it's like that bathtub. You just spent a lot of money for a tub that you're not sure you wanted. Right?"

" 'A lot of money'? I thought it was a few thousand dollars."

"A couple of thousand here and a couple of thousand there adds up ... to a whole lot of money." Josie looked around the large kitchen at the beautiful handmade cabinets and the European appliances. "Even if you can afford it, it's foolish to pay for things you don't care about."

"No one would ever mistake us for Donald Trump," Susan said. "And you're right. It's a stupid way to spend money. I know you didn't say that, but it's what you meant. Maybe if we go over these plans, I can stick to the decisions I've made."

"Good. Ken Cory is probably an honest man, but it's hard to resist making a buck these days. Times are tough."

Susan was busy thinking about that "probably" when Josie Pigeon's next words drove it right out of her mind.

"Frankie lied about being on the phone. He made a call this morning."

"From one of my phones?" Susan asked.

"From the phone in your bedroom."

"You're sure?"

"Yes, I walked into the room while he was making a call."

"Did he say anything to you?"

"No, he didn't see me. He was sitting on the floor, leaning against the bed with his back to the door when I walked in," Josie explained.

"Did you overhear what he was talking about?" Susan asked.

"No. In fact, he was speaking very quietly. Like he was trying to make sure that he wasn't overheard. It was obvious that he wanted privacy, so I just backed out and closed the door behind me."

"That's interesting," Susan said noncommittally.

"We're going to be in your house all day long for weeks and weeks," Josie said quietly. "If you're not comfortable about someone on the crew, it's going to be more than a little difficult for you."

The phone rang before Susan could reply.

SEVENTEEN

"AND THAT'S WHEN THE PHONE RANG AND JERRY TOLD ME that Kathleen had given birth to a nine-pound, thirteen-ounce baby girl."

"And then?" Brett asked.

"And then Ken Cory came into the kitchen to ask me whether I wanted the hardware in the tub to match the faucets we had picked out for the third-floor sink and Josie and I never got any privacy again."

"So this Josie Pigeon didn't ask why you wanted to know about phone calls."

"No." Susan shrugged. "She helped me on the plans for the other two bathrooms and then joined everyone working up in the attic. I called your office and they said you'd be back in an hour, so I went over to the hospital to drop off a gift for Kathleen and then drove on over here."

"What sort of gift?" Brett asked. "I mean, I was thinking that maybe I should send something." He looked embarrassed.

"I took over champagne and a box of imported chocolate truffles. I know how a woman feels after giving birth."

"I was thinking of something for the baby."

"Why don't you take something to Alex? He's going to need a little ego massage with a new sister, and it might be easier for you to find something for a four-year-old boy than for a newborn."

"Who's Alex?"

"You know him as Bananas," Susan said, laughing.

"Oh. It's about time he gave up that silly nickname. And that's a good idea. I'll buy him a toy."

"Kathleen and Jerry don't want him playing with war toys or play guns," Susan added.

"Just because I'm a cop—"

"I'm sorry. I don't mean to be prejudiced," Susan said quickly.

Brett frowned at the notes he had been taking as she spoke. "What do you think about this new carpenter, this Josie Pigeon?"

"She's been so helpful," Susan began. "She offers excellent advice about the bathrooms. I don't like to sound sexist, but she really seems to think of things that the men don't."

"Do you know where she comes from? Has she worked with Cory Construction before? How did she end up working with them on your project?" Brett interrupted.

"I . . . I have no idea," Susan said.

"We should probably find out those things before we start trusting her." Brett looked at Susan expectantly.

"You want me to find all this out?" she asked slowly.

"If you would. If you could."

"When?"

"As soon as possible."

Susan glanced at her watch. "Then I'd better get going. I have no idea how long the crew was planning to work, but I wouldn't think it would be much past six o'clock."

"If you learn anything you'll call me tonight?" Brett asked.

"Of course," Susan said, getting up from her seat in his office and tucking her purse under her arm. "Is there anything else you want me to find out?" She hoped he didn't hear any sarcasm in her voice.

"Not right now," Brett muttered, still writing and paying little attention to her.

Susan drove home reviewing what little she had discovered up to now. Frankie's phone call was certainly suspicious, but was someone else lying? Wasn't it more than possible that a call had been made by another member of the crew as well? There was so much confusion; of course someone could take a few minutes for a private call without anyone noticing. Or could he? She was thinking about this when she arrived in front of her house. The questions were interesting, but not so interesting that she didn't notice that the horde of vehicles had shrunk to one cherry-red pickup truck.

Susan parked next to the large Dumpster, trying to leave room for Jed's Mercedes, got out, and hurried into the house. She was anxious to talk with Josie, having decided to explain straight out what had happened to Simon Fairweather and why she was asking all these questions. Surprisingly enough, Clue didn't enthusiastically greet her entrance. Susan frowned and walked slowly up the stairs, straightening the plastic runner as she went. On the second floor she could hear strange smacking noises above her head. She climbed up to the attic.

Josie was kneeling on the floor, holding a heavy object that was apparently forcing bolts into the wood beneath her. Clue was lying near the top of the stairs, seemingly fascinated by the sight. Susan stooped down and scratched the dog's ears.

"Hi!" Josie said, sitting back on her heels and pushing her blazing hair off her sweaty forehead. "Great dog you've got there. Tell her to lie down and she lies down."

"She does?" Susan asked, amazed by this revelation.

"I'll be done with this in a few minutes, if the noise is bothering you," Josie continued.

"That's okay. I was just going to go downstairs and . . . and start dinner," Susan improvised. "You can hardly hear that thing on the first floor. Say," she added, turning back after she started to leave, "would you like to stay for dinner? It's just going to be stuff on the grill in the backyard."

"Well, I . . ."

"I'd really appreciate it. Jed will be here and you could help me explain all the diagrams we made to him. Of course, if you're busy tonight . . ."

"Not me. I don't even know anyone in town except for the men I'm working with, and I don't think I should try their patience by spending more time with them than actually necessary for a while. Thanks, I'll take you up on that offer."

"It's going to be a simple meal," Susan reminded her.

"No problem. I don't know how to cook myself. But I'm a master of the microwave, and I know the name of every bakery in every town I've ever worked in."

"Then come on down when you're done here. By the way," she added, "what is that thing you're using?"

"Nail gun," Josie explained casually.

Susan watched the metal smash into the heavy plywood and tried not to imagine what it would do to human flesh and bone. "I'll get started on dinner. I'll see you later."

"Great." Josie turned back to her work, and Susan hurried down the stairs to scrounge around in the refrigerator. She wanted to talk to Jed, to ask him to leave the two women alone for a while.

Her husband still wasn't home by the time Susan had laid out everything that could be grilled from her refrigerator and thawed chicken breasts in the microwave.

"Hi!" Josie appeared in the kitchen, Clue at her side.

"Hi! Would you like a drink? I'm having a glass of white wine."

"Do you have a light beer?"

"Sure do. It's in the refrigerator. If you don't mind, you could get it yourself," Susan suggested, busy dipping strips of chicken in a sesame-seed marinade.

"Fine with me. I'm not used to people waiting on me." Josie walked over to the large Sub-Zero and opened the door. "Wow!" she exclaimed, examining the beer and ale selection. "I gather you don't feel it's absolutely necessary to buy American."

"I think there are some bottles in there that aren't imports," Susan protested.

"The finest product of what I think are called designer breweries these days," Josie agreed, picking out a bottle with the image of a blue heron on its label. "Do you mind if I drink from the bottle?"

"Not at all," Susan assured her, laying the last of the

meat on an ironstone platter. "Would you like to go outside? It's probably cooler there. I've got some cheese and
crackers that we can snack on until Jed arrives."

"Great. Shall I bring the dog?"

"If you don't mind her begging."

"This good dog begs?" Josie asked, apparently amazed.
She picked up Susan's wineglass and started out the door.
Susan followed with a tray of snack food.

They settled down on the patio, the food resting on a
small table between them. Clue, miraculously, lay at Josie's
feet.

"Gorgonzola, Cheshire cheddar, Brie with herbs." Susan pointed to the various cheeses. "The crackers are Pepperidge Farm," she added, trying to head off a comment
about her buying habits.

"Hey, I'm not complaining," Josie assured her. "I love
good food. It's just that I can't afford a lot of it. Carpenters
don't make great money and I've got a son in camp now
who's starting boarding school in the fall."

"Where's his father?" Susan asked without thinking.

"Heaven knows," Josie answered, and then volunteered
no more.

Both women were silent for a moment, drinking their
beverages and spreading cheese on crackers.

"I didn't mean to . . ."

"I don't want you to think . . ."

They spoke at the same time, looked at each other, and
laughed.

"You go first," Susan insisted.

"I don't want you to think that I was trashing Ken Cory
this afternoon," Josie surprised her by saying.

"I didn't." Susan paused to swallow her cheese. "What
are you talking about?"

"When I said that you should plan everything out and
avoid making last-minute changes. You didn't originally
plan on having a tub on the third floor, did you?"

"Not really," Susan admitted. "Although I did consider it
earlier, but I thought it was an expense we could do without." She looked seriously at the other woman. "You think

Ken talked me into spending money that I didn't need to, don't you?"

"Look, that's what I'm talking about. This guy is my boss and he has to earn a living. Just be careful about last-minute decisions, they can cost you a lot of money, okay?"

Susan nodded, silent for a moment. "Do you think Ken Cory is honest?" she asked quietly.

Josie frowned. "Look, I have no reason to think he isn't. He did today what a lot of contractors do. He suggested that you make the job slightly larger. Sure, he'll make a bigger profit, but you approved of the suggestion. It's not like he's doing things you didn't agree to or charging you for things that he didn't do."

"Contractors do that?" Susan asked.

Josie shrugged. "Some do. I try not to work for those companies."

Here was the opening Susan had been waiting for. "Have you worked for Cory Construction before?" she asked, leaning forward and picking up a cracker shaped like a butterfly.

"No. I've never worked in Hancock before. Usually I work in resort communities on the summer houses of rich people."

"That must be interesting," said Susan, who loved reading magazines like *Architectural Digest.*

"Framing a wall is framing a wall whether it's a wall in a twenty-room mansion or a tract house in a housing development. But I like my job a lot and I must admit that rich people build houses in beautiful locations."

"How did you happen to be hired by Ken Cory?"

"A friend of a friend knew that he was looking for someone to work on this one short job. I was free . . ." She shrugged again. "And here I am."

Susan got the impression that the young woman was becoming uncomfortable. "Do you live nearby?"

"I'm staying downtown in an apartment over a nail salon, Pink Pinkies Plus. It's a summer sublet. The location is okay. I wish it were a little closer to the deli. I like a good corned beef on rye, but long, painted nails are not a particular obsession of mine." Susan followed her glance down to the short, utilitarian nails on Josie's callused hands.

"How are things going?" Susan asked, not knowing exactly what else to say. She didn't want to sound like she was interrogating this young woman. "Do you think the crew is going to accept you?"

"Yeah. They all seem like pretty nice guys."

"Frankie looks like a fun person," Susan threw out, hoping she might move the topic back to the phone call.

"He does." Josie laughed. "I get a huge kick out of that hair of his. You'll never believe what he told me."

"What?"

"He used buttermilk to start his dreadlocks."

"What?"

"I guess it's pretty difficult to get blond hair to grow into dreadlocks. He says that at first he had to make it really sticky and he used to put buttermilk on it and twist it around and around."

"That doesn't sound very clean," Susan said.

"He's clean now. Neat even, if you don't mind the way his hair looks. And he doesn't use anything on his hair anymore. Apparently after years of working on it, his hair just goes into dreadlocks naturally." Josie took a long pull on her beer. "You're wondering about that phone call?" she asked.

"I . . . I was just wondering whether I missed a phone call," Susan said, glad she remembered the excuse she had given earlier for her interest.

But Josie wasn't having any of it. "Why did you really want to know who was talking on the phone?"

Susan sipped her wine and tried to think of an answer.

EIGHTEEN

"That's some story," Josie commented as Susan finished her explanation and her second glass of wine at the same time.

"Is this the first you've heard of Simon Fairweather's death?" Susan asked, tossing a cracker to the dog.

"No wonder she's always begging," Josie said with a grin. "And to answer your question, no. The crew has talked about little else. But these guys don't feel comfortable around me yet; they tend to shut up when I'm in the room. I'll hear a lot more as they loosen up."

"And do you think Frankie could have made that call?" Susan asked.

"Sounds like it's possible. I walked in on him right before I came down and introduced myself to you, so the time is right. But . . ."

"But what?" Susan asked.

"Well, Frankie doesn't strike me as stupid. Why would he call the police department from your house? Everyone knows that the police have access to phone records, so why make the call from here? Why not wait until he could get to a pay phone someplace else?"

"That's a good question," Susan muttered, trying to think of a good answer.

"In fact, why would Frankie call at all? Why would anyone who's a member of the crew call and make an accusation like that? Now you and the police are going to investigate everyone connected with Cory Construction. What does Frankie—or anyone else—gain by that?"

"A murder investigation always starts with more questions than answers," Susan muttered.

"What do you know about murder investigations? You weren't a cop, were you?" Josie asked, putting down her unfinished beer and sticking out her hand. Clue immediately jumped up and placed her head on the carpenter's lap.

Susan knew it was ridiculous to be jealous. Clue had always preferred whoever was closest to the food. She passed the platter of cheese to Josie, making sure that was the reason for the retriever's allegiance. And then she answered the question.

"I've helped solve a few," she said modestly. "Actually, more than a half-dozen. Kathleen, my friend who had the baby today, was once a police officer and we've worked together."

"Oh. Is that why you hired Cory Construction? Is someone on the crew a suspect in the murder of this Simon Fairweather?"

"I don't think the police have a list of suspects yet," Susan said, realizing that she wasn't actually answering the question.

"What about Frankie?" Josie persisted.

"What about him?"

"Do you think he made that call? You don't think he's the murderer, do you?"

"They're two separate issues," Susan answered. "The person who made that call may just know who the murderer is, like he said. And I don't have any idea if it's Frankie. The call may have been to someone else and be perfectly innocent."

Josie was silent a moment, scratching the dog with one hand and twisting a lock of her own hair with the other.

"Is something bothering you? Are you feeling guilty over telling me about Frankie?" Susan guessed.

"No. Not really . . . well, maybe." Josie stopped fidgeting and spoke up. "You see, Frankie grabbed a few minutes alone with me while we were winding down for the evening."

"And?" Susan prompted.

"And he said it was important, very important, that he talk with me privately." She dug into a pocket of her coveralls and pulled out a grimy piece of paper. "He gave me his phone number and asked that I call him tonight."

"Did he say anything else? Besides that it was important?"

"No, but he looked very serious. I got the feeling that . . . well, that it was a matter of life and death." Josie looked up at Susan. "I don't want to get him in trouble. I don't know him well, but he and Kyle were the only two workers who smiled when I was introduced to the group and Frankie even offered to get me a Coke when I complained about the heat in your attic."

"You might be protecting him," Susan suggested.

"What do you mean?"

"Knowing the identity of a killer could put a person in danger."

"You mean that if he did make the call, he might know something that puts him in danger," Josie said slowly.

"It's a well-known fact that it's easier to kill a second time," Susan said, ignoring the conversation she'd had with Brett just a few hours before.

"I could give him a call, but I wouldn't feel comfortable about this unless I could explain that I told you—and why," Josie said. "I wouldn't want him to be in any danger."

"If you saw him on the phone, perhaps someone else did, too," Susan reminded her.

Josie took a deep breath and flipped her hair over her shoulder. "Okay, I'll do it. Where's your phone?"

"Hanging on the wall in the kitchen. I'll show you."

"I can find it," Josie assured her.

"Do you want me . . ."

"I'd rather be alone," answered the self-assured young woman, then started off. Clue leaped up and followed her new friend into the house.

Susan poured herself another glass of wine and sat back to await Josie's return.

Which took so long that Susan's first impression was that

Josie hadn't managed to get through to Frankie. "Line busy?"

"Uh, yes, for a while, and then when I got through and I explained who I was and all, he . . . he asked that I come over to his apartment. He said he wanted to speak with me." The young woman sat down and scratched Clue behind the ears.

"And?"

"And I told him that I was still here with you—I didn't explain about the phone call or anything else—and he suggested that I talk you into coming along."

"You're kidding!"

"No. He gave me an address." Josie held out a piece of paper. "He said it's an apartment down by the water."

Susan studied it. "This street isn't familiar to me unless it's that little alley down near the place where they sell kayaks. You know, I think that's it."

"Then you'll come with me?"

"I'd love to," Susan said. "Just let me leave a note for Jed."

"You can give me the message in person," Jed announced, opening the gate to the backyard. "Sorry I'm late. I started listening to one of Lou Chandler's long stories and I didn't know how to get away politely. Any news about Kath?"

"Nine-pound, thirteen-ounce girl. Why don't you give Jerry a call? He might be home with Alex by now."

"Where are you going?"

"Josie and I have an errand to run. It won't take long. I was going to grill for dinner."

"I ate two entire bowls of nuts at the club bar. Believe me, I'm not starving. Why don't I get the grill heated?"

"Wonderful. We'll be back in half an hour or so."

"I parked my car behind yours," Jed began.

"Then we'll take my truck," Josie called out, leading the way with Susan trotting close behind.

"Wow. And I thought the Cherokee was a climb to get into," Susan said, stepping into the bright red vehicle.

"People who drive pickups have a lot of names for those

four-wheel-drive yuppie vans," Josie said, not volunteering
to supply more information. "Where do I go?" she asked,
starting the engine.

"Turn left at the end of the driveway. We'll head down
to the water. I think I can find this. I just didn't know anyone lived in that area. I thought it was all commercial."

"Oh, Frankie said that we shouldn't be surprised by the
entryway. His apartment is at the top of a warehouse of
some sort."

"That makes more sense. Then I think I know where
we're going. Just stay straight on this road and turn when
we get to the dry cleaner's on the left-hand side. That road
should take us right to the river."

"There is something else I wanted to mention."

"What?"

"I got the impression that Frankie wasn't alone when I
spoke with him on the phone."

"Oh?"

"Yes, right before he asked me if I could come over to
his place I think he might have put his hand over the receiver and spoken to someone else."

"Any idea who?"

"No, and he didn't say that anyone else was going to be
there."

Susan frowned. "Well, I guess we should just wait and
see. And we don't have long to wait," she added. "We're
almost there."

"I think that's the car Frankie drives," Josie said, pointing to the old green Morris Minor parked on one side of the
street. "I'll pull in behind it and we can find his address."

Susan stared at the street, unable to find building numbers in the midst of the graffiti. "I didn't know there was
anyplace like this in Hancock. It looks more like a street in
the city. In SoHo." In an area that had yet to be gentrified,
she added to herself, stepping down from the truck and narrowly missing a mound of dog droppings. Apparently the
pooper-scooper law wasn't strictly enforced in this part of
town.

"Number 139." Josie peered at the wall by their side. "I think this is it. I'll ring the bell."

"There's a bell?" Susan asked before realizing that the circle at the top of the nine contained a small brass button, which Josie was pressing.

"Josie? Is that you? Just open the door and walk right up."

The voice seemed to come from the sky. Susan glanced around, startled.

"In the window. Up there," Josie said, waving to Frankie, who waved back, his dreadlocks bouncing around his head.

"Come on up," he repeated.

Josie grabbed the metal half-moon that was apparently meant to be a doorknob and the wooden door swung open.

They were faced with a large, open warehouse floor piled high with what Susan guessed were hundreds of cardboard boxes. Josie pointed out a circular stairway to their right that led to the floor above. "That way," she said, starting off.

Susan trotted behind, noticing as she went up the stairs that someone had decorated the banisters with tiny metal animals that got larger and happier as they climbed. Frankie was standing at the top of the stairs, wearing clean jeans and a T-shirt printed with a picture of Iggy Pop. He looked solemn.

"Come on in," he greeted hospitably, opening another door decorated with animals fashioned from shiny metals.

Susan was about to comment on the unusual entrance when she glanced before her at the top floor of the warehouse. Her mouth snapped shut and she stared.

The space had been divided into two areas: the living area next to the door and beyond that a huge sculptor's studio.

"Go ahead and look around," Frankie suggested, seeing where Susan's attention was directed.

Susan walked around the couch and across the Scandinavian rug and headed toward the studio. That space also seemed to be divided in half. On one side there were more animals of copper, brass, cast iron, and tin. There were animal mobiles, animals leaping and climbing across the walls, animal sculptures for tables, animals so large they had to stand on the floor. And many of the animals themselves were exotic fantasies, real enough to be classified by genus but with details that indicated human traits and emotions.

The other side of the studio was filled with large abstract works, reminding Susan of Brancusi and Jeff Koons. In the center of the floor a great shape, almost like a giant marlin, stripped of all detail, stood. A welding torch lay on the floor by its side. Susan realized Frankie was standing next to her.

"Your work?" she asked quietly.

"Yes, the welding stuff. The animals"—he waved at the other figures beside them—"they were done by someone else."

"We're interrupting your dinner," Josie announced. She had remained in the living section of the room and was staring down at a table with the remains of a meal.

"We were almost done. My friend had to leave on an errand. But I was just going to make coffee when you called. Would anyone like some?" Frankie asked, moving over to Josie and beginning to clear the dirty dishes from the table.

"Sure," Josie agreed, helping to clean up.

"You share your studio with someone else?" Susan asked, moving closer to the group.

"Yes. We met in art school," Frankie said, appearing from behind the divider that separated the kitchen appliances from the rest of the room.

"How did you end up doing plumbing?" Susan asked.

"Actually, I started out being a plumber. After I flunked my freshman year of high school, it was suggested that I switch to technical school. I messed around with a bunch of trades there. Even thought about being a carpenter until I took a course in plumbing. I know it sounds strange to people, but I loved it right away."

"Really?"

"I love welding. Always have," he added, reaching across a divider and putting a turquoise platter of dark plums and apricots on the table in front of them. "And I started playing with this type of stuff"—he pointed at a very large abstract hanging on the wall above the door—"right away."

"So how did you end up at art school?" Josie asked.

The scent of coffee began to fill the room. "I was working on a job for a couple who were collectors. I was just knocked out by their collection and I tried to copy a sculpture they had on their patio. Some of the guys on the crew knew about it and the homeowner's wife heard them kidding me. I think she just wanted to be nice because later she said she would like to see what I'd done. I put a small piece in my car and showed it to her and her husband the next day." He got up and began to place mugs and spoons on a wooden tray.

"Turned out her husband was a major contributor to an art college. The next thing I knew I was getting together a portfolio to show the admissions office. And that fall I discovered myself taking basic design and a sculpting class or two."

"But you still do plumbing work."

"The type of stuff I do isn't terribly commercial. I have to earn a living some way. Milk or sugar?"

Both women insisted on black and Frankie continued his story. "My friend . . . actually my roommate's work is a little more commercial."

"Kiss of death. The man called me a commercial artist." A good-looking newcomer stood in the doorway.

NINETEEN

"You see," Frankie said, putting the full tray down on the table in front of them, "I'm gay."

Susan and Josie exchanged puzzled looks.

"So?" Susan prompted.

"So?" He repeated her question.

"I think what Mrs. Henshaw is asking is, what does that have to do with anything," Josie added.

"Frankie knows that you overheard him calling me on the phone today," the other man explained, coming into the room and getting another mug.

"I still don't get it," Susan said slowly. "You were afraid that Josie would find out that you were gay?"

"Not you, actually, but the men I work with," Frankie answered.

"And you think that would be a problem?" Susan asked.

Frankie looked at Josie. "Can you imagine what they would say if they knew I was a homosexual?"

Josie frowned. "I don't know. There have been lesbians on some of the crews I've worked with. They haven't had any more problems than I have—except for an asshole or two—but you run into that type of thing everywhere. Of course, I just got here. You know those guys better than I do."

"Wait a second." Susan got back to what she considered the point. "You were calling your . . . your roommate on the phone and you thought Josie overheard the call?"

"I know she overheard. I saw her reflection in the mirror over the dresser."

"Actually, I didn't hear what you were saying. I just knew that you were on the phone."

Frankie looked confused. "So why were you so serious this afternoon? If you didn't hear what I was saying, what difference did it make—although I know we're not supposed to use the homeowners' phones." He looked at Susan. "Ken makes a big deal about that. But Sean and I had a fight this morning and I just wanted to clear everything up. Normally, I wouldn't have considered breaking the rules."

"It's fine," Susan said. "I mean, that's between you and Ken."

"So now I don't get it," Sean broke in. "If you weren't upset about Frankie using the phone, why are you here?"

"I asked them." Frankie answered the question that had been directed to the women. "Well, I asked Josie if I could speak with her and she was still at work when she called here, so I asked if she would bring Mrs. Henshaw over. I guess I thought I'd better get you on my side if Ken and the guys were going to be on my back—if that makes any sense."

"Sort of. And now that everything's cleared up, I'd better get home to my husband," Susan said, worried that Josie might mention the call to the police department. The less people who knew about that, the better. She put down her mug and stood up.

"I'm the driver." Josie hopped to her feet. "But you know," she added to Frankie, "it's possible Ken won't care about your love life. You might be worrying for nothing."

"That's what I tell him," Sean said.

"Sure. Easy for you to say. You're making a good income from your artwork," Frankie said.

"Yes, your work is wonderful. I'd like to talk to you about that sometime. Maybe you could do a piece for the wall in one of my bathrooms. Not fish, though. Fish decorations in the bathrooms are a cliché," Susan said, moving closer to the door. "We'd better get going," she added to Josie. "Jed will have the grill fired up. And I'm starving." She opened the door. "And we'll keep your relationship a secret whether it's necessary or not," she assured Frankie, leaving the room.

Josie apparently got the idea and with a brief nod at the two men hurried down the stairway after her employer.

"What's up? Are you afraid our dinner is going to burn up?" she said, hopping up into her truck and thrusting the key into the ignition.

"No, it's just that this is what I hate about looking into murders," Susan said. "You get involved in so much that is other people's private business."

"On the other hand . . ." Josie started, backing out of the parking space.

"On the other hand?"

"You probably get all your prurient interests satisfied," Josie said with a grin.

Susan hooted. "You have a point there. But seriously," she asked, "do you think the men on the crew are homophobic?"

Josie shrugged. "I have no idea. I have found that the people I work with are a pretty varied group. The man that I've worked for for years is a major supporter of liberal causes—and certainly no one would think that of a man who owns a contracting company—especially since his favorite form of transportation is a gigantic Harley hog."

"I guess the lesson is that it's a mistake to make assumptions about people."

"Absolutely."

Susan was quiet the rest of the way home, wondering if she had missed something about Frankie or learned anything about Josie.

Josie didn't speak until she turned her truck in at the bottom of Susan's driveway. "You know what? If you wouldn't be offended, I think I'll pass up your dinner invitation. It's getting late and we're going to start at seven tomorrow."

"Seven A.M.?"

"Didn't Ken tell you? The tub for the attic is going to be framed in first thing and the hardware will be here before lunch—Ken is hoping to get the third floor done in a week—believe me, we're going to be working long days."

"I know you're still new and things are kind of tenuous for you, but . . ." Susan paused. "If anyone says anything about Simon Fairweather or the murder or . . . or anything that might be significant, could you tell me? I'll let Brett Fortesque know."

"Who's he?"

"The chief of police in Hancock."

"Wow. You are well connected, aren't you?"

"I guess so," Susan admitted, admiring her own modesty.

"I don't mind helping you out." Josie frowned. "And you're not offended if I turn down your invitation to dinner?"

"No. I think I should hurry up and get to bed myself. Sounds like tomorrow is going to be a big day."

"The first of many," Josie said as Susan closed the door behind her.

Susan headed straight for the backyard, knowing Jed would be there.

And he was, asleep on the lounge, a half-finished gin and tonic by his side and the grill smoking away. Clue was equally tired, merely opening one eye as the gate clicked shut behind Susan.

"Some watchdog," she muttered, once again content to let her sleeping dog lie. "And you know you're a fire hazard, don't you?" she asked, kissing her husband on the forehead.

"I'm just resting my eyes," he said, opening them. They did look well rested. "Have you started dinner?"

"I was just on my way to the kitchen to get the food," she said, deciding that the couple who lies together stays together.

"Great." Jed closed his eyes again. "Oh, wait," he called. "Kyle Barnes phoned a few minutes ago." He looked at his watch and corrected himself. "A while ago. He asked that you call as soon as you get home. The number is on a piece of paper next to the phone."

"Did he say what he wanted?"

"Something about a phone call."

Susan hurried into the house. Had Kyle also been a witness to Frankie's attempt to make up with his lover? Or did he want to tell her something about an anonymous call to the police department? Perhaps this was going to be a confession. She was anxious to get those questions answered, but there were a half-dozen scraps of paper lying on the counter under the phone, as well as a pile of unopened mail that apparently had landed there yesterday after the hall table was swathed in plastic, and it took her a while to locate Kyle's phone number. Then she was forced to wait impatiently for an answer. None came.

Irritated with herself for doing it, she hung up and dialed again. There was no chance she would get an answer, but she felt impelled to try again. Maybe she had dialed wrong, maybe he had just come into the room and would answer this time, maybe—

"Hello?"

"Kyle?"

"Yes, who is this?"

"Kyle, it's Mrs. Henshaw. Susan Henshaw," Susan said, feeling more than a little foolish. "My husband says that you called when I was out."

"Yes, I wanted to speak with you," Kyle answered. "Remember when you asked whether or not I'd been on the phone this morning? I had gone outside to get a nail gun from the truck and you asked if I had answered the phone—"

"If you had been on the phone," Susan corrected him.

"Yeah. Well, I told you that I hadn't been."

"And?" Susan prompted.

"And? Oh, you mean was I lying or anything like that," Kyle said cheerfully. "No, I haven't ever used your phone. Not even to make a call for Ken."

"Then . . ."

"But you must have asked everyone on the crew if they were on the phone."

"Uh . . ." Susan didn't know what to say.

"I just assumed that you did because the guys were talking about it during their break this afternoon."

"Oh. Were they mad that I'd been questioning them?"

"Nah. They already know that you're going to be a push—you're going to be easy to work for. Some of the homeowners make the crew crazy," Kyle said cheerfully.

"How do you know that I'm going to be easy to work for?"

"Well, you don't complain about every little thing like whether or not we covered the paneling in the hallway enough or if the plastic runner is scooting around when we cart stuff in and out of the house."

"Other people mention that type of thing?" Susan wondered if she should be more particular.

"They raise hell. You wouldn't believe."

Susan decided to return to the subject. She would check the hallway after she had hung up. "Did anyone say that they had used the phone?" she asked.

"No, but I think that maybe you should ask again. I think it's possible that someone was lying." Kyle's natural ebullience seemed to have vanished.

"Who?" Susan asked.

"Well, Buns and Frankie were talking, but it wasn't really what they said but how they said it," Kyle replied.

Susan thought he was reluctant to betray his co-workers. "I know this all sounds stupid. And you're right that I'm not fussy about most things." Probably not as much as she should be, she thought, remembering the cost of the hall carpeting. "But this phone call is really important to me. It's a private matter and I don't want to explain," she was inspired to add, "but if you know that someone on the crew was talking on the phone today, I really need to know about it."

"I'm the youngest guy on the crew and I'm accepted and all that, but . . . well, you know. Sometimes I have to try hard to be one of the crew. I have a year of college behind me and these guys mostly learned their trade from their families, although I think someone said that Frankie went to a community college or something like that."

"You're saying that your background is different from theirs."

"Yeah, I mean I'd never tell these guys that my parents belong to the field club or that I'm saving up to go to Europe in the winter. They're struggling to pay their mortgages. You know?"

"Yes, of course. That's very sensitive of you," Susan said, wishing he would stop explaining how sensitive he was and tell her about the phone call.

"Yeah, well, then you understand why I don't want anything I tell you to make the guys think less of me or anything."

"I won't tell anyone what you tell me," Susan assured him, wondering if he was actually going to tell her anything after all this.

"Yeah, I appreciate that. Well. The guys were talking about the job and you and your house and all. And Buns and Frankie were sitting together sharing a six-pack of Coke and one of them said something about how strange it is that you asked about phone calls when you weren't all that particular about other things."

"Like the carpet and the walls," Susan said, trying to understand.

"Yeah, right. And then Art—I'm sure it was Art because I remember him taking off his headphones for an answer. And that means it's real important to him. Well, Art said that you should've asked Ken about the call. He said Ken would be the only person who'd dare make a private call on a homeowner's phone without asking permission."

Well, that gave her something to think about.

TWENTY

SUSAN WOKE UP THE NEXT MORNING WONDERING IF SHE HAD been transported from Connecticut to California. Surely only a major earthquake could cause such noise and shaking. She leaped up, smashing into the end of the antique sleighbed that had once been the prized centerpiece of her guest room—until she was forced to sleep on it. Her toes were permanently curled these days.

"What was that?" Jed asked.

"I have no idea," Susan answered, rubbing her bruised shin. "I really smashed my leg here. Maybe you should get up and check."

"Sounded like something broke," Jed muttered. "It will still be broken when I get up."

"I can't lie here in bed when heaven knows what is going on around me," Susan insisted, straightening up and limping over to the pile of clothing on the floor. "I really hate wearing clothes two days in a row."

"I thought you were going to move our stuff in here yesterday," Jed said, sitting up slowly.

"I was a little busy yesterday—and exhausted last night." Susan reminded herself that she couldn't kill her husband; she'd have to find an entirely female jury if she wanted to stay out of prison. "Where are you going?"

"Across the hall. I can't wear dirty clothes to work."

"Would you get some jeans and a shirt for me?" Susan pleaded. "I don't want to go out there in my robe and I'd really like clean clothes. I'll move everything we need in here first thing today," she promised.

"You don't have to worry about my stuff. I'll try to get home early tonight. Maybe we could go out to dinner," he added, tying his robe around his waist. "Or I have a better idea. Why don't you come into the city for dinner? It's August. I can probably get reservations anywhere. Where do you want to go? Aquavit? Arcadia? Le Cirque? Or we could go down to the Village—"

"Jed, I'm going to be busy. I've got to see these sinks and toilets, and I want to go out to the tile place that Joe—or was it Joel?—told me about. I definitely plan to visit Kathleen at the hospital. And we've got to start thinking about hardware."

"Hardware? You mean nails and stuff? I thought Ken took care of all that."

"No, I mean towel racks and soapdishes and toilet-paper holders. And lights. I have to look at lights. And I was thinking last night before I fell asleep that we should check into built-in wall heaters versus ones placed in the ceiling. And laundry hampers. Why shouldn't we have built-in laundry hampers, maybe in the hall linen closet as well as in the bathrooms. And—"

"I'm going to be late for work," Jed announced, disappearing out the door.

"And I have to figure out who might have called the police station yesterday . . . and who either hated Simon Fairweather enough to kill him or who hates someone in Cory Construction enough to hope that he's a suspect in this murder," she muttered. "And I really want to go see Kathleen at the hospital."

"What did you say?" Jed reappeared, piles of clothing in his hands. "By the way, Josie is working in our bathroom. She likes my robe. Apparently her father once had one just like it."

"What's that?"

Jed looked down at the clothing he had just dumped on the end of the bed. "The clothes you asked for."

Susan merely smiled. He tried. Just because he couldn't tell winter clothes from summer ones didn't mean he wasn't a good husband. "Is Josie the only person in there?"

"Yes."

"Then I think I'll go find something a little cooler than this wool shirt," Susan said.

"I have to get going," Jed insisted. He was almost dressed. "Call me if you need anything. I should be in the office most of the day."

"Fine." Susan kissed her husband and crossed the hall to their bedroom.

Josie, a tape measure in her hand, came out of the bathroom as Susan entered the bedroom. "Hi."

"Hi. You sure start early," Susan commented, heading over to the closet and opening the door.

"Don't say I didn't warn you. Seven A.M. on the dot."

Susan made a mental note to start setting the alarm for six-thirty. She dressed in her large walk-in closet while chatting with Josie. "Are you going to be working here or in the attic today?"

"Mostly up there, but I'll be coming down here while the plumbing is beginning. Kyle and Art can handle the framing themselves and a third person just gets in the way. You know," she added as Susan came out of the closet wearing leggings and a large T-shirt, "the men were talking about you when I came in. In fact, I think part of the reason that I was sent down here was to get me out of the way so that they could continue their speculations."

"About me?"

"Uh-huh. Seems they were wondering what sort of phone call could have been so important that you questioned everyone about it and the only conclusion anyone could draw was that you were expecting a call from your lover. It was even suggested that you were worried that he might hear a strange man answering the phone and think that you were two-timing him. Buns wondered if that meant you were three-timing Jed. I left at that point in the discussion."

Susan slipped her feet into some sandals and frowned. "These men don't know what a dull life I lead," she muttered.

"You think investigating murders is dull?"

"No, but—"

"Mrs. Henshaw, ma'am." Buns was leaning against the doorway, leaving a long smear of grease on the white woodwork. "We need you upstairs."

"Oh." Susan grabbed an elastic band from the top drawer of her dresser and pulled her hair back into a ponytail. "What do you want me to do?"

"You have some decisions to make," Buns said, hiking up his pants and turning back toward the attic stairs.

"I'll be right up," Susan called to his departing back. "Could you come with me?" she asked Josie. "Please."

"In a minute," Josie answered. "I don't want it to look like I'm second-guessing the rest of the crew, but I'll be up as soon as possible. And just remember: You can wait to make a decision. This is a big job. There's always other work to be done."

Susan sighed. "Okay. I'd better get going. By the way," she added, "what was that loud noise this morning?"

"You better ask about that upstairs." Josie turned and went back into the bathroom.

Susan ran up the stairs; now that she was fully awake, she was curious to see what progress had been made. The night before, the attic had looked so orderly with the walls beginning to take shape and the wood flooring laid down nice and smooth. Today . . . She arrived at the top of the steps and stopped immediately.

Evil elves must have been very busy while she slept. The entire attic was a mess. The walls that had been marked with two-by-four pieces of lumber were no longer standing. The wood, pipes, and long dowels were scattered around the floor and leaning up against walls. Susan noticed that a table saw had been set up on a trunk that had accompanied her to her freshman year of college. Nearby, boxes and discarded sports equipment were covered with sawdust. Long sheets of some sort of white material were protected by shrink-wrapped plastic and propped up in front of the window. The old toilet lay on its side, dripping filthy water. The new toilet was being used as a chair by Ken Cory.

There was probably a sink around somewhere, but Susan had something else to worry about.

"That's not the bathtub I ordered," she announced, staring at the monstrous white ceramic square that took up a large chunk of the floor.

Ken looked up from the diagrams he had been studying and smiled. "Looks huge, doesn't it?"

"It—"

"Everyone says that," Buns announced. "Don't worry. Most of that tub is built in."

"It's stained," Susan insisted, moving over for a closer look.

Buns bent over, too. "Nah. Look at this. Wipes right off."

It did. And then it rubbed off onto the wall as he braced himself to grope around under the eaves for an elusive length of copper pipe. Susan bit her lip and didn't say anything. It was no big deal. She'd just repaint when they finished. "What happened to the walls that you built yesterday?" she asked, pointing to the empty space.

"You changed your mind and added a tub. We had to take them down to get the tub in place," Kyle said, smiling at her.

Susan sighed. "You had some questions to ask me," she said to remind Ken why she was there.

"We need to know if you want lights in the ceiling over the tub," Ken said, "and if you're planning on having a separate fixture over the sink. Remember, you and Jed agreed to buy all the electrical fixtures."

"I haven't had time to choose."

"We just need to know the location so we can get the wires in place before the walls go up. Angelo is going to be here any minute now."

"Can't you do this later?" Susan asked, remembering Josie's suggestion that she could wait to make decisions.

"Sure can. But it will be more expensive," Ken said, smiling again.

Susan had no idea how she was going to visualize the lighting locations without knowing what the lights looked like, but she gave it her best shot, listening to suggestions and generally agreeing with all that was said. "I guess I'd better go to the lighting store first thing this morning," she added.

"Good idea," Ken agreed, nodding his approval.

"Am I supposed to actually buy the lights myself? Pick them up and bring them here?"

"Unless you can teach them things to walk by themselves," Buns said in a jovial voice.

"But what about the other stuff? Wires and everything?" Susan protested. "I don't know anything about that."

"Angelo takes care of all that. Don't have to worry yourself about that stuff," Art said. His headset hung around his neck and he seemed to be communicating with the outside world today.

Susan got the impression that he would like to tell her not to worry her pretty little head about this particular thing. Although he might not describe her appearance that way, she thought ruefully, wondering when she was going to find time to run to the club and wash her hair. "I'd better get going," she added. "I'm not going to be necessary for anything, am I?"

She heard a snicker or two in response to her question, but her attention was drawn to something else. "Isn't that edge of the tub broken?" she asked, pointing at the corner where a large chunk of metal seemed to be damaged and bent.

"Nah. It's fine," Buns insisted, getting up and pushing a large piece of cardboard around the offending sight. "Nothing for you to worry about."

Susan smiled weakly and left the room. She was going to walk the dog, have a deliciously greasy breakfast at the diner downtown, then go and do some serious shopping.

An hour later she was standing in the Brightly Lit showroom and realizing that her day wasn't going to be easy. In the first place the hash browns (or possibly the ranch omelet) had given her indigestion. In addition, there were more kinds of recessed ceiling lights than she had ever imagined. The salesman who directed her to bathroom fixtures had

bragged that they carried over a hundred different models—
what he hadn't mentioned was that most of them were
hideous.

It took her almost thirty minutes to choose ceiling fixtures. She liked them so much that she decided to use the
same model in all three bathrooms. Feeling extraordinarily
efficient, she had placed her order for the lights and was
examining brass wall sconces when she felt that someone
was staring at her.

She turned and discovered Patricia Fairweather standing
behind her. Susan didn't know what to say.

But Patricia leaped right in. "Hi," she said, smiling. "You
know, I thought these were appropriate mourning clothes
for running errands, but I think I was wrong." Patricia
looked down at her black jeans and black T-shirt. "I feel
like a geriatric heavy-metal fan."

Susan laughed as she knew she was supposed to. "I think
you have to shave your head."

"Funny you should mention that. I was thinking of getting my hair cut."

"You're kidding." Patricia's long, straight hair was as
much a part of her as her strong artist's hands.

"I guess I'm looking for a symbol of a new life."

Susan nodded. "Without your husband."

"That and other things."

"Ma'am. Ma'am." The salesman was trying to attract her
attention.

"Yes?" Susan asked.

"The lights you ordered, ma'am."

"Yes. You know, I think I need ten, but did you find out
if I can return some if I'm wrong about that?"

"Yes, ma'am. You can return them. But that's not the
problem."

"Then what is?" Susan asked, realizing that Patricia
Fairweather was still by her side.

"They're out of stock. They have to be ordered from the
warehouse."

"And how long will that take?" Susan asked, all her attention drawn to the question at hand.

"Between a month and sixty days."

"You know what that means," Patricia said. "If I were you, I'd choose another style."

Susan frowned. "You know, I think you're right," she told the other woman. "I guess I'd better check out some more," she told the salesman.

And when she looked around again, Patricia Fairweather was gone.

TWENTY-ONE

"AND WHEN I TURNED AROUND, PATRICIA FAIRWEATHER was gone," Susan said, picking a dead rose off the floor by Kathleen's hospital bed.

"So what did you do about the lights?"

"Well, I figured I had three choices: wait sixty days for them—or probably longer, you know how these stores are; pick out different lights; or go to another store, which might not have the lights either. But then I had an inspiration. I copied down the information hanging from the light on display and called Jed. He's going to go down to the Lower East Side after work and see if he can pick them up there." She pulled a notebook from her purse. "Damn, I lost the list I made this morning!" she said, writing furiously before she forgot what she had planned to do.

"What else are you going to do today?" Kathleen asked, moving around to try to make herself more comfortable.

Susan looked down at the list she had just completed. "It's not what I want to do, it's what I have to do. Every time I change my mind, it costs us money. And I have to go to that bathroom design showroom out on the highway, a tile store downtown that the men who are laying the tile on this job recommended, and to every lighting store in the area until I find fixtures."

"I thought Jed—"

"That's for recessed ceiling lights. I have to find lights for over the sinks in both second-floor bathrooms. I did buy something that isn't too ugly for the attic."

"Lunchtime, ladies." A perky nurse's aide entered the room, a large tray held in front of her ample chest.

"Thanks," Kathleen said politely as the tray was deposited before her. She waited until she and Susan were alone again before removing the cover from the food. "You know, I ate a lot of dreadful meals while I was a police officer, but this stuff . . ."

Susan reached across and, taking the cover from Kathleen's hand, hid the meal. "I know exactly what you mean. No hospital is known for its food. That's why I brought this." She pulled a large canvas carryall from under the chair where she had stowed it. She moved the hospital tray and put a paper bag and a white bakery box in its place.

Kathleen opened her goodies. "Oh, Susan, you shouldn't have. A sandwich and my favorite salads from the deli and"—she peeked under a corner of the box—"and mixed Italian pastries from DiBonni's! And I didn't even thank you for the chocolates and champagne you sent last night."

"Don't thank me. Just get lots of rest. You're going to need it. And I'd better get going. The nurse at the desk scares me to death and she was very direct about visiting hours for nonrelatives. Also I want to get a peek at your beautiful baby before they kick me out of here."

Kathleen, her mouth full of corned beef, nodded and waved her goodbye, and Susan, after visiting the viewing area of the nursery, headed back to her car to finish her errands.

She pulled a chopped liver on rye from a bag on the passenger seat and bit into it as she steered the car from the hospital's parking lot. First things first. But what was first? The towel racks? Sinks? Tiles? Sinks and toilets, she decided. Besides, the bathroom showroom was closest to the hospital. She hurried to finish her lunch before she got there.

Susan entered the large store and was immediately accosted by a salesman. "May I help you?" he asked, appearing from behind a shiny black shower stall.

"Yes, I—"

"You have something smeared across your T-shirt," the man continued.

Susan glanced down. "It's chopped liver," she said, knowing exactly what it looked like.

"Are you here because you need a shower?" he said, smiling at his own witticism.

"Actually," Susan said, deciding that it was time to get to the point, "I'm here to look at some sinks and toilets that I have on order. And to pick out those glass things that go around showers."

"Tub enclosures. What's your name?"

"My name?" That seemed a little rude.

"I'll look up the order in the computer if you give me your name."

"Oh. Henshaw. The order was probably placed in my husband's name. Jed Henshaw."

"I'll go look it up. The tub enclosures surround all the showers and tubs in that section." He waved his hand. "And there are more against the rear wall. Also, of course, we can design something just for you if you don't find what you like here. We are known for our custom work. I'll be right back."

Susan wandered around the large sales floor, examining glass enclosures as she went. But the salesman returned almost immediately. "There has been no order placed in your name," he announced.

"Oh, that can't be possible. Ken Cory told me—"

"Oh, you're using Cory Construction. That explains it. I'll be right back with your printout."

"I—" But he had hurried back to his computer and Susan decided to wait. She had just spied the sink she'd picked out, anyway.

"Ah . . . you've found your sink."

"It's too shallow," Susan said, placing her hand in the porcelain interior. "It didn't look like this in the catalog. I can pick out another, can't I? That's what Ken told me."

"Yes. Let me see, your order doesn't go out for a few weeks. There will be no trouble at all. It's a good thing you came in today."

"Ken insisted on it," Susan said. She wandered among the sinks, turning on taps that didn't work and trying to decide between brass and chrome.

"Sounds like Cory Construction is back on its feet," the salesman said casually.

"What do you mean?" Susan asked, stooping down to peer at the pedestal of a large forest-green sink. "Does this come in white?"

"Yes, of course. There's also a matching toilet. Right over there."

"I like them. What's the price?"

"About twenty percent less than the set you chose originally."

"Let's order these then," Susan said. She'd be sure to point out to Jed that she was saving money every step of the way. "What did you mean when you said that it sounded like Cory Construction is back on its feet?" she asked again.

"From what I'd heard, Simon Fairweather had almost shut them down," the salesman answered, writing in the large notebook that he carried. "You said white, didn't you?"

"Yes. What about Simon Fairweather and Cory Construction?"

"Well, I only know the gossip, but from what I hear, for the last few months Simon Fairweather had almost refused to accept any work that anyone on the crew did. Hiring Cory Construction meant that your job was never going to be done."

"I don't understand."

"It was simple. Simon Fairweather personally inspected all the jobs that were done by Cory Construction."

"And?"

"And he worked very hard to avoid approving any of the work the company did—from the early stages of a job, every single time an inspection had to be done, the work was not approved without extensive reworking and revisions."

"Could Simon Fairweather do that?"

"Yes, he certainly could. And did until the day he died.

Most people in this town stopped hiring Cory Construction about three months ago."

"You're kidding."

"Well, at least for jobs that required inspection. They might have done some decorating—you know, painting and the like—but they haven't done much building around here that I know of."

"How did the people who hired Cory Construction know this was going on?"

The man shrugged. "Can't say I'm sure of that. Once in a while someone would come in here and mention it. In fact, one of my colleagues was just telling me about a woman who came in last week to try to return a bathtub. I don't know the whole story, but Cory Construction screwed up her job about halfway through and she fired them. But she had already ordered some of the bathroom fixtures and Ken Cory didn't cancel the order. One of her kids accepted delivery on the fixtures for a thirty-thousand-dollar bathroom—"

"Right before she got the bill from Ken Cory explaining that he expected to be paid fully for a job he wasn't going to be allowed to do." They had been joined by another salesman.

"You're kidding!" Susan exclaimed.

"Mr. Bordon had, after all, signed a contract."

"Jack and Eleanor Bordon?" Susan asked. "I knew Ellie wanted to get her bathroom redone—"

"We really shouldn't be talking about our clients," the man who had been helping her said quickly.

"I would never pass this along to anyone else," Susan assured him, hoping they wouldn't stop talking. "You see, I'm concerned because Cory Construction is working for me," she explained to the new arrival.

"Now that Simon Fairweather has died, you don't have anything to worry about, do you?"

Susan thought about that statement while she was doing the rest of her errands.

She picked out a wonderful clear-glass surround for the master bath and a standard tub enclosure for the main bathroom. The man who had waited on her politely refused to answer any more questions about Cory Construction or the Bordons. His colleague had disappeared. But she did get the feeling that they both considered her a suspect in Simon Fairweather's murder. Who benefited after all? She did. She was going to acquire three remodeled bathrooms. She decided that she was suffering from low blood sugar and headed for the nearest bakery.

Two slices of sour-cherry strudel and a creamy napoleon later, she had found the hardware store, fallen in love with chrome faucets for the master bath and chosen traditional brass and porcelain for the family's bathroom, and was wondering exactly what had happened six months before to turn Simon Fairweather against Cory Construction.

She picked out a long rectangle of chrome wires fashioned in Italy to hold soaps and sponges and anything else (bath salts? candles? glasses of wine?) over her extra-long bathtub. She discovered quadruple showerheads that would spray in all directions. And decided that she should call on the Bordons just as soon as possible.

Her next stop was the tile store, which lived up to the Joes' accolades.

She ordered white tiles with a watery iridescent finish for the master bathroom and spent a wonderful few hours discussing possibilities for the family bathroom with the tile artist. And she decided that she didn't know enough about Simon Fairweather. Not nearly enough.

But first things first, she reminded herself, parking her Cherokee in the street in front of Jack and Ellie Bordon's home. She would have parked in the cobblestone circular drive if a massive overflowing Dumpster hadn't gotten there first.

Susan locked her car and jumped out, hurrying up the flagstones that led to the entrance of the faux English-country cottage the Bordons had purchased a couple of years ago.

"Susan Henshaw, what are you doing here?" Jack Bordon exclaimed as he opened the door. "Ellie was just talking about calling you."

"You're kidding!" Susan followed her host into the hallway, remembering just in time that the tiny, colored panes in the stained-glass windows permitted almost no light to permeate them and that there was a large, dark antique trunk just waiting to remove chunks from the shins of the unwary. "What about?"

"Cory Construction."

Sometimes things just fell into your lap if you waited long enough, Susan gloated silently.

"Ellie is in the living room. We were just having cocktails. Maybe you'll join us?"

"Of course," Susan agreed before remembering that the Bordons were big fans of amontillado, fino, and manzanilla sherry. Oh, well, it had been a long day. She didn't need anything stronger.

"We've been experimenting with single-malt scotches," Jack surprised her by saying. "Would you like to try one of them?"

"Sounds good," Susan said, peering into the gloom of the Bordons' living room and spying Ellie lying on a large maroon leather couch with her feet across a sleeping basset hound. "Ellie. Hi," she added as her friend opened one eye and apparently looked in her direction.

"Susan. We were just talking about you. Come and sit down, you poor thing."

Susan wondered if there had been a death in her immediate family that no one had told her about. Could anything else deserve such commiseration and sympathy?

Ellie sat up and patted the cushion beside her. "Sit here. We need to talk."

"About what?" Susan asked, glad she was wearing old clothes. Apparently basset hounds shed almost as much as golden retrievers.

"About how Cory Construction is going to ruin your life."

TWENTY-TWO

"I REALLY DON'T THINK CORY CONSTRUCTION IS GOING TO ruin my life," Susan protested, accepting a thistle-shaped glass of amber liquid from Jack Bordon. "They're just re-modeling my bathrooms."

"Your bathrooms? You're letting them work on more than one?" Ellie asked in a horrified voice.

"Three, actually. Let me explain," Susan answered, and started to tell the story of her home's plumbing disaster.

"Susan, you don't know what a disaster is until you in-vite Cory Construction into your home. Come, let me show you something," Ellie insisted, interrupting Susan's story.

"Bring your drink along," Jack added as they all stood up. "You may need it."

"What do you want me to see?" Susan asked as they all tramped through the hallway (this time the trunk acquired a small piece of her shin as she passed) and up the broad stairway to the second floor.

"Do you remember the bathroom at the top of the stairs?" Ellie answered her question with a question.

"Not really."

"It was designed by the previous owners. In violet and white. With purple and white violets on every surface, if you know what I mean."

"Wallpaper . . ."

"And the tiles on the walls and floor, etched into the lights over the sink, enameled in the surface of the sink itself—"

"And on towels and shower curtains, even on the bathmat," Jack finished his wife's story.

"Yes, but those were different—they were easy to get rid of," Ellie said impatiently. "But the rest called for something more drastic. And, we figured, since we were going to have to change the sink and all the tiles—"

"Why not just remodel the entire thing? It will be just as easy," Jack finished her story in jovial terms. "Well, that's what we thought at the time," he added in response to his wife's glare.

"That is what we thought at the time, but we were entirely mistaken as you are going to see," Ellie added, reaching out and throwing open a door at the top of the stairway.

Susan peered into the darkness. "I can't see anything."

"Wait. There's a light here somewhere." Ellie reached around the corner into the room and pressed on a switch attached to a heavy orange extension cord. The room did not exactly spring to life, but a 150-watt bulb, which was tied to a rough ceiling beam, brought its unbroken glare to all four corners.

"What a mess!"

"A mess? You call this a mess?" Ellie mocked her statement and Susan realized that she had had too much to drink. "A mess is what you have when this exists for a week or two. Even a month of this is a mess. Six months is a disaster. And that's what we've been living with for six months. That damn Dumpster in the middle of our driveway. A garage full of . . . of plumbing shit that will never be used. Only one bathroom in the entire house that works. We can't give parties, can't have company, can't live a normal life because of what you refer to as a mess."

"I only meant—" Susan began.

"We know what you meant," Jack said quietly, putting a restraining hand on his wife's arm and turning out the light with the other. "You see, we have no idea how long we're going to be living like this and, I have to admit, it's gotten to both of us."

"I don't understand."

"We're suing Cory Construction," Jack said quietly, leading both women back downstairs with promises of fresh drinks. "And we have to leave everything in place until the case comes before the court."

"And that's only part of the story," Ellie added, hurrying ahead of the other two when further drinks were mentioned. "We had to stop work originally because our esteemed building inspector's office wouldn't approve any further construction. That was six months ago. So we fired Ken Cory and tried to return the garbage in our garage, but no one would accept returns, and we'll have to take a huge loss if we try to sell it to another contracting company or a jobber. It's been a disaster. We gave up a month ago, put the dog in a kennel and went to Europe for three weeks. We just got home yesterday."

"Then you don't know that Simon Fairweather is dead!" Susan exclaimed, resuming her seat on the couch and picking up her glass.

The next few minutes were spent busily mopping expensive single-malt scotch whisky off the basset hound, who had been sitting underneath Eleanor Bordon's arm when Susan made that announcement. As the Bordons worked, Susan continued the story of the murder.

"Guess it's a good thing we were away when Fairweather was murdered or we'd be suspects in the case," Jack continued jovially.

"Not really," his wife contradicted him. "His death doesn't help us. We're still stuck with that mess upstairs and in the garage. Our lawsuit is against Cory Construction, not Simon Fairweather. The only person who is going to be helped by Fairweather's death is Ken Cory—and maybe Patricia Fairweather, if you believe the rumors about their marriage."

"What rumors?" Susan asked quickly.

"I once heard something about him hitting her during a fight," Ellie said.

"Where? Who did you hear it from?" Susan asked quickly.

Ellie seemed surprised by these questions. "Down at the club, I think. I was complaining about Cory Construction and how it couldn't get approval for any work from the building inspector's office and someone—in my aerobics class, I think—said that Patricia Fairweather's husband was a real skunk, that he beat his wife."

"Do you remember who?"

"You know, I do remember. It was Caroline White. She and Patricia did some volunteer work together—League of Women Voters or something—and she said that Simon had given Patricia a black eye. She was smart enough to hire Hancock Contracting when they had the addition built on the side of their house, I know that."

"So—" Susan tried again.

"But there were one or two other people in my class who had been skunked by Ken Cory."

"Who?"

Ellie nodded. "Lacy Knight and Debbie Sanderson. Do you know either of them?"

"I'm not sure. Wasn't there a Debbie who won the hand-ball championship down at the club? Tall and thin? A brunette?"

"Exactly! What a memory you have, Susan."

Susan glanced down at the third glass Ellie had emptied since her arrival but didn't say anything. "I don't think I know who Lacy is. Tell me about her and Debbie. Did Cory Construction work on both their houses? Did the work ever get completed?" She had visions of unfinished construction dotting the landscape all over Hancock.

"Yes and no." Ellie frowned and looked around the dimly lit room. "I'm getting hungry. Maybe we should have something to munch on with our drinks."

Jack took the hint and stood up. "I'll get us all some cheese and crackers, shall I?"

Ellie smiled. "That would be lovely, dear." She turned back to Susan as soon as he had left the room. "Jack is sweet, but there are some things he doesn't need to know. Like why I chose Cory Construction instead of another company."

Susan was becoming confused and said so.

"Well, why did *you* pick them?" Ellie asked.

"Because they had free time and no one else even bothered to return my calls," Susan explained.

"Well, of course, now things are different for Ken. He's just lucky that there are some people in town who haven't heard about his problems with the inspector's office and are interested in hiring him. But a few months ago the word wasn't out. At least, I didn't know anything when contractors were putting in bids to do the work on my bathroom."

"So why did you hire him? Did he give you the best price? Had you heard good things about his work?" Susan asked.

"Not really," Ellie admitted, looking at the door her husband had used to leave the room. "I guess I hired him because he flattered me. He certainly didn't give me the best price, although his estimate wasn't the most expensive I received."

"But?" Susan encouraged her to continue.

"Well, he told me how much he loved my house and everything I had done with it." Susan remembered the comments Ken had made about her hallway. "He practically raved about the needlepoint pillows I had made for this couch." Susan remembered how impressed he had been with Chrissy's stenciling. "They're not here now," Ellie explained. "The dog took a strange dislike to them and chewed them up. But Ken was just so sweet and he looks so nice—I thought it would be worth a little more money to have him do the job. After all, he was going to be working in my house. You know how it is."

"I do."

"But please don't tell Jack how foolish I was. I just told him that Cory Construction had a good reputation and made the best bid—neither of which was true, but I didn't know about their reputation when I hired them."

"What about Lacy and Debbie? You said they had bad experiences with Cory Construction, too," Susan was saying as Jack returned to the room with a platter of Brie, olives, and three types of crackers. She was impressed. Jed seemed unable to locate things like crackers in the kitchen.

She was fairly sure he knew that cheese and olives were kept in the refrigerator.

"Lacy hired Cory Construction about the same time I did. They were just going to do a small job: rebuilding a stairway to her attic and insulating it and installing a floor. You don't know her? Well, she has twin boys—eleven years old," Ellie continued when Susan shook her head. "And she was thinking that they could use the area as a play space and maybe, when the kids got older, she would have the entire room finished and turn it over to one or both of them as a bedroom."

"And it didn't get finished?" Susan asked, thinking of the bathroom over her head.

"It didn't get started. Simon Fairweather wouldn't approve the initial plans. And it was all Ken Cory's fault. You'd almost think he didn't want the work."

"I don't understand. What did he do?"

"What do you know about the Universal Building Code?" Jack asked, popping a cracker piled with cheese into his mouth.

"Nothing. Except that Jed was telling me that Hancock uses it, whatever that means."

"Well, in the case of Lacy Knight it meant that she didn't even get to begin to refinish her attic the way that she wanted to," he answered.

"But it was all Ken Cory's fault," his wife repeated. "If Ken had just filed the plans and said that the space was going to be used for storage, everything would have been all right."

"But he didn't do that?" Susan asked, hoping the story would become clearer as it became longer.

"No, he drew the plans, and when they were submitted, he explained that the attic was going to be used in the future as a bedroom for two children. So, of course, the plans were turned down." Ellie leaned back against the couch as though she had just made everything crystal clear.

Jack recognized Susan's confusion and explained. "You see, there are certain qualifications that rooms must meet for different uses. Like grounded outlets have to be installed in all bathrooms. And the windows in rooms where people sleep have to be of certain dimensions so that they can serve as exits in case of fire."

"But bedrooms have a lot of different window sizes—" Susan began.

"I know what you're thinking," he interrupted. "The bedrooms in this house have small casement windows with tiny panes. I doubt seriously if they're up to code—and they don't have to be. Each building must meet the code in effect at the time it is built. The code changes—is upgraded and probably becomes better in terms of safety—but only new or remodeled spaces are required to meet the current code."

"Oh." Susan nodded, thinking that she understood at last. "So the attic would have had to have lots of changes to be considered as a bedroom in this day and age."

"Expensive changes," Ellie added. "Like doubling the size of all the dormer windows, and there are ten of them, five across the front of the house and five across the back. And the roof is hand-cut slate. Lacy said it would have cost a fortune."

"And if Ken Cory had submitted the plans stating that the work was being done to create extra storage space?" Susan asked.

"They would have passed," Jack answered.

"Unless Simon Fairweather found some other excuse to turn them down," his wife disagreed.

"And the same thing happened to Debbie Sanderson?" Susan continued her questions.

"Not quite, as I understand it," Jack replied.

"Well, the result was the same," Ellie argued. "Her backyard is even worse than our bathroom."

"Debbie was having an extension added to the back of her house," Susan said, thinking she had heard something about this.

"They were having a huge extension added. I saw the plans and it was going to be wonderful. The architect had designed a large octagon with built-in couches and bookcases and glass on five sides. Then there was a wooden deck attached that repeated the shape of the building and steps that led down to a similarly designed flagstone patio with a fish pond placed in the middle of it."

"Sounds fabulous."

"We'll never know. The entire thing turned out to be such a mess that Debbie says it was actually responsible for her divorce."

"What happened?" Susan asked.

"Cory Construction started to dig the foundation before the plans were approved by the building inspector's department. And when Simon Fairweather found out about it, he insisted that the entire project be stopped."

"For how long?"

"I believe Debbie said that his exact words were 'until Hancock has a new building inspector,' and she didn't think he was talking about retiring."

"What does that have to do with the Sandersons' divorce?" Susan asked.

"Debbie signed the contract for the project without her husband's knowledge. He said he wasn't going to pay for work that he didn't order done and that, apparently, wasn't going to be completed anytime in the near future. And he just walked out the door and never looked back. At least, that's how Debbie sees it."

"And what is she going to do?" Susan asked.

"I have no idea. They're in the middle of negotiations over the terms of their divorce. He refuses to give her anything, except the house, which is large, expensive to run, and has water flooding into the basement from the ugly dirt hole that is now in their backyard. Debbie says she can't afford to fill it in and there is no way she's going to be able to sell it like it is."

"Unless she can convince a prospective buyer that it's a swimming pool," Jack Bordon added with a smirk.

"So what are you going to do now?" Ellie asked, an identical expression on her face.

"I'm going to go home, change my clothes, and go to church," Susan answered, standing up.

"Good idea. Prayer never hurts," Ellie said.

TWENTY-THREE

$\int$ IMON FAIRWEATHER'S FUNERAL WAS BEAUTIFUL. THE HANcock Episcopal Church was filled from the doors to the altar with bouquets of white flowers tied with miles of wide white satin ribbons. In the pews mourners sat elbow to elbow, sharing hymnals since there weren't enough to go around. Susan had slipped in after the service began, intentionally arriving late to avoid standing around before the service and talking about a man she couldn't even remember meeting. Now she got the feeling that everyone else in town had been his close friend. She frowned and listened as Buck Logan, Hancock's mayor, explained what she had missed.

". . . one of the finest members of our community. Not only was he diligent in his work as Hancock's building inspector—a position he held for almost thirty years—but his volunteer work for the community is well known by everyone. How many years did he single-handedly run the Community Chest fund drive? How many times did he say yes when the volunteer firemen were looking for someone to help erect the Christmas tree on the town commons? How many Halloween parades for our smallest children did he help judge? How many Easter eggs were hidden and then found under the auspices of this particularly devoted citizen of our lovely village? And who was ever more ready, willing, and able to assume high office in one of the many clubs to which he belonged?" Buck looked over the large congregation as though expecting an answer from man, if not from God. "Who else but Simon Fairweather?" he ended when no one spoke.

"So who would kill such a saint?" someone in a pew at the back of the church whispered loudly.

"Almost anyone who knew the bastard!" came the anonymous reply.

The man next to Susan snorted his amusement and his wife smacked him in the ribs with her elbow. Susan tried to concentrate on Buck's continuing tribute.

"Although he had no children of his own, all Hancock's children have and will continue to benefit from the conscientious way Simon Fairweather carried out his professional duties and his personal obligations. And now we'll have a word from another dear friend of mine and a dear friend of Simon Fairweather's, the president of the Hancock Community Chest."

Susan watched and waited as Simon Fairweather was eulogized by at least half of Hancock's most boring men. She was in the middle of singing the final hymn when she realized that no one had mentioned Simon's personal life, and that, in fact, this was the first funeral she had attended where not one member of the family spoke.

Not that Simon had much of a family. His aunt was sitting in the first pew, too old and possibly too senile to pay much attention to either the service or her surroundings. His wife, Patricia, was the only other family that Susan knew of and certainly no one expected the dead man's wife to speak at her husband's funeral. The wife's job was to greet the mourners after the service and possibly to entertain them later in her home. At least Susan hoped that was what Patricia Fairweather was going to do. She hadn't even seen the widow yet. She closed the hymnbook and joined the general exodus toward the rear of the church.

And that's when she spied Patricia Fairweather. She was standing in the doorway of the narthex surrounded by a group of tall, blond people. They looked so much like her that it was impossible to imagine they were anything but closely related.

"They must be the Storm sisters," a neighbor of Susan's

whispered in her ear. "I've always heard how much they looked alike when they were young. I guess that didn't change much as they aged."

"The men," Susan asked. "Were there any brothers?"

"No, those are the husbands, I think."

"All three sisters were attracted to men who look like Norse gods?" Susan asked, incredulous.

"Don't all women like men who look like Norse gods?" came the reply.

No one disputed that.

Susan continued on her way to say a few words to the widow. She passed some friends and many neighbors and found herself wondering if she would rate a funeral half this size if she died in her sleep tonight. As at many funerals she'd attended, the talk was about everything but the deceased. One couple was arguing over an apparent snag in their divorce settlement. There were more than a few people exchanging stories (horrors or brags) of their summer vacations. Three women were even exchanging favorite recipes for barbecue sauce. Susan passed through the crowd, smiling at those she knew and eavesdropping on those she didn't, until she was at Patricia Fairweather's side.

"I'm so sorry," she murmured.

"Thank you." Patricia looked straight into Susan's eyes and then glanced down. "You will be coming over to the house afterwards, won't you?" she asked quietly.

"Of course," Susan assured her, thrilled that she was to be included in the group. Not that she was morbid or wanted to intrude on anyone's grief; she just expected that she would find out more about Simon Fairweather there than anyplace else at the present time.

"So I'll see you at the Fairweathers' house?" asked the neighbor who had spoken to her earlier as Susan headed down the steps of the church and out into the humid August heat to the parking area behind the rose garden.

"You were invited, too?" Susan asked undiplomatically.

"Everyone who came to the funeral was asked as far as I could tell. Don't tell me you expected this to be an intimate little gathering, Susan Henshaw. You know Hancock better than that. I just hope I can manage to stay away from Buck Logan—that man is so obnoxious in an election year. You'd think there was actually someone else in town who wanted his job from the way he campaigns."

Susan smiled politely and hurried toward her car. If everyone there was heading over to the Fairweather house, it was going to be difficult to get a parking place. She started the car, relieved when the air-conditioning began blasting cool air. She had become only too aware that her best black summer suit was more appropriate for spring than an August day that was promising to be in the high nineties.

There was going to be food, Susan realized, pulling up in the driveway behind the caterer's vans. In her rearview mirror she spied other guests arriving, getting out of cars and, apparently in unison, deciding a more casual approach to dress was appropriate and tossing their jackets back into their vehicles. Susan followed suit.

And then she followed the line of guests heading into the backyard, where a buffet brunch had been set up on the edge of the mossy green lawn. Susan accepted a cup of coffee from a uniformed waiter and wandered around, trying to keep her heels from puncturing holes in the immaculate lawn and find a friend to speak with at the same time.

She was admiring a blowsy purple clematis growing over an ornate trellis when someone came up behind her.

"What I don't understand is, if no one liked him, why is his funeral turning into the social event of the season?"

Susan turned and discovered Debbie Sanderson by her side. "Debbie! I was talking about you recently. . . ." Susan didn't know how to finish that statement.

"What about me? How my husband has actually had the lack of imagination to run off with his secretary? How my children are refusing to live with either their father or myself and trying to con their grandparents into paying tuition at one of the most expensive boarding schools in the country? How I had slightly too much to drink at the field club's Fourth of July party and fell into the kiddy pool wearing a gauze dress that became completely transparent the second it hit the water? About how—"

"About the remodeling job on your house," Susan interrupted before she was forced to listen to every embarrassing thing that had ever happened to the woman. "How it was left incomplete due to a mistake made by Ken Cory. You see," she added, "I hired Cory Construction to work on my house. In fact, they're there right now."

"When did they start work?"

"About seven o'clock."

"I mean, when did they start working on your house?"

"A couple of days ago. Why?"

"Right before or right after Simon Fairweather was killed?"

"Right after."

"Then you're okay."

"What do you mean?" Susan asked, puzzled by the direction this conversation was taking.

"If he had been killed right afterwards, you'd be a suspect in his murder, wouldn't you?"

"I don't understand."

"Susan, you're supposed to be so up on everything in Hancock. Surely you know that Simon Fairweather has been screwing up jobs for Cory Construction for at least the last six months, maybe for the last year."

"Yes, I heard that's what happened to your addition—"

"Not exactly," Debbie interrupted. "What happened with my addition is that Ken Cory somehow misunderstood someone in Simon Fairweather's office. He thought the plans had been approved when they hadn't. So he went ahead and hired someone to dig a huge hole in the backyard right next to the foundation of my house. And then when Simon Fairweather found out that the work had begun without his official sanction he stopped the entire project."

"He just said 'I don't approve' and the work had to be stopped? Just like that?"

"Not quite. He claimed that the addition needed to be

granted a variance in the local zoning laws and that a variance had not been applied for."

"Weren't those things Ken Cory should have taken care of automatically?" Susan asked. "I know that I've had those little yellow sheets of paper stuck up in my window from the first day of the project."

"What are you having done?"

"Bathroom remodeling."

"Oh, nothing major," Debbie said with apparent disdain. "That type of stuff can be done with a trip to the building inspector's office. Throw a few dollars on the desk and get your permits. Extensions require more than that, a lot more."

"Like what? You mentioned variances?" Susan asked.

"According to the zoning laws in Hancock, Connecticut, a house can only cover a certain percentage of the land that it is built on."

"You mean, like a house can only cover a third of an acre-size property? Something like that?"

"Sort of."

Susan got the feeling that Debbie wasn't all that sure of her facts. "So your addition was going to make your home larger than it should be? And that's not allowed?"

"Oh, it's allowed. You just have to go through a long, time-consuming, and, of course, money-consuming process of getting every neighbor within a certain distance to agree to the whole thing. Then you and your builder and your architect have to go in front of the planning board and give them your plans and the opinions of the neighbors and then Simon Fairweather decides whether or not you're going to be allowed to do what you want to do with property that you already own."

"Not Simon Fairweather," Susan argued. "The planning board makes that decision, surely."

"In Hancock, Connecticut, what Simon Fairweather says goes. He runs that planning board like he does his own office. Ken Cory assured me of that from the very beginning."

"How did Simon do that?"

"He's . . . he was . . . one of the original dictators."

Susan frowned. "I don't get it. How did one man become so powerful?"

"I don't get it either," Debbie said. "And I don't want to get it. I'm so sick of worrying about Simon Fairweather that I could scream. And maybe," she added, "it all comes down to what we were saying just a few minutes ago."

"What?" Susan asked, looking around. The backyard was filling up with guests. If she was going to taste one of those delicious-looking cheese Danish, she'd better get in line, she reminded herself as Debbie continued to talk.

"If no one liked him," Debbie repeated, "how come there are so many people at his funeral?"

"You're here and you certainly didn't care for the man," Susan reminded her.

"I thought it was going to be a viewing. You know, with an open casket. I just wanted to make damn sure he really was dead."

TWENTY-FOUR

It was pure luck that the next person Susan ran into was Simon Fairweather's secretary. She stood out in this large gathering of mourners by being the only person present who was wiping tears from her eyes.

"Allergies," the middle-aged woman explained. "From the moment the first stalk of goldenrod blooms by the side of the road until the first frost, I am a slave to my allergies."

"That must be dreadful," Susan said noncommittally. They were side by side in front of a table piled high with tiny pastries and Susan was trying to choose between raspberry Danish and a miniature cheese croissant. She settled the problem by taking both. And then a third. After all, lemon was one of her favorite flavors.

"Simon was always so concerned about my allergies. He even brought large boxes of Kleenex to the office in the early fall."

"You worked with Simon Fairweather?" Susan asked, becoming interested immediately.

"For the past twenty-six years. I always thought he would be the one to give me my thirty-years-with-the-village gift, but I guess that was not to be." A loud sneeze punctuated this statement, and Susan reached out to support the plate that was tipping precariously from the other woman's hand.

"Why don't we find someplace to sit down?" Susan suggested. "Perhaps in the shade?"

"I'd like that."

Susan led the way through the crowd toward a couple of chairs formed from branches and twigs, which were off by themselves near a small herb garden.

"Simon told me about these chairs," the other woman said, sitting down. "He made them a few years ago. I'd always wanted to see them."

Susan sat down, too, and introduced herself while shifting her weight to keep an outlaw branch from poking her in the kidney.

"It's nice to meet you, Susan. I'm Evangeline Forest. Everyone calls me Evie." Evie rummaged around in her capacious patent-leather purse and finding the pink handkerchief with tatted edges that she had apparently been looking for blew her nose before continuing. "Over the past few years I've heard a little about what you do. Are you helping Chief Fortesque investigate Simon's murder?"

"Yes, I am. Well, not right now, of course," Susan lied. "This isn't really the place for me to start asking a lot of questions."

"I don't mind. I haven't been as upset about Simon's death as I thought I would be. I mean, we didn't have a very personal relationship."

Susan thought about twenty-six years in the same office and those boxes of tissues, but she didn't interrupt.

"We worked together, but I never felt that I understood the man," Evie continued, blowing her nose again.

"What did you do for Simon?"

"I ran his office," Evie answered proudly. "Oh, not to begin with. I began as a secretary. Back in the old days we were the entire office, just Simon with me as his secretary. We used to work out of one room down at the municipal center. We had that tiny office where everyone now goes to get dog licenses, can you believe that?"

"You're in a larger space now?" Susan had been to the mayor's office, the tax office, and, of course, the police department, but she had no idea where the building inspector worked.

"We're up above the town council chambers. We have the entire second floor," Evie said proudly.

"You're kidding. That really is a large area if it's the same size as the meeting room."

"It is. And I can tell you that we need it."

"But Hancock is such a small town," Susan said.

"True. But the building inspector's office is always very busy. Think how many of your neighbors have improved their homes in the past few decades," Evie reminded her.

Susan chuckled. "Almost all of them," she admitted. "Some more than once."

"Every time someone changes a leaking toilet they have to apply for a permit," Evie explained, nodding her head.

"You're kidding!"

"Well, that's the law. But you would be surprised how many people try to get away with breaking the law."

"Surely just replacing an old toilet . . ." Susan began. She didn't know about everyone else, but she had no idea she'd needed a permit for such a small job.

"Simon always said the law was the law."

It was difficult to argue with that.

"And that made my job much easier," Evie continued.

"What do you mean?"

"I started out as a normal secretary—straight out of high school. I typed letters, answered the phone, took notes during meetings of the town planning committee, you know the type of thing."

"But that changed?"

"Well, the office got so much bigger in the eighties. Instead of a few requests for permits a day and probably one or two variances applied for a week—at the most—things changed. Not only did half the people in town want to expand their houses or upgrade their kitchens or whatever, but builders started coming in and buying up old houses. Some of them were remodeled and some were bought to be torn down. Sometimes two or even three new homes were built in place of one. The paperwork was enormous. So another secretary was hired and then about ten years ago a third."

"But you're the senior secretary."

"Yes, and I've had enough experience to do a lot of the routine work without any problem."

"Like what?"

"Like accepting fees and handing out permits for simple remodeling jobs. Or taking down information that's needed to apply for a variance. Or looking up old covenants—you'd be amazed how many homes in Hancock are built on land that is covenanted."

"I don't know what that means," Susan admitted.

"It means that you buy land on which a past agreement restricts the use of the land in some way."

"Like what?" Susan asked.

"Well, there are covenants that prevent land from being subdivided. You know, so that someone can't build another house on their large lot. There are covenants that require all the building in a particular area to be done in a certain style. That's pretty uncommon these days, though," Evie added.

Susan agreed. Hancock was a veritable melting pot of housing styles.

"There used to be covenants against things like selling your house to a member of a minority."

"You're kidding!"

"No, that type of restrictive covenant was pretty common before the early sixties, but of course it's illegal now. There are also records of various rights of way that our office keeps track of," Evie added, starting to sniff again.

"Like driveways that go through other people's properties," Susan said, having a friend who had lived with this situation for the past few years.

"Exactly. And there are a lot of questions of previous use, grandfathering and that type of thing."

"Like what?"

"Like doctors' and dentists' offices in homes in residential areas. Back in the fifties neighbors didn't object to that type of use. But now every time a house like that is put on the market, there are neighbors who insist that the office be removed. And that's difficult if it's been there for decades."

"And you give out information about this type of thing."

"Sometimes. Of course, if I don't know about the situation, people can always go look it up at the county offices.

But a lot of the time I'm just the first face that anyone sees in the building inspector's office. I tried to take some of the burden off Simon."

"What sort of burden?"

"Well, most of the contractors are unreasonably impatient. They file building plans with us and expect approval or disapproval immediately."

"How long does that type of thing usually take?"

"No offense, but you sound like some of the contractors in town. The whole point, Simon would tell you if he were alive, is that we don't know how long it will take to examine the plans until the plans are actually in our hands."

"I don't understand."

"That's because you haven't spent almost thirty years dealing with building and remodeling plans. Believe me, the variety is limitless. A house can be a mansion like the one in *Gone With the Wind*—"

"Tara," Susan supplied the name.

"That's right. Or it can be a one-room geodesic dome."

"In Hancock?"

"A permit was issued for one last week. Of course, we had to have an out-of-town engineering firm examine the architectural drawings and all of the specs."

"Is that usual?"

"It's what Simon always did when the plans or materials were something he wasn't familiar with, like that underground house over near the field club. That was built about twenty years ago and the technology was experimental. The U.B.C. didn't cover that type of construction then, so Simon called in more than a few experts to make sure the design was feasible and safe. He was always making sure that Hancock was protected from lawsuits."

Susan shook her head. "I don't understand. Who would sue the town over something like that? The town didn't build it."

"If a plan wasn't safe and there was a fire—or the roof fell in on a sleeping baby because no one checked to make sure there was a load-bearing wall where it should have been—if something like that happened and the building inspector's office had approved the plans or, even worse, given a certificate of occupancy to the unsafe building, Hancock could very well be sued by the family who owned the home. And Hancock would probably lose a suit like that. It would be devastating for a town this size. That's why Simon was always careful. He didn't care how many enemies he made, all he cared about was getting the building built safely."

"That's certainly admirable," Susan said, wondering if it would be tactful to ask how many enemies he had made and if Ken Cory was one of them.

"Of course, that's what I told Chief Fortesque," Evie continued. "It wasn't Simon Fairweather's job to be popular, it was his job to be conscientious, firm, and fair. That's what he always said. He had an artist paint a sign that hung on the wall over his desk. It said ' 'Tis Better to Be Honored Than to Be Loved.' "

"Were there many people who considered Simon Fairweather their enemy?" Susan asked.

Evie nodded seriously and moved her chair inches closer to Susan's. "He said there were a lot of people in town who would be happy when he was dead."

"Really?" Susan looked around at the gathering and wondered if any of these people were secretly thrilled by this serious occasion.

"Then, of course, they could go ahead and build their shoddy buildings without Simon Fairweather peering over their shoulders."

"Did he?"

"Did he what?"

"Did he peer over their shoulders?" Susan asked, wondering whether or not Simon had been paranoid. "I thought he just went out and inspected buildings when it was time to have a final inspection done."

"Not on your life! In the first place there are numerous inspections done on all new buildings. The foundation has to be inspected before the floors are poured. Then the concrete is examined. There's a framing inspection that is done after the framing is finished, including the roof framing.

That's when the rough electrical, plumbing, and heating inspection is done, too. There's also an inspection done after the walls, both interior and exterior, are up. And then there's a final inspection before a certificate of occupancy is granted."

"So—"

"But that's not all. A building inspector can decide that other inspections are required, that tests of building materials are needed, that someone should check out a building every step of the way. In fact, a building inspector could be on a building site once a day. Even for residential buildings."

"You mean private homes."

"Yes."

"Don't builders mind all that looking over their shoulders?" Susan asked.

"Some do and some don't. But it really didn't matter to Simon. It was Simon's job and he did it."

Susan was silent for a while, eating her pastry while Evie sniffed into her handkerchief and stared unselfconsciously at the people milling around the lawn. "I see Mrs. Fairweather decided that jeans weren't an appropriate outfit for her husband's funeral," she commented.

Susan decided to ignore how catty the woman sounded. "I think she always looks wonderful. I don't know her well, of course. But I've seen her around town over the years and I took a pottery class with her in the spring."

"Oh, so you're artsy-craftsy, too."

"Well, I'm not as good as Patricia," Susan explained. "She says it's not true, but she really is an artist, you know."

"Simon always said artsy-craftsy." Evie continued to use the word that somehow offended Susan. "He never said a word against her, of course. He was a loyal husband. But sometimes he would talk about the women in Hancock who have too little to do. The housewives who add family rooms when their families are never home to use them. Women who would explain that they just had to have saunas in their bathrooms no matter what the fire code is because their arms hurt so much after long tennis games at the club. And, you know, I used to wonder if he wasn't thinking about his wife and her artsy-craftsy pretensions."

Susan tried to work up some sympathy for this woman's obvious bitterness. After all, Patricia Fairweather was talented and wealthy and didn't have to earn her own living. But, on the other hand, it was Patricia Fairweather who had the reputation for being an abused wife, not Evangeline Forest. She had just decided to ask Evie about that when Patricia joined them.

TWENTY-FIVE

"I WAS HORRIBLY EMBARRASSED. I'M SURE SHE OVERHEARD me talking about her. I felt like a fool."

"She's probably forgotten all about it," Brett Fortesque suggested. "Today was probably very traumatic for her. Remember, that funeral must have been a strain no matter how little real feelings were left in the Fairweathers' relationship."

"She did seem genuinely upset," Susan said slowly, stirring sweetener into a tall glass of iced tea. "I thought it was a little strange, in fact. Most people are less emotional by the time the funeral comes around, and Patricia was very together right after Simon's murder."

"Interesting," Brett commented, picking up a French fry and, after dipping it in catsup, returned it, uneaten, to his plate.

"Yes, I thought so."

"I spoke with your ceramics teacher," Brett said, not adding that the woman had confirmed Susan's poor performance in class. "She admitted knowing that Simon had beaten his wife. More than once, she said. But Patricia insisted on keeping the information private."

"I just wish—" Susan began.

"Your teacher also spent some time wishing that she had done something. But really, it was up to Patricia Fairweather," Brett insisted. "And guess who else I spoke with? The Fairweathers' cleaning woman. Well, I spoke, but I'm not sure she understood me," he added ruefully. "She doesn't speak English very well. But she did confirm

Patricia's story about how we got the wrong message. After spending time with her, I'm surprised we got any message at all."

Susan only smiled.

"Did you happen to have a chance to speak with any of the family?" Brett asked the question so casually that Susan knew it was the reason he had grabbed her after the reception and suggested this lunch that neither of them was hungry enough to eat. "I didn't want to do it at the funeral; it might have seemed a little insensitive."

"I spent a few moments with one of her sisters." Susan picked up a sweet potato chip and stuffed it into her mouth. Why did she always eat the fattening stuff?

"The one with the house in Montauk?"

"She did say she lived on the tip of Long Island," Susan said. "You got her phone number from Patricia. Didn't you call and talk to her?"

"Yes. She said that Patricia was staying out in Montauk when her husband was murdered. We didn't discuss anything else," Brett said. "What did you two talk about?"

"Oh, you know, social things. She mentioned growing up in the house her sister was living in now and I said something about how different the house was, how much work Simon Fairweather had done on it over the years. And she said yes, he had, and that Hancock had changed tremendously since she was a little girl. And she asked how long I had lived here—"

"I'm not all that interested in what you told her," Brett admitted gently.

"Okay. If you want to know if she said anything like 'Did you know that bastard Simon Fairweather was beating my sister and I'm glad he's dead,' the answer is that nothing like that came up. I was already feeling a little embarrassed about the personal nature of my conversation with Evie. After all, a funeral is no place to investigate a murder."

"Susan," Brett said.

"But I did overhear the family talking about getting together for dinner tonight at Patricia's house. And I just might think of a reason to stop over."

"What sort of reason?" Brett asked.

"Something a little artsy-craftsy," Susan answered mysteriously.

"Did you find out anything more about Simon Fairweather from talking with Evangeline Forest?"

"She certainly is loyal to her employer," Susan said. "She said you had already spoken with her. Did you get the impression that their relationship was anything more than professional?"

"Not really. Though I did wonder if maybe she wanted it to be something more," Brett admitted.

Susan nodded. "I wondered the same thing. But most of our conversation was about Simon's job and the way he did it. I found that interesting."

"In what way?"

"Well, in the first place, I had very little idea what a building inspector does. You know, the whole approval process and how many choices he has over the way he does his job. Like how many inspections must be carried out at each site and all that."

"A building inspector is a very important person in town. And most people don't realize how much is left up to his discretion. He has to see that the terms of the building code are carried out, but how he goes about it is pretty much his decision."

"So I gather. It didn't sound like he did his job very well to me," Susan said. "Jed always says that a good manager hires good people and then he lets them do their work in peace."

"But Simon Fairweather didn't hire the people that work on the houses, the homeowners do. And the contracting business has long been known as a place where people can get rich quick and then get out of town. Simon Fairweather's job was to make sure that didn't happen."

"You sound a little like Evie Forest. She apparently thought her boss was some sort of saint protecting us all from buildings that would crash down on the heads of innocent infants."

"Simon Fairweather was a pain in the ass, no doubt about it. But he did accomplish what his job was supposed to do. Sometimes that means you won't win a popularity contest. No one knows that as well as a cop."

Susan picked up her avocado, bacon, and tomato sandwich and took a big bite. Chewing gave her an excuse not to speak until she had thought of something to say. But the only thing that came to mind was another question. "Do you have any information that anyone else in town was mad enough to kill him?"

"There were some other people whose plans for a dream home were wrecked by Simon's insistence on following the rules, but nothing and no one who struck me or any of my men as unreasonable. There is some recourse if you don't agree with the building inspector's decisions, you know. You don't have to kill him."

"I didn't mean to imply that murder is an answer to anything."

"In this case there's also an appeals process and anyone can request a hearing before the board of planning. Simon didn't have the final say in everything."

"But someone said"—Susan was beginning to have trouble keeping her information straight—"that in some towns the planning board was just a rubber stamp of the building inspector's office."

"Not true in Hancock. I had a man going through the files down at the building inspector's office. Simon Fairweather didn't always get his own way. He lost on little things like whether someone could put up a treehouse in their backyard for their children without having it inspected and on big things like subdividing the land down by the old mill. But," Brett continued seriously, "there is nothing that anyone in my office can find that is similar to the relationship between Cory Construction and Simon Fairweather. There is not a single instance of his stopping a building project completely except for the one that Ken Cory's men worked on. And it is certainly true that hiring Ken Cory meant that Simon was going to be carefully looking over your shoulder. But—before you ask—there isn't a clue as to why Ken Cory was singled out by our anonymous caller."

"They're not incompetent, are they?" Susan asked. She held her breath, hoping to hear the correct answer.

"No. There have been some fly-by-night companies that came into town, but they didn't stay long. Simon got after them and the only legal problem that I know about was a company that offered Simon a bribe if he would accept some shoddy work."

"He didn't take it."

"He turned in the man who did it as well as the owner of the contracting company. They were prosecuted, of course. Bribing a government official is serious stuff."

"It's true that I haven't heard anything about his being dishonest," Susan mused, licking mayonnaise off her finger.

"I don't think you're going to. We're looking into that, of course."

"So what this boils down to is that our first guess was correct. If it wasn't his family who did it, it was probably Ken Cory or someone on that crew."

"It looks that way," Brett agreed. "It certainly does."

"I suppose you could say that eliminating suspects is progress," Susan murmured.

"We always do," Brett assured her. "Otherwise the entire force would have days when Prozac seemed like the only answer. Too bad Kathleen is going to be indisposed for a while."

Susan bridled. "You think I can't look around for a while by myself, do you?"

"Well, even the best can't be in two places at once," Brett said.

"True. But you haven't met Josie Pigeon yet," Susan said.

"Who is Josie Pigeon?" Brett asked.

"My fly on the wall."

"What?"

"She's my spy. She's a carpenter that Ken Cory hired to help out with my job. I thought I told you about her."

"How do you know that she's not the member of the crew that the caller referred to? How do you know that someone doesn't think she's a murderer? Just because she's a woman, you trust her," Brett protested.

"Because she just joined the crew two days ago," Susan insisted. "She's not like everyone else. There's no reason for her to have anything against Simon Fairweather. She only arrived in town a few days ago. Until now she's been working in a resort community at the shore. That's why I trust her. Besides, right now everyone on the crew is discriminating against her."

"Where did you say she used to work?"

"At the ocean someplace. Why?"

"Is it possible that it's Montauk?" Brett asked. "Does her arrival have anything to do with Patricia Fairweather and her sister?"

"I certainly don't see how," Susan insisted, wishing that she had thought of that before this.

"Well, maybe you'd better find out before you put your trust in someone you don't know," Brett suggested angrily.

"Why are you getting mad at me?"

"I'm not mad at you. I just think you're being foolish. And you could end up in danger."

Susan stood up. "I'm fine, Chief Fortesque. Although I thank you for worrying about me. I have things to do this afternoon, so I'll leave you now. Thanks for the lunch."

"You're welcome," Brett said, motioning to the waitress to bring him their check.

"I'll let you know if I discover anything about the murder," Susan said, walking away.

"I certainly would appreciate it if you did so," Brett said to the empty seat across from him.

TWENTY-SIX

SUSAN RETURNED HOME TO DISCOVER THAT JOSIE WASN'T there. An unhappy woman whining loudly about the men who had betrayed her indicated that Buns was controlling the radio for the afternoon. "She's gone to the lumberyard, ma'am," he answered when Susan insisted on knowing Josie's location. "Art needed someone to check out the most recent order and she wasn't doing anything more important."

Susan smiled her thanks and hurried out of the sweltering attic. "Any idea when the air-conditioning will be back on?" she asked over her shoulder.

"Nope. Might check with Angelo. He's doing something with the wires down in your bathroom."

"Thanks. I will," Susan said, hurrying off to find the electrician.

Angelo Ferraro wasn't on the second floor; Susan found him in the middle of the kitchen surrounded by dozens of open cardboard boxes. Clue was by the electrician's side, gnawing a large cardboard tube. "You buy these things?" Angelo shouted over the sound of a disco hit that Susan had hated ever since she first heard it—back in 1974.

"I picked them out at the store in town."

"You got these things at Hancock Electric?"

"No."

"At Brightly Lit?"

"No, they were out of stock. My husband bought them in the city. He had to go all the way down to the Lower East Side."

"Too bad."

"What?" Susan wondered why he couldn't turn down his radio before speaking.

"I said too bad."

"Why?"

"They all have to go back."

"What! No, they don't! I love them."

"You better love them enough to have a fire in your bathroom 'cause that's what's gonna happen. No way to ground these mothers. They're a disaster waiting to happen. And where are the wall heaters? Didn't Ken tell you that we were going to be installing the wall heater in the attic first thing today? The walls are prepared and I pulled the wires last night. I thought we were all ready to go."

Susan turned around and walked out of the room. It was that or start screaming. And who knew when—or if—she might manage to stop.

"Oh, and you got a call from a man at a tile store this morning. He needed to know right away what color to use for the background or something like that. Said for you to call back. I think Frankie's got the number."

Susan was beginning to understand how Buns's favorite singer felt about men as she searched for Frankie. A persistent reggae beat drew her to the bathroom in the hallway. Frankie was soldering copper pipes hanging from the ceiling.

"Hi. I thought the upstairs bathroom was going to be finished first," Susan commented as he switched off the flame.

Frankie reached over and turned down his radio before answering. "The pipes are all connected, ma'am," he said, smiling at her.

Susan grinned back, feeling like she had found a friend among the enemy camp. "I'm sorry if I was being stupid. I don't know anything about plumbing. I understand you have a phone number for me. There was a call from the man who is making our tiles," she added.

"Oh, sure. Right here." Frankie fumbled through the pockets of his jeans until he found a small slip of paper. "It may be a little late to call, though. I think he said he was leaving early today."

Susan sighed.

"Don't let this get to you. It's a big job and everyone is going to be telling you that their part is the most important and that it has to be done immediately. Don't you believe it. Everything will get done whether you run around like a chicken with your head cut off or not."

"Thanks. I'll try to remember that."

"Hey, Frankie, Buns said to tell you you got a phone call from someone named Sean. He asked that you call him back as soon as possible. Something about dinner plans," Kyle Barnes called out, sticking his head in the doorway. "Hi, Mrs. H. Did you talk to Art yet? He wants to know exactly how long you want the towel racks to be. The ones under the countertop."

Susan took a deep breath.

"Just remember what I said," Frankie reminded her.

"I'll try," Susan promised. "I have to go out again for a few hours, but I'll figure out the racks and call the tile man first. Say, do either of you know where Josie is living?"

"She said something about being in an apartment above a florist's shop, didn't she?" Kyle offered.

"Or was it a dry cleaner's?" Frankie asked.

"I'll find it," Susan said, remembering the silly name of the nail salon. "If I leave a message for my husband, would someone see that he gets it?"

"No problem," they answered in unison as Susan headed up the stairs. She would talk to Art, call the tile store, and spend some time studying those permits that were hanging in her living room window. Then she'd go see Patricia Fairweather.

And by the time she'd done all that, maybe Josie would have returned to her apartment and they could talk.

She hurried through her chores, deciding to take Clue along on her travels. Sometimes having the animal along was a pain in the butt, but she had found that occasionally dogs opened doors that would otherwise remain closed.

And sometimes they barged right in, she was reminding

herself an hour later as Clue's leash slipped from her hand and her pet flung herself into Patricia Fairweather's house.

"I'm so sorry," Susan apologized to the tall woman who had opened the door.

"Is she friendly?"

Susan knew exactly what was being asked. "Almost impossibly so. She loves everybody—and especially other dogs," she added as Clue reappeared with a large chocolate lab by her side.

"Ghiradelli has been starved for some company. Would it be okay if I closed the two of them in the backyard for a while? They can eat up the pastries that were dropped on the lawn while you talk with my sister. You're here to see Patricia, aren't you?"

"Yes," Susan admitted, aware of the fact that Patricia's sister didn't remember their previous meeting after the funeral.

"I'll take them outside and go get her. Why don't you wait in the living room?"

Susan did as suggested and a few minutes later found herself being entertained by the owner of the labrador retriever. "My sister was in the shower. She says she'll be out in a while if you don't mind waiting?"

"Not at all."

"It may take a while. She was washing her hair. Getting it dry is something of a challenge."

"I was glad to see that she hadn't cut it," Susan commented, leaning back on the couch. "She was saying she might."

"She's been talking about whacking it off for years— whenever she's in a bad mood. But she never does. I'm glad myself. I can't imagine Pat-Pat with anything but long hair."

Susan grinned. " 'Pat-Pat'?"

"Yeah, it's what we called her when we were kids. Terrible, isn't it? You live like an adult for years and then your family comes around and tells all these tales about you."

"True. I'm Susan Henshaw. And I don't think I remember your name."

"I'm sorry. I should have introduced myself. I was assuming that we had spoken at the service or in the backyard this morning. I'm afraid I've met so many different people in the last twelve hours that I'll never get them all straightened out. I'm Lillian Weed. I'm Pat's older—actually, her oldest sister."

"We did talk for a few moments after the funeral," Susan admitted. "You're the sister with the house in Montauk. The one Patricia was staying with when her husband was killed." Susan realized she wasn't being very tactful, but this was what she had come there to talk about and she had never dreamed it was going to be this easy.

"Yes. I'm her alibi."

Susan opened her mouth and nothing came out.

"Don't be shocked. That's what Pat has been calling me for the last few days. Apparently the chief of police came by and asked her why she had decided to change her plans for an Alaskan cruise at the last minute and practically accused her of flying back here and murdering her husband. So it was a lucky thing that she was staying with me at the time. Although, of course, it was a ridiculous idea."

"Why?" Susan asked.

"In the first place, why would Patricia want to kill her husband? They might not have had a marriage made in heaven, but if they had been terribly unhappy, they could have gotten a divorce. Murder wasn't necessary. Besides, why wouldn't a wife just poison her husband's oatmeal or something? Certainly Patricia wouldn't have killed Simon with an automatic nail gun. What an ugly thing to do! My sister is a charming, cultured woman. If she had been going to murder her husband she would have done it with some class—absurd as that sounds."

"If this is the type of thing my sisters say about me, what are my enemies saying?"

"If your own family can't trash you, who can?" Lillian answered back, the grin on her face identical to the one displayed by Patricia Fairweather.

Susan looked from one to the other, delighted by the family resemblance.

"Susan Henshaw is the woman I was telling you about who helps the police solve murders in Hancock," Patricia said pointedly to her sister. Susan was surprised by how serious she looked.

"We have murders—plural—in Hancock these days?" came the amused reply. "And to think I was desperate to leave here when I was a teenager because it was so dreadfully dull."

"It's not all that funny when it's your husband who was murdered," Patricia reminded her dourly.

"That man was dreadful, Pat-Pat. You should have divorced him years ago. Heaven knows why you didn't. I certainly didn't wish him dead, but if that was the only way we could get him out of your life, then I'm not going to sit around and pretend to mourn the bastard."

"Lillian!" Patricia turned to Susan with a frown on her face. "Please excuse my sister. She's always been known as the one in the family with absolutely no tact."

"I call a monster a monster. You're well rid of him. And you know it."

Susan saw how upset Patricia was becoming and decided it was time to break into the conversation. "I'm not just the person who helps Brett solve murders, I'm also a struggling craftsperson. I took a pottery class with your sister last spring," she explained to Lillian.

"And did very well."

Susan knew that was just a polite lie; no one would call her work anything but inept, but she continued. "I was wondering if you would work on a commission for me. I know this might not be the best time, but I would sure appreciate it if you would make one of those beautiful porcelain baby sets for my friend Kathleen's new baby girl.

"You see, I want to get her something special. Not special like from Tiffany's special, but special like unique. And I remembered the cup and bowl that you were making for one of your nieces' babies . . ." She let the statement drift off. It was an excuse to get in the door. She didn't really care if the answer was yes or no. In fact, she had already bought Kathleen's baby an eighteenth-century English porringer—the child could always sell it and use the money to hitchhike around Europe when she was a teenager.

"I never saw the mug you made Bettina's baby," Lillian exclaimed.

"I can show you something similar," Patricia said, looking curiously at Susan. "That's what you came here for?"

"I guess this is the wrong time. I was going to mention it this morning, but . . ."

"It's an excellent time, Pat-Pat. You need something to occupy your days and starting up a business is just the thing to keep you going until this whole mystery is cleared up."

"Sure. And if worse comes to worst, I'll just try to get committed to a prison that has a good crafts workshop."

"My sister the pessimist," Lillian said, standing up. "Please ignore her, Mrs. Henshaw. There is no way she's going to be arrested for the murder of her husband."

A phone ringing in another room interrupted them.

"Would you get that for me?" Patricia asked her sister. "It might be the press again and I'd rather not talk to them."

"Certainly."

As Lillian Weed hurried toward the sound, Patricia turned to Susan and grabbed her hand. "I need to speak with you. Alone. Do you know a little restaurant over on Ivy Lane called the Seagull's Retreat?"

"No, but I can find it," Susan assured her.

"Then I'll meet you there for breakfast tomorrow morning."

"Couldn't we meet sooner?"

"My family won't be leaving until then," Patricia insisted. "Please, tomorrow at nine."

Susan could only agree.

TWENTY-SEVEN

CLUE WAS HAVING A WONDERFUL DAY. FIRST A THRILLING hour spent racing around with a cheerful companion on a lawn liberally studded with delicious lumps of sugary dough. Then a long nap in the back of Susan's Cherokee. And now three tiny white kittens to lick as they clung to her silky coat.

"I cannot believe that dog. Apparently she's never heard that dogs and cats are natural enemies," Josie said, handing Susan a bottle of light beer. "I suppose I should have gotten you a glass," she added, making no move to do anything about it.

"I can't believe you adopted three kittens at once," Susan answered, taking a sip from the dripping bottle. "You do know that they're going to grow up into three cats, don't you?"

"I work long hours. They'll keep one another company. How much difference can there be between one and more than one? I'll just have to clean out the litter box more often."

"I guess," Susan said.

"Besides, I miss my son. These little guys will keep me company."

Susan smiled. She hadn't had time—yet—to miss her own children. "Did you hear anything interesting from the crew?" she asked, coming to the point of her visit. "I've been thinking about you all day. I hope I didn't make you more unpopular than you already are with the rest of the crew."

"No, actually I used the fact that they don't particularly like me to elicit some information about the guys." Josie sounded particularly proud of herself.

"How did you do that?"

"Well, I figured that Frankie knows we're investigating, right? At least he knows that you are and that I was hanging around with you. But he also wants to keep his sexual choice private, so he isn't going to talk about that visit to his apartment."

Susan nodded slowly. "I've been thinking about that. But, you know, I'm not so sure that his lifestyle is a secret. I heard Kyle give Frankie a message about a phone call from a man about dinner. It wouldn't take a huge effort to translate that into the truth."

"Yeah, well, I've been thinking about that, too, and it struck me that maybe Frankie was being a bit paranoid about the whole sexual thing. I've worked on crews that were homophobic, but I've also worked with men and women whose sexual preferences weren't particularly Middle-American and they haven't had a lot of problems. Actually, I think Frankie would get more kidding about his unusual artwork than who he sleeps with. There probably aren't a whole lot of carpenters into abstract sculpture." Josie picked up one of the kittens, laid it in her lap, and petted it absently as she spoke.

"So you started asking questions with Frankie," Susan prompted.

"Not really, I just went up to the attic where everyone was working—"

"Except for you?"

"Except for me—as usual." Josie frowned. "And I said to Frankie that I had heard he'd been with Cory Construction longer than anyone on the crew except for Art."

"And?"

"And everyone started arguing about how long they'd been working on this particular crew—just like I thought they would," she added proudly.

"And?"

"Well, as far as I can tell, the progression goes like this:

Art Young and another carpenter—George Somebody—were hired by Ken Cory when he started the business. So Art is the only one of the two originals employees left."

"What about plumbers and the like? Frankie and Buns? And Angelo?"

"Well, when Ken started his business, he just hired a couple of carpenters and he subcontracted for other people to do the rest of the work as needed. Later, when he got a reputation for working on kitchens and baths, he connected with Buns. Frankie came later. Angelo doesn't work with Cory Construction all the time. He has his own business and comes in when he's needed."

"But they've all been working with Cory Construction for at least a year."

"Definitely. Except for Kyle. He hired on at the beginning of summer when the workload got heavier. They had been shorthanded ever since George died, but Ken had been filling in, and it doesn't sound like Cory Construction was actually overburdened with work until recently. And then there's me, of course."

"Did you find out if the Joes always work with this crew?"

"No, but I think you could probably assume so. There are a lot of variables in contracting work: the job itself, the homeowners and their lifestyle, different designs—things like that. Contractors like to work with the same people over and over. They get to know the styles of the outside workers and vice versa. It makes things easier for everybody."

"Sounds like you didn't have trouble getting that information then."

"Not at all. Nothing like what happened when I mentioned Simon Fairweather. Those guys really hated that man."

"Well, then . . ."

"Of course, hating the building inspector is practically a full-time hobby on some jobs," Josie went on.

"Because they have so much power."

"Exactly. I see you're catching on to the business."

"You mean . . ."

"I should say what happens on a lot of construction sites. Although it does sound like the relationship between Simon Fairweather and Cory Construction was rather extreme. At least, it's the first time I've heard of such animosity being carried from job to job. To be honest, when I first heard about it, I just assumed that you'd hired an incompetent contractor and that I was working for one."

"But you don't think he's incompetent?" Susan asked, hoping for the answer she wanted.

"Not at all. Ken is a little greedy, but contractors got used to really big money in the eighties and some have had a tough time scaling back. Besides, to be honest, this is a very wealthy neighborhood. It's pretty obvious that you—and your neighbors—can afford to have big things done on your houses."

"But still . . ."

"But you still want to get the best you can for your money. I know."

"So you're saying he charges too much?"

"He's expensive, but so are a lot of contractors. The best always are. Ken just likes to add on to the job. And lots of small additions can really increase the cost—and hide profit. But we've talked about this before and I don't see what it has to do with Simon Fairweather's murder."

"Why not?"

"Because the building inspector's job is to see that everything is done right—done to code. And that has nothing at all to do with the cost of the work."

"So the inspections don't ever increase the cost of the job," Susan said.

"Actually, that's not quite true. Some contractors save money by cutting corners, and it's the building inspector's job to make sure that isn't done. And a job that is done twice—even if it was done wrong the first time—costs more than one that was done once."

"Is that what happened with Ken Cory and his crew?"

Josie sat back against the couch and flung her hands in the air. "I have no idea. And no matter how much the guys on the crew talked, I couldn't get a handle on it."

"What do you mean?"

"Well, as far as I can tell, the problems with Simon Fairweather began a while ago—maybe nine months or even a year ago. I know that there was some sort of problem with a job late last fall because Buns made a comment about Simon Fairweather trying to keep them from being with their families for a four-day weekend at Thanksgiving. I didn't catch the story, but I'm sure about the timing. And there was a major problem with a foundation last spring."

"That must be Debbie Sanderson's house," Susan commented.

"Well, if she's a friend of yours, you better warn her to get that thing filled in now that Simon Fairweather isn't around to stop it. If a hole full of water sits up against the foundation all winter, freezing and thawing, it could crack the back wall of her house and imperil the entire structure."

"I'll mention it," Susan promised, wondering how she was going to phrase such a dire prophecy. "Anything else?"

Josie petted her kitten and thought for a moment before speaking. "Look, I'm only hearing one side of the story, but . . ."

"But what?"

"It sounds to me like Simon Fairweather had it in for Ken Cory and his men. The stories they're telling sound like unjustified harassment pure and simple."

"Really?" Susan breathed. "Are you sure?"

"That's just it. I can't be sure because I've only heard one side of the story, but unless these guys have all gotten together to tell the same lies, Simon Fairweather was acting in an unprofessional manner."

"Too bad we can't find out the truth," Susan muttered.

"We'll all know next month though, won't we?"

"What do you mean?" Susan asked.

"There are going to be hearings about all this, aren't there?"

"I have no idea what you're talking about," Susan admitted.

"Oh, the guys were talking like it was a big story in town. I just assumed that you knew. Your town has a planning board that homeowners and builders can appeal to if they don't agree with the decision of the building inspector—most towns handle the appeals process in a similar manner. But this is a small town and the people on the board are volunteers who go away for the summer, so the planning board doesn't meet from late May until after Labor Day. According to Art Young, the first thing on the agenda when vacation is over is a case that has to do with Cory Construction and Simon Fairweather. Of course, no one knows what will happen now that Simon is dead. Art seems to think that whoever takes over the building inspector's office will just withdraw their side of the argument."

"Can that be true?"

Josie shrugged. "It's possible. Art seems to know what he's talking about. If you can't believe a man who knows the names and lengths of the twenty longest rivers in the world, who can you believe?"

Susan frowned. "You mentioned George Porter."

"The other carpenter on the original work crew."

"Exactly. Did anyone happen to tell you about his death?"

"Not exactly. I think Art said it was an accident."

"A terrible accident the way Buns tells it," Susan agreed.

"What happened?"

"He touched a live wire with one of his tools. Apparently he was electrocuted." Susan didn't feel any need to repeat the description of the man as a piece of fried meat.

"In the spring before Kyle was hired," Josie said.

"Right. The question I have is: Was it an accident? You know, it seems a little strange to me. The first thing any of the workmen did when they arrived at the house was turn off the power. I assume that's standard procedure?"

"Well, it sure should be."

"Then—"

"Things aren't always the way they should be," Josie continued. "Sometimes people forget to turn off the power. Sometimes the wrong circuit breakers get turned off. Sometimes someone thinks someone else has done something that they either forgot to do or just plain didn't know needed doing. Not many people work for very many years without touching a live wire. It can be a truly hair-raising experience," she added, fluffing up her unruly red curls.

"But George was killed," Susan said.

"It happens. Not often, but it happens."

Both women were silent for a moment, watching the animals cavort on the floor. "You know what I think?" Susan said finally. "I think maybe we should try to find out why George Porter died. Maybe it was a freak accident. Or maybe we have two murders instead of one here."

"I was afraid you were going to say that," Josie admitted.

"You thought the same thing?" Susan asked.

Josie nodded her head in agreement. "Yes. In fact, I was so worried about it that I asked some questions about George."

"Do other people think it might have been murder?"

"Not that type of question. I thought you would want to look into that yourself. Besides, the guys were talking about his death as though it never occurred to them that it was anything other than an accident."

Susan was confused. "So what questions did you ask?"

"I found out where he lived."

"Where?"

"In an apartment over the hardware store."

"Was he married?"

"His wife died a little over a year ago. He lived with an adult daughter. Art stays in touch with her. Her name . . ." Josie paused and went through the pockets of her overalls before she found the piece of paper she was looking for. "Her name is Patsy Porter. This is her phone number. I thought you might want to give her a call or something."

"I sure do. Where's your phone?"

"Kitchen." Josie pointed out the way.

It took Susan only a few minutes to call. She returned to find Josie on the floor, roughhousing with the animals.

"She agreed to see me tonight," Susan said.

"Do you want me to come with you?"

"Maybe she'll think it's a little strange if two unknown women appear at her door this late."

Josie glanced down at her watch. "It is a rather unusual time to make a social call, but maybe that's the way you rich suburbanites live." She grinned. "After all, you don't have to get up early like us poor working people."

"You've figured out a way to work silently?" Susan asked, smiling back. "Because unless you have, I think I'll be getting up pretty early for the next few weeks."

"A few weeks? You're getting my nomination for optimist of the year," Josie kidded as Susan stood up and called to her dog. "I could keep Clue here for you," she offered.

"Thanks. But I'll leave her in the car. That way I won't have to come back and bother you tonight."

"Anything you say. Maybe I'll be able to find out more about the crew tomorrow."

"That would be great," Susan said, wondering about the serious expression on Josie's face. It wasn't at all typical of the young woman. "You know, sometimes looking into the personal and professional lives of people who find themselves in a murder investigation is a little depressing. You don't have to do this, you know."

Josie frowned. "I guess I should have thought of that a while ago."

"Then don't—"

"I'm fine," Josie said, putting a wide grin back on her face.

Susan would have believed her if she had seen the usual gleam in those remarkable green eyes.

TWENTY-EIGHT

The woman who opened the door to the apartment was not aging gracefully. Susan guessed her age to be in the late thirties, but her style was that of an old woman. Her hair was pulled back into a thin bun; the lines on her face were undisguised by makeup; the flowered housedress she wore was popular among farm women in the fifties, but Susan would have had a difficult time knowing where to buy one like it today.

"Patsy Porter? I'm Susan Henshaw."

"Mrs. Henshaw. How nice to meet you. Please come in." Patsy stood back to permit Susan to enter.

"Thank you, I . . . What an interesting apartment."

"It's exactly the way it was when my mother died. She inherited many of these things from her mother," Patsy said proudly. "It hasn't been easy to replace some items as wear and tear took its toll, but I go to flea markets on weekends and manage to find some things. And my father used to bring home furniture that people were throwing out when they remodeled. You would be amazed what some people consider worthless. That lamp next to you, for example."

Susan looked at the curly iron floor lamp with the pink ruffled shade. She wasn't surprised it had been discarded. Although, now that she thought about it, without the shade . . .

"Of course, I had to work to find the shade. It came from a used furniture shop in Darien." Patsy interrupted Susan's visions of redecorating. "Sit over there." She pointed. "Then you'll get the breeze from the floor fan."

"I think my grandmother had an ottoman fan like that," Susan said, sitting down on a knotty-pine couch slipcovered with itchy plaid fabric ruffles.

"My father kept that one running ever since I was a child. He always believed in fixing things instead of throwing them out or replacing them with something cheap. Of course, that became more and more difficult for him to do after my mother died. He was so distraught over her death," Patsy explained proudly, sitting down across the room from Susan. "Would you like something to drink? Maybe some iced tea? Or Sanka?"

"No, I'm just fine, thank you," Susan answered, wanting to get on with her questions but not knowing how to start.

Apparently Patsy had no such problem. "You're here to find out more about my father, aren't you?"

Susan had been thinking of beginning with some polite small talk. "I—"

"You believe that he was murdered, don't you?"

"I—"

"I know who you are. You're the woman who investigates murders in town. You're here to talk with me about Dad's death."

"I'm—"

"I can't tell you how relieved I am. I've been telling everyone that it couldn't have been an accident. Dad wouldn't have had an accident like that. 'Safety first,' he always said. It was his motto. He wouldn't have gone into a wall where there were live wires. He would have turned them off. Someone else must have turned them back on. But you must know that. That's why you're here, isn't it? You're going to find the man who killed my father and bring him to justice."

"Please wait. I can't do anything until you tell me what happened to your father. And even then I may not be able to do anything. But begin at the beginning. First you have to tell me about your father's death. Everything you know."

"I—"

"From the day that he was killed," Susan insisted gently.

"I don't know." Patsy looked around the room, obviously confused.

"Why don't you start with who told you that he had died."

"The doctor at the hospital. But you don't mean that, do you?" Patsy asked, obviously upset at the memory. She took a deep breath and continued. "You want to know how I knew he was hurt. You see, I work at the hardware store downstairs—in the housewares department, of course," she added, seeing the surprised expression on Susan's face. "And I was on my midmorning break in the back room when Mr. Young found me."

It took Susan a few seconds to catch on; previously she hadn't heard Art Young referred to with such respect. She nodded, encouraging Patsy to go on.

"I was shocked to see him, of course. Mr. Young comes into the store from time to time, but my department is separated from the lumber and tools and things like that and I couldn't imagine any reason for him to be there.

"But he immediately told me that my father had had an accident and that he had come to take me to the hospital. I . . . I guess I was confused because I said that I couldn't leave without telling my boss. But, of course, I didn't know that my father was dying, might already have been dead at that point."

"So you went to the hospital with Art Young?"

"Yes. Mr. Young insisted it was urgent and didn't even give me time to get my purse. We keep them locked up when we're working because sometimes customers wander into the back rooms."

"And when you got to the hospital?"

"We went to the emergency room and a man there—he was so young that I thought he couldn't be a doctor but he said he was—he came up to me and told me that my father had died." She stopped talking and looked down at her hands, which were crossed in her lap.

"And?"

"And that's how I found out that my father had died."

"How did you discover the circumstances around his death? That he had been electrocuted?"

"Well, they had to tell me immediately because they had to explain why they wouldn't let me see him. They thought his burns would shock me, I suppose."

Susan had visions of being in this hot sticky room for the rest of her life. "They told you it was an accident, didn't they?"

"Yes, of course. But once Mr. Young explained what had happened—the circumstances—I knew it had to be murder. My father simply did not make mistakes like that."

"Did you tell Mr. Young that?" Susan asked.

"Of course. And he agreed with me that my father had been an extraordinarily careful worker."

"But even the most careful worker makes mistakes."

"Not my father. You didn't know my father, Mrs. Henshaw. He wasn't like other men."

Susan decided to try another tactic. "But why would anybody want to kill him?" she asked.

"I have given that a lot of thought," Patsy answered seriously. "A lot of thought."

"And?"

"Why are most people murdered? For someone's gain. Right?"

"Yes, but—"

"And who had the most to gain from my father's death?"

"Yes, who?" Susan asked, wondering if Patsy was asking a rhetorical question.

"I am his only heir," Patsy stated flatly.

"So . . ."

"So the crime was not committed for monetary gain. We can eliminate that."

"Then . . ." Susan started wondering where, if anyplace, this was going.

"Then it couldn't have been personal. My mother died over a year ago and my father had remained faithful to her memory. There were no other women in his life. And no other family except for me. His life was his work." She leaned toward Susan. "It must have been something professional."

Susan wasn't quite so sure about this deduction, but she wasn't going to argue. "Do you have any idea what someone he worked with would have gained from his death?"

"They must have been trying to keep him quiet. What else?"

"Quiet about what? Did your father know something that made him dangerous to someone else? Had he mentioned anything like that to you before he died?"

"Nothing specific . . ." She paused. "You'll be discreet, of course?"

"Of course," Susan assured her seriously.

"My father said strange things were happening at work."

Susan almost looked around for the orchestra that was going to punctuate that statement. "Like what?"

"He didn't tell me."

Susan sighed and leaned back against a calico pillow. "He said that strange things were happening and then he didn't explain what they were?"

"You must understand. My father believed in protecting the women in his life. For instance, my mother never knew how much money he made. He said she should buy what she needed to keep the family running and he would tell her if she was exceeding their income. Of course," she added, seeing Susan's eyebrows go up in surprise, "I've always felt that I should be self-supporting even though I've always lived at home."

"Well, if you've lived with your family, maybe you noticed a change in your father before he died?" Susan asked gently.

"Now that's an interesting question. I can tell you've had a lot of experience at this type of thing. The policeman who talked with me after Dad's death never asked anything like that."

Bingo. If Brett had been interested in the death, it might have been something other than an accident. She'd check that out with him later. "Did you notice anything?" she repeated her question. "Any changes?"

"It was obvious that he was worried. He would come home and have a couple of beers and just pick at his dinner. And that happened even when I made his favorite meatloaf with mashed potatoes and gravy."

"How long had he been acting like that?"

"I don't know. A few months maybe."

"And you have no idea why?"

"Sometimes he would talk about how things were changing in the world and I would get the feeling that he was talking about work, but that's really all I can tell you and it's just a guess."

"Did your father ever mention Simon Fairweather or the building inspector's office?"

Patsy nodded. "I thought about Dad when I heard that Simon Fairweather had been killed. He didn't like him." She looked up at Susan. "I was taught not to speak ill of the dead."

"You know I wouldn't ask unless it was important. And I'm not just gossiping."

"Dad hated Simon Fairweather."

"There seems to be a lot of hostility toward the building inspector from the men working in my house. Maybe that's just normal," Susan suggested.

"It was more than that. Dad said that Simon Fairweather wanted to take away his job."

"Take away his job? Those were his exact words?"

"Yes. You must understand that my father loved his work. He was proud of every single building that he ever built. When I was young, he always took my mother and me to see the homes he had worked on once they were completed. And years later, when he would drive by one of those buildings, he would point it out and describe something unique about that project or tell a story about the work. But for months before Dad died, every time Cory Construction started a job, something happened and the job was stopped."

"Why?"

"I have no idea. But it was causing Dad a lot of unhappiness. I know that. And he had gone to Simon Fairweather about it."

"Really?"

"Yes. He kept saying that he was going to and I would say, 'Go talk to him, Dad. You always taught me to speak up when something was bothering me. Go to Simon Fairweather and talk with him about whatever is wrong.' "

"And he did?"

"Sure enough. The week before he died, he went down to the municipal center and marched right into the building inspector's office and insisted on some answers."

"And did he get them?" Susan asked quietly.

"Dad refused to leave until he got them," Patsy Porter replied. "But, unfortunately, he never told me what happened. He just said that Simon Fairweather hated him. You'd be interested in that conversation, wouldn't you?"

"Definitely. Did he seem to feel better after that meeting?"

"You know, I don't think so. He was even more distracted and unhappy, if anything. It's so sad to think that his last week was miserable. Dad was one of those men who took a lot of enjoyment from the world and from what he did. It shouldn't have ended like that for him."

"No, of course not," Susan agreed sincerely.

"Dad said that something awful was going to happen."

"What do you mean?"

"The night before Dad was killed, he told me that someone was going to die . . ."

"He must have had a reason even to be talking about death," Susan prompted when Patsy stopped in the middle of her sentence.

"I don't remember. Frankly, I was so shocked by Dad's murder that I sort of forgot what had happened before he died. Later I remembered that we had had this strange conversation over dinner the night before he died. See, I didn't understand why he didn't feel better after talking to Simon Fairweather and I asked him about it. He refused to explain—I think he just didn't want to worry me. That's the way Dad was: Always protecting the little woman."

"But he said something about someone dying," Susan reminded her.

"That's all he said. He said that he had a lot on his mind these days, that someone was going to die."

"And that's it?"

"I'm afraid so. He didn't mention any names. I know he didn't think that the person who was going to be killed would be him. Are you still going to see if you can discover who killed Dad?"

"I . . . Of course," Susan answered, the only way she could. She had no idea if this death was connected to Simon Fairweather's murder, but she was fairly sure that Brett would let her see the official records. And that, she decided, standing up, was the place to start.

She thanked Patsy for her help and, after some polite appreciation of the most hideous watercolors she'd ever seen, made her way out of the apartment.

Her Cherokee was parked on the street in front of the hardware store in a spot too convenient to have ever been available when she had a heavy load to carry. Clue was waiting patiently in the back.

"Come on, sweetie. Just a quick walk over to that big pine tree on the corner and we'll be on our way." She grabbed one of the blue plastic bags in which her *New York Times* was delivered and stuffed it in her pocket.

Susan was familiar with the saying that you can lead a horse to water but you can't make it drink. However, she had personally experienced how many times a dog can sniff and circle an area before doing what it had been led there to do.

At least ten minutes had passed before Susan had coaxed Clue back into her car and was turning around to find the exact location of the covered wastebasket she had noticed earlier.

That's when she was attacked from behind.

TWENTY-NINE

" . . . So I smacked him——or her——with it."

"You hit a complete stranger with a plastic bag full of dog shit?"

"I hit the person who grabbed my shoulder with the only weapon I had available," Susan called out indignantly from the shower.

There was only silence from her companion.

"Are you laughing at me?" she yelled.

"I'm trying hard not to, and it's not as though I don't appreciate your creativity, but it is pretty funny," Brett called back through the partially opened bathroom door. They were both having trouble making themselves heard over the sound of water running. "Why don't I just go and see if I can find you a big garbage bag for your clothes?"

"Great! More than one, if you can. I'm not even sure double-bagging will contain the smell. And I have no idea what I'm going to do about the inside of my car," Susan muttered to herself, scrubbing her legs with the only clean washcloth she'd discovered in the police chief's poorly stocked linen closet.

"Did you say something?" A man walked in the door.

Susan screamed and grabbed for a towel with NYC POLICE ATHLETIC LEAGUE stamped on one end.

"Hey. No need for privacy. It's me. Your husband." Jed pulled open the shower curtain and grinned at his soapy wife. "Brett called about fifteen minutes ago and explained the situation. I came right away. I brought you clean clothes. And that bottle of Issey Miyake perfume that you love so much."

Susan sighed. "Good thinking. I smell like a used pooper-scooper left in the sun too long."

Jed looked around. "Something in here sure reeks. Where's Clue, by the way?"

"There's a tiny yard behind here. She's running around out there. I don't know how we're going to get her home. I sure don't want to get in my car and we don't want to put her in your car until she's had a bath."

"Susan, what happened?" Jed asked.

"Why don't you just leave my clothes there on the john and go ask Brett. I told him the whole story. He can fill you in. And take my dirty clothes—they're lying on the floor wrapped in a towel. Don't unwrap them! Just take them out and stuff them in the bags that Brett was finding for me. I'll be done in here in a few minutes."

Actually, it was more like ten minutes. Susan couldn't resist scrubbing up and rinsing off one more time. She was positive that she still smelled, but her nose was so stuffy there was no way to be sure. She entered Brett's living room with an embarrassed smile on her face.

But there was no one there. She walked across the sparsely furnished room and peered out the sliding doors to the patio. Brett and Jed were on their knees trying to subdue a very wet and slippery dog. She backed up quickly before they spied her and asked for help. She'd done enough for one evening, she decided, sitting down on Brett's couch and closing her eyes.

But the men returned almost immediately and her break was over.

"Brett told me about your unusual methods of defense," Jed said, sitting beside her and slipping his arm around her shoulders. "I'm glad you're okay," he added seriously.

"I know I'm repeating myself, but are you sure you didn't recognize your attacker?" Brett asked, sitting on a chair across from the Henshaws.

"No, but unless he or she has showered recently, I'll bet anyone could pick them out in a crowd—with their eyes closed. I smelled terrible and I just got some of the fallout.

That bag split right across the back of his—or her—neck. That person must stink.

"I have men out all over town, checking to discover if anyone has run into a very smelly person this evening—particularly any member of Cory Construction's crew—but, of course, they're only going to find the ones that are at home and who answer their door. Someone could be showering and we'd never know."

"You never told me that we might be hiring a murderer when you chose Ken and his men to work on our house," Jed said accusingly.

"I knew you'd feel like that, so I didn't mention it," Susan admitted. "Besides, you met Ken before we signed the contract. You picked them out as much as I did. But no one told me that one of the crew members was killed last spring," she added, looking at Brett.

"There's no proof that George Porter's death was anything other than an accident."

"But you did look into it. His daughter said she had been interviewed by a policeman."

Brett nodded. "Two of my men spoke with her at different times. She insisted that her father would never have made a fatal mistake like the one that took his life. But we had no reason to accept that. All the men on the crew admitted that accidents happen to the best of people. And I checked that out with other contractors. They all said the same thing. And some of them had some pretty hair-raising stories of their own to tell. Construction can be a very dangerous business."

"As Simon Fairweather found out," Susan muttered.

"Well, that wasn't quite the same thing," Brett said. "After all, he was found dead in his office, not on a building site."

Susan frowned but didn't answer immediately. "You're saying you have no evidence that George Porter was murdered."

"I also have no evidence that he wasn't," Brett said. "I've been wondering if the two deaths were related, too. In fact, I have the file home for the night," he added, nodding at the pile of papers sitting on his Formica dinette table.

"Could I . . . ?"

"Of course. Stay where you are. I'll even get them for you," he offered.

"And I'm going to use the phone, if you don't mind," Jed said.

"Feel free," Brett told him, handing Susan the stack of papers and sitting down next to her in the spot Jed had just vacated. "Do you want me to go through this with you?"

"Fine. But you must have suspected murder when you sent someone to speak with Patsy, right?"

"No. We always check out accidents. And we probably wouldn't even have gone back a second time if she hadn't insisted that her father had been murdered. You can see that the officer I sent was skeptical," he added, handing her a typed report.

Susan took the time to read carefully through the pages. "Are you sure this isn't just a bit sexist? I mean, the man practically says that Patsy Porter is a flake."

Brett took the offending statement from her hand and glanced at it. "This was written by a woman. And Patsy Porter was acting a little strange at the time. But that's not unusual in a case of sudden death. However, she was interviewed a few days later also and her story hadn't changed—that's why we checked everything out with the other carpenters and with members of two other contractors in Hancock. They all agreed that an accident was more than possible. See. Here." He handed her more papers.

"Interesting. You know, reading through this I'm surprised that Art Young wasn't more upset by George's death."

"Should he have been?"

"Well, they had worked together for years. Wouldn't you be upset under the circumstances?"

"How I would feel and how someone else would are two different things. When you're a cop, you learn quickly that people act differently, especially in crisis situations. Besides, just because they worked together doesn't mean they had developed a close personal relationship."

"But less than twenty-four hours after his co-worker died Art is quoted talking about finding a replacement for him,"

Susan protested. "Doesn't that seem a little insensitive to you?"

"Sounds to me like he had a job to get done," Brett answered.

Susan shuffled through the papers. "Sounds like he already had Kyle in mind for the job, though, doesn't it?"

"I wouldn't say that," Brett disagreed.

"Look here," Susan insisted, pointing at the middle of one page. "Your officer asked Art Young how Cory Construction was going to get along without a second carpenter. And Art said that he knew about a good carpenter who was looking for work."

"I did that interview," Brett said. "And I remember the conversation, but you're making it rather ominous. It was no big deal. I asked, more in passing than anything else, what was going to happen to their work without George and Art commented on another carpenter he knew who was free. Susan, it's hard to imagine that conversation happening any other way with any other carpenter."

"And how do you know he was talking about Kyle Barnes?" Jed spoke up.

"I don't, of course, but I intend to find out." Susan picked up the notes and began reading again. She was aware of the fact that the two men were exchanging looks over her head, but she wasn't going to let that bother her. She was beginning to unravel the threads of this particular puzzle and she had no intention of becoming distracted by their attempts at superiority. "There's something else interesting here," she muttered, sniffing the air. There was still a certain smell in the room. Maybe she should change brands of dog food.

"What?" Brett asked.

"Well, for one thing, Ken is a trained carpenter, so how come he didn't just pitch right in after George died? It says here that Art was working alone when you interviewed him. And if Ken had been helping out, there wouldn't have been such a rush to find a replacement carpenter."

"Ken doesn't seem to be doing any of the carpentry on our house either," Jed reminded her.

"Do you think that's strange?"

"Not necessarily," her husband said. "I just assumed that he was busy planning and ordering materials and ... and whatever else there is to do right now on the project."

"Besides," Brett reminded them both, "you're talking about last spring, and at that time Cory Construction was starting projects that Simon Fairweather wouldn't allow them to complete. At least that's what your wife has been telling me," he told Jed. "What I'm trying to say is that maybe there was no immediate reason for another carpenter to start working. And maybe Ken was very busy with other things like protesting everything that the building inspector was doing to the planning board."

"True, things are different now that Simon is dead," Susan mumbled, looking over her shoulder. Surely the smell was getting stronger? "But the question is," she continued, "how were things different after George was killed—no longer on the scene?"

Jed shrugged. "They needed another carpenter to take his place."

"Hmmm."

"What are you thinking about?" Brett asked Susan.

"I'm wondering what really happened at that meeting between George and Simon Fairweather that Patsy told me about."

"It's going to be hard to find out now that both men are dead," Brett said.

"Is there anyone else who might know?" Jed asked.

"Patricia Fairweather" was Brett's suggestion.

"Perhaps, but she didn't seem to know very much about her husband's work. Maybe she wasn't interested or maybe he didn't bring his work home from the office—or, more likely, he was rarely home," Susan added. "Remember, he was out at a meeting the night she left for vacation and Patricia implied that that wasn't an unusual occurrence."

"Someone in his office—" Jed began.

"Of course, his secretary! What's her name?" Susan asked.

"Evangeline Forest," Brett said. "You've met her?"

"We spoke at the funeral yesterday. She was quite willing to talk about Simon."

"Doesn't surprise me. She must miss him. Some of the people down at the municipal center say that she's had a crush on the man for years.

"You know, the police department and the building inspector's office are alike in some ways: They're the two largest departments in the building and they're both separated from the other offices—the tax collector, the department of health, the mayor's office, the parks and recreation department, and the like. We have a wing to ourselves because we function twenty-four hours a day and we have a small holding cell. The building inspector's office is upstairs—above the city council chambers. It's a large area and busier than anyplace in the building beside the police department."

"I think I'll be seeing it for myself in the morning," Susan said.

"Maybe after you shower again," Brett suggested gently. "I know your bathrooms aren't working, so if you want to use this one again . . ."

"There are flashing lights out front," Susan said, standing up.

"Must be the tow truck I called," Jed answered.

"Why did you call a tow truck?" Susan asked.

"Brett suggested it."

"Your car is going to be towed to a garage that specializes in cleaning autos. They'll air it and spray it with deodorant, and if that doesn't work, they'll replace the carpeting and upholstery. We use them after accidents and disasters," Brett explained.

"Disasters?" Jed repeated the word as a question.

"Cars that get caught in floods and fires. It's a tossup as to which smells worse: mildew or smoke. Of course, your wife's car stinks worse than either of those things." He chuckled and looked at Susan.

"Sue?" Jed tried to attract her attention. "Are you with us?"

"Sorry." She rubbed her eyes. "I'm tired. I think I'll take you up on that offer to use your shower again and then I'll go home and get to bed."

THIRTY

Susan woke up the next morning realizing that she was never, ever going to become accustomed to living in a house while it was being remodeled. A huge crash seemed to cue Jed to roll in her direction.

"That reminds me," he muttered. "What made that loud noise yesterday morning?"

"Probably the same thing you just heard," she answered, and pulled a pillow over her head. She didn't want to admit that she had failed to discover the answer to that question. She squeezed her eyes closed, trying to ignore the voice in her brain reminding her that there were a lot of questions that needed answering—and none of the answers were going to be found there in her bed.

"Are my suits in the closet?" Jed was now sitting on the edge of the bed.

"Excuse me?"

"My suits. My shirts. You said you were going to move our clothing across the hall," he reminded her.

"I had a busy day yesterday."

He stood up. "Would you like me to get something for you to wear while I'm at it?"

"Don't worry about me. I can put on the things I wore last night. After all, I only wore them for a couple of hours." She swung her legs over the side of the bed, narrowly missing the footboard. "I'm meeting Patricia Fairweather for breakfast."

"Please, hon, drop Clue off at the dog groomer's before anything else. Brett and I did the best we could, but . . ."

"I don't have a car! How—"

"I already thought of that. I called Jerry last night and I'll go in with him. You can take my car. I'd better get going."

Susan noticed that he didn't bother to kiss her goodbye. That might have bothered her if she hadn't been in such a hurry herself. Jed was right: First things first. She would stuff Clue in the car and throw herself on the mercy of the owner of the Pampered Pooch, then she would set out in an orderly fashion to solve the murders—plural.

She dressed quickly and hurried out of the house, waving to Art Young and Frankie as she passed them. She knew if she stopped they would think of things to ask her that would take time and, most likely, leave her with even more problems than she had right now.

Jed's car was usually off limits, so Clue considered the trip to the dog groomer's a real treat. Susan dropped the dog off and drove over to the restaurant. Patricia was sitting in a window seat waiting for her.

"Hi," Susan said, sitting down across the table from Patricia. "I like your shirt." She offered the compliment hoping to get the conversation going.

Patricia seemed to have forgotten the reason she had asked Susan to join her there. She looked down at her clothing and sighed. "I seem to wear black jeans and a dark shirt every day since Simon died. It's silly, really. No one expects a widow to wear mourning anymore. And I'm not the type of person to put on a public show about anything," she confessed, as a young waitress approached. "I keep thinking that people might not think it's appropriate for me to wander around in torn jeans and a Greenpeace T-shirt like I used to." She frowned. "It's just not like me to worry about such things. I guess Simon's death has upset me more than I thought it had."

Susan had no idea what to say about that after the waitress had left and they were alone again. "You two were married for quite a while," she muttered, looking at the wheat germ and raisin muffin in front of her. The Seagull's Retreat was a tiny health-food restaurant so she didn't have much hope for the baked goods, but the muffin turned out to be excellent. Susan had never even noticed the place before. She guessed that Patricia, from the greetings the staff had given her, was a regular.

"Yes. We were" was all Patricia said.

New Age music tinkled in the background, so Susan figured that what she was experiencing couldn't actually be called an awkward silence. She decided to try again. "Do you think you'll stay in that large house? Now that you're alone?" she added when Patricia didn't respond.

"It's my family home," she finally answered, rather vaguely. "I suppose I'll stay there. I've always been there, after all."

"And you have your studio all set up," Susan reminded her.

"Yes. There is that," Patricia admitted. She seemed more interested in breaking a large slice of zucchini-carrot bread into tiny pieces than talking, so Susan ate her food and looked around the restaurant.

The café was only big enough for seven tables and a long counter that displayed baked goods and bowls of fruit, but the walls were covered with prints, posters, and even framed poems. "This is an interesting place," Susan said, not expecting a response. Patricia seemed to be getting more upset as her husband's murder receded farther and farther into the past.

"The art on the walls changes monthly," Patricia answered slowly, not bothering to glance around. "But . . . but I didn't ask you here to talk about art. I need to tell you something. Something about Simon that no one knows." She paused and looked around the room. "In fact, I didn't even know it until a short while ago. A very short while ago," she added quietly.

"When?" Susan asked.

"Yesterday afternoon," Patricia admitted, and then fell silent again.

Susan realized that she was going to have to ask questions if this conversation was going to go anywhere. "Why don't you start at the beginning," she suggested, as she always did. She expected to hear a story beginning less than twenty-four hours before, but the time frame Patricia Fairweather was concerned with was measured in years.

"I suppose this all started about three years after Simon and I got married," she began. "When I was growing up, there was a small peach orchard behind the house. It was wonderful. I was the youngest child and I guess I was lonely. I used to go out among the peaches and imagine all sorts of things. It was really a magical place for me. The blossoms in the springtime were fabulous. But the smell of the ripe fruit hanging from the branches around this time of year—I think I liked that best."

She sighed at the memory and continued. "But we needed money. Simon was working as a general contractor, and he was making a decent living but not enough to support the lifestyle that he wanted. And I have to admit that my family home was costly to maintain and we were in the midst of remodeling. Simon was looking for cash and he got it by subdividing the orchard and building two houses there."

"It must have been a real loss for you." Susan commented.

"Yes, but that's not what I'm trying to tell you about. Simon used the profits from selling off those houses to buy some land down by the river, and he built three homes there and sold them at what we thought was an enormous profit. He was happy with the result and we had some extra cash for the first time since our marriage. But Simon wanted to be someone important, not just a general contractor, and when Hancock's building inspector died, Simon was thrilled to be asked to take the job."

"Really?"

"Yes. He had worked with the inspector while he was building those five houses and during our remodeling, of course, and I just assumed that he had found something that he wanted to do with his life."

"And that wasn't true?"

"Well, maybe in the beginning. The job was wonderful for him. Hancock was in the process of changing from a lovely small town into a wealthy suburb. There were so many opportunities for Simon to act important. He could hold up projects over minor technicalities. He could strut around the houses of millionaires like he owned them. He was courted by contractors and members of the community who were busy cashing in on the housing boom of the late seventies and eighties."

"Was he building houses himself at the same time?"

"No, and I think that was the problem." Patricia drained her cup of tea and looked straight across the table at Susan. "You see, his timing was bad. He was building houses in the late sixties and early seventies before the market boomed. He made an honest profit—actually it seemed like a fortune to us at the time—but it wasn't anywhere near the amount of money that people were making for doing far less only ten years later."

"So?"

"So he became dishonest," Patricia explained very quietly. "I didn't know it at the time. I guess I've been very foolish."

"Maybe it would help if you told me about it," Susan suggested gently as windchimes and an oboe once again became the only sounds in the room.

"The building inspector has a lot of opportunities to make money illegally if he's so inclined," Patricia began slowly.

"Like in New York City, where we're always hearing about them being paid off to approve unsafe structures and ignore building-code violations," Susan said, thinking she understood at last.

"No. He didn't do that. I don't think Simon would have even considered anything that made the buildings unsafe. What Simon did, I think, was pick a particular contracting company and make them pay him to allow them to work in town." She pulled her hair together and began making one long braid over her shoulder. "Looking back, it all makes sense. You see, these companies were making the type of profit that Simon had never even dreamed of. And they had long waiting lists of people who wanted work done.

"Poor Simon had had to dredge up jobs that paid very little and then when that job was over, go out and find another. Suddenly there were literally lines of people who wanted building done and who were willing to pay premium prices for the work. And Simon was out of the business. He also preferred being an important official rather than a carpenter with dirty fingernails. So he found a way to make being a building inspector pay."

"And they paid him—what would you call it?—bribes so they could work?"

"Exactly. And there was so much money around that they went ahead and paid. One after the other. Some were probably perfectly happy to toss a small percentage of their profits in the direction of the building inspector. As you said, it had been going on in New York City for years. And the few that objected discovered that they couldn't get permits issued or inspections done on time. Those that didn't get the hint had their jobs shut down. But . . ."

"But?" Susan prompted when Patricia didn't continue.

"What's the expression? What goes around comes around? Life changed. A recession came along that made the contractors as hungry as Simon had been and recently one of them refused to pay up."

Susan finally realized where all this was leading. "Ken Cory."

"Yes, I think so," Patricia's voice broke and a tear slipped down one cheek. "I hate to tell you this. I . . . I just couldn't keep it to myself."

"You did the right thing," Susan assured her. "In fact, you really should have told Brett right away."

"Oh, but I didn't know any of this until right before you came over yesterday!" Patricia insisted. "I never would have accepted living on money that was gotten illegally. Never. And that's why Simon never told me any of this. He understood I would find his actions completely unacceptable."

"Of course."

"Of course that doesn't change the reality of the situation. I did live for years on the earnings of illegal activity.

I'm going to have to find some way to atone for that . . . or something."

"But how did you find out about this?" Susan asked, less interested in Patricia's feelings than in the facts.

"My sister and I were going through the desk in Simon's bedroom. We were looking for insurance papers," she explained, almost as though the activity wasn't completely understandable or acceptable. "And in a folder at the bottom of the last drawer we found pages of notes and figures. It took me a while to sort it all out. But when I did, I realized what had been going on."

"Are the names of the contracting companies there?" Susan asked, thinking of Cory Construction.

"Not as such. There are numbers and initials to identify the companies. It might be possible to figure it all out if you had records of all the building that has gone on in town for the past twenty years or so."

"Is it a lot of money?"

"Maybe not to everybody, but for us it was. As much as fifty thousand some years. And never less than twenty-five."

"And tax-free," Susan muttered to herself.

Patricia nodded. "You know," she said, "I'm partially to blame for all this. I never got involved in our finances. Simon handed me the money that I needed to do what I wanted. I never questioned where it came from."

"I don't see how that makes you responsible. I don't question Jed about where our money comes from. You just assumed that your husband was acting ethically and legally. Like lots of wives."

"I suppose. But I keep thinking that I should have been paying more attention. That I should have known. We . . . we lived very separate lives and I accepted that. But I had no idea that Simon was doing anything like this."

Susan could see that Patricia was close to falling apart. "And you haven't told Brett Fortesque anything about this?" she asked, hoping to return to a less emotional topic. "This could have something to do with your husband's murder."

"I . . . I know that," Patricia said, taking a deep breath and sitting up straighter. "That's why I wanted to see you. I was hoping you would tell him. I just don't think I can bear to talk about this with someone I hardly know."

Susan thought for a moment. "These records that lay all this out . . ." she began.

"They're in my car," Patricia said, apparently anticipating her suggestion. "I could get them for you and maybe you would give them to Chief Fortesque."

"I suppose I could do that," Susan said slowly. "But he's going to insist on talking to you about all this."

"Yes. I . . . I know that. I just want to spend some more time with my sister first. It's important. She's probably going to leave for Montauk today."

"Then why don't you just give me the records and I'll take them to Brett," Susan suggested. She had heard enough tinkling bells and windchimes for one day—for a year, in fact.

THIRTY-ONE

BRETT HAD WARNED HER ABOUT HOW MUCH HAPPENED IN the office of the building inspector, but Susan was still surprised by the activity behind the double doors of the building inspector's office. She was even more surprised when Ken Cory stepped out of the crowd and greeted her.

"Mrs. Henshaw. Susan. What are you doing here? I thought we agreed that I was handling all the paperwork for your job."

"That's not why I'm here. I had to see someone who works in the office," she explained, sniffing deeply.

"Catching a cold?" Ken asked.

"I think it's an allergy." Susan didn't want to admit that she was trying to detect any telltale odor clinging to him.

"Have a Kleenex." Evie Forest thrust a flowered cardboard box across the counter.

"Thanks." Susan tried to blow her nose and ended up honking loudly.

"Did you come here to see me?" Evie asked.

"Why?" Ken began.

"I thought you'd know the name of a good allergist," Susan said inspired.

"Sure. I have to do some work here, but we close at noon for lunch. You can wait for me in my office if you'd like."

"Great," Susan said. She turned back to Ken Cory. "I guess I'll be seeing you at home."

He merely nodded his reply and Susan followed Evie down the hall and into a small office. "Is that Simon Fairweather's office?" she asked, nodding at the closed door nearest to Evie's. Bits of the yellow tape the police had used to cordon off the room were still stuck to the woodwork.

"Sure is. Go on in and look around, if you'd like. I have to get back out there."

"I'll be fine here," Susan assured her, her hand on the office doorknob.

She entered the office and Evie hurried back down the hall.

Fifteen minutes later the two women were together in Evie's office.

"Sorry about the mess," Evie said, moving a large pile of papers off the spare chair so that Susan could sit down. "We've been getting behind ever since Simon died. And I don't suppose it's going to get better until there's a new man in his place."

"What happened when Simon was on vacation? Or sick?" Susan asked.

"I don't remember Simon ever being ill. And when he took a vacation, we just waited for him to return."

"You're kidding!" Susan said with more surprise than she felt. No wonder Simon had managed to keep his illegal dealings a secret. He'd been the only person who had done his job and his secretary had been so enamored with the man that she would never suspect anything illegal.

"Hancock isn't a very large town, after all," Evie said. "And we always knew when he was going to be out of town so we could plan for it. The contractors were never seriously inconvenienced by Simon's vacations. He saw to it that everything got done in a timely manner."

Unless he was trying to extort money from one particular contractor, Susan added silently.

"Did you really want the name of my allergist?"

"No, I wanted to ask you some questions, but I didn't want Ken Cory to know."

"Of course, Cory Construction must be full of suspects in this case," Evie said complacently.

"Well, some of them," Susan admitted. "And I need to know the way your office worked when Simon was alive."

"Of course. Where do you want me to start?"

"What happened when someone came in to see Simon? Did you screen people or keep track of his appointments?"

"No. Never. Simon believed in being available to the people. He was a servant to the community. He said that time and time again. And he had an open-door policy. If anyone wanted to see him, they saw him. Unless, of course, he wasn't in his office."

"Which was frequently?"

"Well, he had to carry out his inspections on-site, didn't he?"

"Of course."

"And he was also very active in civic affairs. Well, you were at the funeral. You heard what the mayor said about him. He was a very busy man."

"But your office is right next to his. You must have seen who was coming and going sometimes."

"I don't believe in prying. I'm a worker and too busy with my job to be watching what isn't my business."

Evie's voice was beginning to take on an offended tone, so Susan resorted to flattery. "Naturally," she said. "I'm sure Simon couldn't have done all this without you."

"That's exactly what he was always saying."

"But I really need to know if you noticed two particular visits from members of Ken Cory's crew. Like George Porter back in the early spring."

"Of course, the man who cut through the 220 wire. Simon was very upset about that. He said that any carpenter who did such a stupid thing shouldn't be working in Hancock."

"And you saw George visit Simon's office sometime before he died?"

"No" came the disappointing answer. "That is, I might have, but I certainly don't remember it now."

"Do you happen to remember who visited Simon Fairweather in his office the day before he died?"

"That's different. I'll never forget that day—it was our last together, you see."

Susan just nodded and Evie continued.

"Simon was very busy that day. I've already told the police about it."

"But did anyone from Cory Construction visit his office that day? Probably late in the afternoon?" Susan asked.

"You're asking about that carpenter, right?"

"Art Young or Kyle Barnes?"

"I don't know anyone called Kyle Barnes. Art has been working on houses in Hancock for years. I know him."

"And he visited Simon that day?"

"Late that afternoon, just like you said. In fact, he was still in the office when I left for the day."

"Really? You're sure about that?"

"Of course I am. I went in to tell Simon that I was leaving and he was sitting there. I couldn't miss the man, could I? Of course, I didn't know then that that was the last time I would see Simon."

Susan pushed the box of Kleenex across the desk toward Evie.

"Don't worry. I'm not going to sit here and bawl my head off. That would be entirely unprofessional. I still try to keep Simon's standards."

"His office is immaculate."

"His office was always immaculate. And, of course, the police cleaned up any mess in there before they opened the office for business."

"You mean blood and . . . and everything," Susan said.

"Yes, and, of course, all Simon's scribbles."

Susan remembered the note that had been found in Simon's hand linking her name with Cory Construction. "Did he doodle when he talked?" she asked.

"Oh, yes. It was even something we joked about. I used to tell him that you could figure out what he was thinking by what was on the scrap of paper closest to his hand."

"Did you happen to notice if he was scribbling while he was talking with Art Young? The last time you saw him?"

"No. I didn't notice anything. There was probably a

sheet of paper nearby, but I didn't see one. I would probably have noticed if there hadn't been one. You know what
I mean?"

"Like the dog that barked in the night," Susan muttered,
standing up.

"What?"

"Nothing. Just thinking about an old Sherlock Holmes
story," Susan said. "I'd better be going. A friend of mine is
bringing her baby home from the hospital today and I want
to check on her."

"I hope I helped you."

"You did. I think I'm getting closer to an answer all the
time," Susan said. "Sometimes all you need is the missing
piece." She headed down the hall and back to her car.

The ride to the Gordons' home took less than five minutes and when she got there she was no closer to a solution
than she had been before. But she knew that the answers
were there, right below the surface. All she needed was a
final clue for everything to fall into place. At least that's
what she told herself as she rang the doorbell.

Kathleen's mother answered the door, the baby tucked
lovingly in her arms. "Susan, how nice to see you again.
Kathleen is upstairs in her bedroom, resting. We're heading
out to the backyard to get some fresh air, aren't we, lovely
lambkins?"

Susan was fairly sure that she wasn't the lambkins being
addressed. "I'll just go on up and see her," she said, reaching out and patting the baby on her soft, fuzzy little head.

"Kathleen's upstairs," Mrs. Somerville repeated, turning
so that the baby was beyond Susan's reach.

"I'll go on up," Susan repeated, then did so. "Kathleen?
It's me! Susan."

"Come on up. I'm in the nursery."

"Hi," Susan said, entering the room indicated. "Your
mother said you were in bed resting."

"She hopes that I stay there and leave the baby to her,"
Kathleen explained, bending stiffly in an attempt to peer
under the new cherry dresser.

"You may not need complete bedrest, but you shouldn't

be doing that less than a week after giving birth," Susan insisted, dashing to her friend's side. "What are you doing anyway?"

"Looking for an electrical outlet. We had one added to this room and now I can't find it."

"Sit down in the rocking chair and I'll find it for you," Susan instructed. "What do you want to plug in, anyway?"

"A radio."

"Nice, then your daughter can listen to classical music. It's supposed to increase an infant's IQ, although I have no idea how they test that type of thing."

"I don't want Alice to listen to classical music. Or rock. Or anything else. I want to listen to all-night talk radio. I discovered when I was nursing Alex that it was one of the great perks of motherhood."

"Alice?"

"Alice Emily Gordon. Like it?"

"I sure do!" Susan exclaimed. "And I've found the outlet. Just let me move this dresser and I'll plug it in. Then you'll be all set for the two A.M. feeding."

"Great." Kathleen yawned. "Just the thought of it makes me sleepy."

Susan spent a few more minutes moving furniture, and then, setting the Sony on the edge of the dresser, she pressed the on button. A loud male voice filled the air.

". . . that seventy-eight percent of all accidents happen in the home. So remember—"

"You don't have to shout," Kathleen admonished the anonymous announcer, reaching out and turning down the volume. "And where are you going? You just got here!" she asked, realizing that Susan was heading out the door.

"Call the police station and tell Brett to meet me in his office," Susan called back over her shoulder. "I think I just figured out who killed Simon Fairweather."

THIRTY-TWO

BRETT HAD CALLED THEM ALL TO THIS MEETING IN SIMON Fairweather's office.

"Not bad." Frankie looked about appraisingly.

"The best office in the building," Brett said. "Mainly because Simon built all these shelves and cabinets around the walls."

"Nice work," Art said, running his hand over the dark wood. "Hard to find chestnut this fine these days."

"Is the wall hanging your work?" Susan, sitting on the desk next to Brett, asked Patricia Fairweather. Patricia was leaning against a window, shredding a tissue, and she only nodded nervously.

"Notice the quote over Simon's desk," Evie insisted. She was prepared for any nasal eventuality with an unopened box of tissues under her arm. Susan glanced at the words, but Ken Cory spoke before she could say anything. "Why are we wasting time in this place? My crew and I have a large job to get on with, as you well know."

"We're here because this is where Simon Fairweather was killed."

"Are we revisiting the scene of the crime with hopes that someone will break down and confess?" Frankie asked, sounding interested.

"No, we're here because Simon Fairweather was murdered here rather than someplace else," Susan said, moving forward on the edge of Simon's desk. "Remember those public service announcements that declare that something like seventy-eight percent of all accidents happen in the home?" Susan looked around at her audience. Some were interested, a few were obviously nervous. "There was one playing on the radio a few hours ago and it finally struck me that I had missed something significant. Why was Simon Fairweather killed in his office?"

"Why not?" Buns asked.

"Because it could have been made to look like an accident if it happened on a job site," Susan explained.

"Like George Porter's death," Frankie said, nodding his head. "I have to admit, that one sure looked like an accident to me."

"That type of thing just happens once in a while," Josie agreed. "There was no reason for anyone to think it was anything else."

"It was an accident," Brett said.

"But it was an accident that led straight to Simon Fairweather's murder," Susan said.

"I don't see how." Art spoke up, looking around nervously. "It didn't have any effect on us—except we needed a new carpenter."

Everyone in the room glanced at Kyle Barnes.

"Hey, guys! I didn't kill anyone!" he protested, brushing his blond hair off his forehead. "I came to work to get together some money so I could travel around the world for a while, not to murder Simon Fairweather. I didn't even know who the man was until two months ago."

"I'm sorry," Susan said. "I didn't mean to imply that you had anything to do with Simon's death."

"So you're saying that Kyle and Josie aren't suspects in the murder because they weren't working with the rest of us when the conflict began between Simon Fairweather and Ken," Buns said, scratching his neck with filthy fingernails.

"Not exactly."

"Look, I told you—" Kyle started to protest, beginning to sound angry.

"Why don't you just wait until the entire story is finished," Brett suggested, moving over behind the young carpenter.

Kyle glanced nervously over his shoulder, but he shut up.

"You're awfully quiet," Susan said to Josie.

"I didn't know anything about all this. Honest," the young woman protested. "I got offered this job. And I took it because I needed the money so badly. This is the first year my son's wanted to go to camp. I barely manage to support him during the year. Camp is a real luxury, one that I couldn't afford working for my old boss."

"Hey, it's not like Ken pays better than anyone else," Buns said. "Unless, of course, he pays women extra."

"That doesn't seem too likely, does it?" Frankie said, standing up for Josie. "Considering how prejudiced you all are, how unwilling to accept anyone different from yourselves."

"Hey, who are you talking about? We're not like that," Buns protested. "Just look around this room. Does this look like a . . . a what-do-you-call-it . . . a homogeneous group?"

"Well, not really," Frankie answered slowly.

"They know you're gay, man. And they could care less," Kyle said impatiently. "You've got nothing to bitch about here."

"Just don't start wearing dresses to work and we'll get along just fine." Joel spoke up. "Even Uncle Joe."

"Uncle Joe wants everyone to do their work to the best of their ability," Joe told them.

"Your uncle Joe can speak for himself. And what he wants is to find out if he's been working with a murderer," the older man said, managing to include both his nephews in one outraged glare.

"Well, now that we've gotten some of the confusing issues out in the open, why don't we try to make some order of all this, something I've been trying to do for the last few days," Susan said seriously.

"You see," she continued, "this is the first time I've tried to solve a murder where everyone talked openly about hating the victim. And that was a big problem to begin with. Instead of hiding their dislike after the murder, everyone volunteered to tell me how thrilled they were that Simon Fairweather was dead. Even people down at the club were quick to offer stories about how the building inspector had made their lives or the lives of their friends just a little more complicated.

"Of course, it was really the job that most people hated, not Simon Fairweather himself. No one likes to be told what they can and can't do with their own property, and it was Simon Fairweather's job to do just that. And every time he refused to sign off on an illegal project, every time he refused to bend the rules, every time he did exactly what the town of Hancock paid him to do, he made another enemy.

"There was a dartboard with his picture on it at the tile shop. And to bring up his name in the locker room down at the club was to be regaled with tales of work stopped and permits denied. Of course, the killer had to hate Simon Fairweather the man, not just Simon Fairweather the building inspector. But it was sometimes difficult to separate the two.

"And then, of course," Susan continued, "everyone knew that Simon Fairweather played favorites with the contracting companies. At least that's what it looked like from the outside."

"And, in fact, according to the information that Mrs. Fairweather has given us—information that she just discovered—it turns out that it wasn't just the general impression. It was true." Brett spoke up. "Simon was making extra money—a lot of extra money—by forcing one contracting company at a time to pay him off. Or else he would see that they went out of business."

"You mean . . ." Ken Cory seemed to be so surprised that he was speechless. "You mean, it happened to other guys?" he asked when he had finally regained his composure.

"Yes. I've had men on the phone all morning checking it out ever since we were given the information. Cory Construction was just the last in a long line of companies that was told to either pay up or get out," Brett assured the man.

"Of course, your company was a little different," Brett continued. "In the first place, there aren't as many contractors around these days. The economy has changed." He shrugged. "And I suppose there isn't as much space left vacant to build new homes on. You see, Simon Fairweather didn't just go after any company. He was very careful about those he chose. And, we think, although we haven't checked them all out yet, that the other companies were from out of town. Most of them were from places closer to New York City, places that had accepted payoffs as just one of the costs of doing business." Brett stood up and looked sternly around the room. "Things like that aren't done in Hancock."

"Cory Construction has always been located here." Buns spoke up for the first time in a while.

"That's right. And in the nineties there isn't a lot of work; most people chose to hire locals, so Simon Fairweather didn't have the luxury of picking on an out-of-town contractor."

"So he stuck a pin in a book and came up with Cory Construction?" Frankie asked.

"No. I don't think Simon Fairweather did anything without thinking about it. But, you see, Ken is vulnerable, more vulnerable than other contractors, I'd imagine. Because he is known to have had affairs with the women he worked for. Women whose husbands might not be so happy to pay his high bills if they knew he was sleeping with their wives."

Susan remembered what Natalie McPherson had told her about herself and Ken and nodded. His crew members were grinning broadly.

"But there was something else different about Ken Cory, wasn't there?" Brett asked, turning to the men.

They all stopped smiling and looked at one another.

"It was George Porter, wasn't it?" Brett asked Ken quietly.

"Hey, that was an accident, man," Angelo said. "I'm an electrician. I know about those kinds of accidents."

"That's not what I'm talking about right now," Brett continued, still staring at Ken. "You didn't want to fire him and Simon was pushing you to, right?"

Ken nodded his head slowly. "Yeah, George had been with me from the beginning. Art and George and I used to work 'til all hours of the night to get jobs done. But things changed when George's wife died. He became forgetful and incompetent." Ken looked at Art Young. "I know you were trying to cover up for him, but the problems were obvious to me—and to Simon Fairweather, I'm afraid.

"Simon said he wouldn't approve our work unless I fired George. I suggested that George retire, but he said it would kill him not to work. What could I do? George was a good worker who had been with me from the beginning. I couldn't hurt him at that time of his life. I refused to fire him. So Simon asked for a payoff. I refused that, too, and threatened to make his request public."

"He even talked to George Porter about it," Susan added. "Patsy Porter said that her father had been claiming that Simon Fairweather wanted him fired and that he went to his office to talk to him about it a short time before he died."

"Poor George," Ken said. "That must have been horribly humiliating for him. Well, I wasn't going to have any part in it. And I wasn't going to pay Simon Fairweather off. But he had dug up that stuff you were saying about those women and he threatened to make it public. Well, that would have ruined me. I didn't pay. But I didn't talk. And Simon started refusing to accept any of our work." Ken sighed. "It was a miserable time. And then George died. . . ."

"An accident," Angelo insisted.

"Yes, it was," Susan said. "But like so many accidents, it was caused by someone else."

"I did it." Art Young stood up and faced the room. "I caused my friend's death."

"No," Susan said gently. "You didn't do it. Simon Fairweather just let you think that you did. It was really his fault."

"Manslaughter, probably," Brett agreed quietly.

"What? I didn't do it? And that man . . . I talked to him the night before he was killed and he . . . he let me believe that it was my fault." It was obvious to everyone that Art was near tears. "I thought for sure I had told George to disconnect that electricity the day before. And then, when

George went through that wall, I could hardly believe it. Obviously George had forgotten to do it. There was nothing I could do and everyone thought it was just one of those accidents." Tears were flowing down his cheeks, and Frankie, closest to him, reached over and put his arm around the older man's shoulders. "I worried about how I would make it up to him. We were buddies, you see. I worried each and every second. And then I got this idea that I could try out for *Jeopardy!* again. And this time I'd get on and win a lot of money. And I'd give it to that sweet little Patsy. George would have liked her to have something."

"It was a lovely idea, but it wasn't your fault," Susan said. "George was supposed to turn off the power and cut those lines the night before, right?"

"Yes, but they should have been checked out . . ." Art began, and then looked up at Ken. "There was an inspection due to happen. They should have been checked by Simon Fairweather before any work was done."

Ken nodded. "But Simon had long ago stopped bothering to even come to a Cory Construction worksite since he wasn't going to approve anything that we'd done. I knew that, but you guys didn't."

"So in many ways it really was Simon's fault that George died. If Simon had been doing his job—"

"George would still be alive," Art finished quietly.

"But I still don't know why you went to see Simon Fairweather the night that he was killed," Susan said.

"I wanted to talk to him. I'd started a few letters to him, but I never could get the words right." Susan remembered the note she had seen hanging out of his tool chest the day they'd met. "I thought I should visit him in person and tell him that George's death was my fault. We—the guys on the crew and me—all knew that Simon was after Cory Construction and I thought maybe that was my fault, too. So I went to confess, but he just sat there and doddled on the sheet of paper in front of him." Art took a deep breath and exhaled loudly. "And to think that all the time I was talking to him, he knew that George was dead because of a mistake he'd made, not because of something I'd done. If he weren't dead, I'd take my nail gun and kill him myself."

"But it was the nail gun that you left behind that was used to kill him," Brett said. "And it was that nail gun that almost convinced me that the murderer had to be a member of the crew."

"Except," Susan said. "Except if Simon was going to be killed by a member of your crew, wouldn't it be more logical if the murderer made it look like just another fatal accident? After all, as the man on the radio said, 'Seventy-eight percent of all accidents happen in the home.' "

"And you're suggesting that my husband should have been killed in my home?" Patricia Fairweather asked.

"In your home?" Josie spoke up, shaking her red curls, which were more unruly than usual, and looking at the woman. "I don't understand. Who is your husband?"

"Simon Fairweather," Ken Cory answered for the woman. "This is Patricia Fairweather."

"No." Josie stood up and faced Susan. "This is the woman who paid me to come to Hancock and work for you."

THIRTY-THREE

"This *is* Patricia Fairweather," Susan insisted.

"Wait a minute. You said this woman paid you to come to Hancock and work for Ken?" Kyle asked. "You didn't get your job just like the rest of us did?"

"No, I . . ." Josie looked at Ken and then at Patricia and frowned. "Obviously, I don't understand exactly what is going on here, but maybe I should tell my part of this story."

"Please do," Susan requested, sitting back down on the desk with a loud thump.

"It happened last week. I was working on this house that we were beginning to work on out in Montauk and this woman"—she nodded toward Patricia—"came across the road to talk to me.

"That's not all that unusual. Neighbors frequently drop in at the beginning of projects. They're naturally curious about the work being done in their neighborhood, about the people who are working there, and whether or not the final result is going to meet their standards. Well, this woman—"

"Why don't you call me Patricia?" Patricia suggested gently. "It will be easier all around."

"If you say so," Josie agreed, sounding as if she wasn't convinced. "Well, Patricia hung around for a while and asked some questions about the house I was working on and then she asked some questions about me. That's not all that unusual, either. There aren't a lot of female carpenters out there. I suppose we're still something of a curiosity. And so she started asking questions and I answered.

"And I told her something about myself and how I

needed more money for my son's camp expenses. He has a scholarship to camp, but his clothing and equipment were so expensive that I was completely broke.

"And then Patricia Fairweather—and that's not who she told me she was—said that she would pay me to move to Hancock, Connecticut, for a month until my son came back home on Labor Day. That she would rent me an apartment and pay a fee on top of my regular salary if I would work for a contractor there and try to discover exactly what was going on with the members of the crew."

Josie stopped talking and looked at Patricia. "But I didn't know that it was a murder that we were talking about. I thought there had been some funny business in a contracting company, but nothing like a murder," she repeated. "I never would have come if I had known what I was getting into."

"That's why you were so willing to help me out. You were already investigating for Patricia," Susan said. "I never guessed."

"And that's why you stayed on the fringes of the group—always wanting to go off and work by yourself," Frankie said. "You wanted to listen in, but you didn't want to get too involved."

"That's true. Especially when I realized how serious the situation was," Josie admitted. "But I was feeling so guilty. I'm not much of a spy, I guess. I like what I do and I like working with people. I had really gotten in over my head, just for a few extra bucks."

"But Ken must have known," Susan said. "He didn't just happen to hire you. It must have been arranged between him and Patricia."

"You're right there," Ken said. "I was desperately afraid of losing my company. I had finally gotten together my courage, decided the hell with it if a few men in town got mad at me for sleeping with their wives. Hell, it was their wives' fault, too. And I filed a protest with the planning board. But when Simon found out, he convinced me that he controlled the planning board, too."

"That's just not true," Brett said. "The corruption stopped

with Simon Fairweather. Those people on the planning board are honest—as you'll find out in a few weeks."

"But I didn't know that. And when I got a call from Mrs. Fairweather suggesting that I could hire this young woman to find out if anyone in my company had killed her husband—"

"Wait, when did you talk with Patricia?" Susan asked Josie.

"I'd better answer that," Patricia said. "I spoke with Josie early in the morning the day after my husband was killed."

"We started work at seven A.M., as usual," the young carpenter agreed.

"So you didn't kill him either," Frankie said, looking around the room to see if he had missed any possible suspects. "But if it wasn't someone on the crew and it wasn't you . . ."

"I think I'd better explain," Patricia said slowly. "It's the least I can do. In fact, right now it's the only thing I can do. It is, I'm afraid, a long and sordid story. And some of you already know parts of it."

"Why don't you start at the beginning," Susan suggested.

And Patricia took her suggestion. "You see, I grew up in Hancock. I was the youngest of four sisters and we lived in the house that I live in today. Except that when I was a child, I hated that house more than almost anyplace on earth—we all did. By that I mean my sisters and myself. My mother never expressed an opinion, not about that or about much else. My father was a tyrant and he had her and his children completely under his thumb. My sisters left home for college and never came back. I was the youngest and I stayed here. There wasn't anyone left to give me moral support and I was too weak to leave alone.

"And then, when I was in my late teens, Simon proposed to me. We'd known each other for years. Hancock wasn't a very large town back then and pretty much everyone knew everyone else. Simon was older than I was, and although I didn't know him well enough to love him, I thought he was offering me a chance to escape my family.

I was seriously mistaken. What had actually happened was that my father had offered Simon a way of moving painlessly from the wrong side of the tracks to the top of the hill. Painless, that is, if Simon didn't mind marrying his youngest daughter. Then we could move into this great mansion with my parents and all would be well—for a man who liked to control the lives of those around him.

"But my father had a heart attack and died. I know how insensitive this sounds, but his death freed me from years of terror and obligation to a man I had grown to hate. And it was a stroke of luck for Simon, because he got a house that he could use to parlay himself into being a major figure in town. As Hancock grew, so did Simon's importance.

"And during this time, I was trying to find myself. That sounds very psychobabble silly, I know. But when you're raised the way I was, it is very difficult to know exactly one's own identity. I was lucky, though, and one of my sisters gave me a wonderful present: tuition to a class at the art center in town. I found something that added meaning and beauty to my life. That class changed my life.

"Meanwhile Simon and I just toddled along in our marriage. The only thing we did together was plan and work on the house. For Simon the house was a professional showpiece. For me it was turning the darkness of my childhood and youth into something bright and beautiful. We continued that way for years.

"But Simon was becoming mean and bitter. He was always jealous of the people in town with more money and power than he had and it was only getting worse, not better. And one night he started hitting me."

"When was that?" Brett asked.

"About a year ago," she said. "I realize now that he was in danger of losing all the extra money that he had depended on to allow him to hobnob with the important and wealthy people in town. I didn't see that at the time, of course."

"And it went on until his death, didn't it?" Susan asked gently.

"Yes. I . . . I didn't want anyone to know," Patricia said.

"You didn't tell anyone?" Susan asked.

"Just . . ." Patricia had been getting more upset as each moment passed and she finally broke down.

"Your sister?" Susan asked gently. "I'm right, aren't I?"

"Yes. She'd suspected for months. When I decided not to go on the cruise it was really because Simon had gotten mad and hit me. I went to Montauk and told her about it."

"And she came here and found Simon working late in his office. Someone had left a nail gun there. And she killed him, didn't she?" Susan asked gently.

Patricia, in tears, could only nod her head.

"And where is she now?" Susan asked, seeing that Brett was already heading for the door.

"I . . ." Patricia took a deep breath and made an effort to continue. "She left late last night. I . . . I got back from our breakfast and went up to the room she was staying in. But she wasn't there. This note was on the pillow." She held it out to Brett with a shaking hand. "It says . . . it says she was going to go for a long swim in the water off Montauk. It says she was going to see what the lighthouse looked like from a few miles out at sea. It says goodbye."

No one spoke. The only sound was Patricia's sobbing.

THIRTY-FOUR

One Week Later

"I HAD WONDERED EXACTLY WHY YOU WERE SO HAPPY TO help me look into the murder."

"What did you think?" Josie asked, pouring some beer from her Bud Light can into Clue's open mouth.

"I had no idea," Susan admitted, picking up the pile of towels she had been folding neatly. "I did finally realize that you had made the phone call to the station saying that a member of the crew was a murderer."

"That was pretty stupid. I was worried about you. Patricia said that she wanted me to investigate the men on the crew, but she didn't say anything about murder. And I hadn't known about the note that connected you and Ken Cory to Simon's murder that was found in Simon's hand."

"Patricia had told Lillian that I investigated murders. She probably saw the initials on the nail gun, what Simon had already scribbled on the paper on his desk, and added my name, thinking she was adding a suspect or two. Of course, she had no way of knowing that Ken Cory's men really were going to be suspects or that I was going to be in immediate need of a contractor," Susan explained.

"Well, once I got here and found out what the true situation was, I just felt like the police should get involved and look after you. Of course, I had no idea at the time that you were an experienced detective," Josie added, her characteristic grin on her face.

"As you are now," Susan pointed out.

"I am going to go home tomorrow and return to work for my old boss." Josie tossed her head in a gesture Susan had come to recognize as an expression of her happiness. "It's not an exciting life, but it's my very own. I'm leaving murders to someone else."

"Does this mean that the third-floor bathroom is almost finished?" Susan asked.

"We finished this afternoon. Just let the men clean up."

"You're kidding!"

"Hey, those guys aren't sexist at all!" Josie insisted. "They said they'd mop up the place . . . as long as I took everyone out to dinner tonight."

Susan laughed. "But there is something else that you want to confess, isn't there?"

"How did you know?"

"Your hair."

"My hair?" Josie once again repeated the impossible task of trying to smooth it down.

"It always looks like it's going to take off into space, but that day in Simon's office I thought it was going to levitate by itself."

"That's what my hair does after it's been washed and rinsed a half-dozen times," Josie admitted.

"And then I realized that you were the only person who knew I was going to visit Patsy Porter," Susan continued.

"You know that I didn't mean to scare you like that, don't you?" Josie asked, sounding worried. "I was feeling so guilty about all the lies. I just wanted to talk to you. I thought I'd confess what I was doing in town. When I reached out to get your attention, I never thought I'd get socked with Clue's manure."

"If you'll forgive me, I'll forgive you," Susan offered with a hug.

Later That Evening

"Wow! You're a genius. This room looks wonderful!" Jed stood in the doorway and admired the third-floor bath. No longer did the eaves seem low. Now they were interesting angles that defined the room. Unused porcelain gleamed. The walls were freshly painted and the tiles on the floor unscuffed. Long towel racks held fluffy new linens and large shells displayed piles of scented soap. "Maybe we really should add a guest room up here," Jed enthused. "This is great."

"What a good idea."

"After we pay off the bills from this project," he continued.

Susan knew what that meant: There was no reason to start planning now. Besides, she had to worry about the other bathrooms. She kept calling the man who was making the tiles and he wasn't giving her any answers. Maybe she should drive there, she thought, sliding her hand across the smooth, shiny rim of the bathtub—and running into a lump. "Jed, there's a scratch here," she cried out dramatically, flinging herself down on the floor and examining the spot more closely.

"This is the dent I saw when the tub was delivered," she muttered. "I told them it was damaged and they ignored me."

Jed sat down on the tub's rim and examined the spot. "It's just a tiny dent."

"I know, but—"

"And to replace the tub, all the tiles would have to come down. And possibly the wall—"

"Probably the wall," Susan corrected him. "I remember when it went in."

"Do you like the room? Are you happy with everything except for this?" he asked gently.

Susan smiled. "Very. It really looks nice, doesn't it?"

"Can you live with this?"

"Yes. I have other things to do. I'd better get down to the tile man if I want the other bathrooms finished before the kids get home," she added, following her husband down the stairs.

Three Weeks Later

Susan cut the ribbon that hung across the doorway. "Ta da!" she exclaimed, and moved out of the way so that her children could enter and admire.

Except Chad seemed to have something different on his mind. "I've been living in the wilderness for five weeks. As nice as this looks, now that I'm finally in a bathroom I'd like to do something other than admire it!" he said, and hurried up to the third floor.

Chrissy strolled slowly around the room. Despite the oppressive heat of late summer, she was proudly wrapped in a new outfit of Spanish suede. The heels on her boots tapped loudly on the new tile floor.

"Do you like—" Susan began.

"Who did the tile work?"

"A man, an artist, really, who was recommended to us by the people who laid the tiles. See how the tiles are painted to resemble a field of flowers."

Chrissy emitted a long, and almost but not quite, despairing sigh.

Susan got the impression that her daughter was sure that her parents would never, ever learn. She was just not sure what there was to learn.

"They're okay. A little suburban, of course, but what else can you expect?"

Susan and Jed smiled weakly.

Three Weeks Even Later

"I thought you were going to take a bath in your wonderful, new extra-large bathtub," Jed commented as his wife headed down the stairs in her terrycloth robe.

"Just getting some stuff," she muttered.

Jed chuckled and leaned back against the wall to await her return.

"Look what I found in the refrigerator! Cold champagne!" she said a few minutes later, a bottle and glasses in her hands.

"Two glasses?" Jed grinned. "Does this mean you're expecting company?"

"Jed ..." She paused. "I'd really like to soak for a while."

"I know. You go ahead and enjoy your first bath. I'll have a glass of that stuff in the bedroom while you turn yourself into a prune—a sexy prune."

"You'll open the bottle for me?"

"Sure." He took it from her and followed her into the bedroom. Gardenia-scented steam was billowing out of the bathroom door. "That tub isn't going to overflow, is it? We don't want another flood."

"No. But it does take an awfully long time to fill." Susan put the glasses up on the dresser and turned around.

"Where are you going?"

"Forgot the votive candles," she muttered, vanishing out the door.

Jed was struggling to open the bottle and didn't bother to comment.

Fifteen minutes later the tub was full, the bathroom warm and steamy, a thin crystal flute of champagne waited on the metal shelf, and a half-dozen white candles shimmered on the iridescent watery surfaces of the room. Susan checked out the water temperature, dropped her robe on the floor, and got in, stretching luxuriously and slowly, slowly leaning back into the bubbles until she felt her head sink under the water.

"Jed," she sputtered, spitting water out of her mouth and wiping bubbles from her eyes. "Jed!"

"What's wrong?" he cried, dashing into the room.

"The tub! My perfect tub!"

"What's wrong?"

"It's too long. I can't lie down and keep my head out of the water. It's ... it's like a coffin."

Jed chuckled, then started to unbutton his shirt. "Don't think of it that way. Think of it as a tub built for two," he suggested.